Permelia Cottage

Permelia Cottage

A Novel

Carole Lehr Johnson

INK MAP PRESS

Permelia Cottage

Published in Pollock, Louisiana, by Ink Map Press
www.inkmappress.com

Cover Design by Victoria Davies
Cover Photography by Carole Lehr Johnson
Interior Design by Morgan Tarpley Smith

Scripture quotations are from the New King James Version of the Bible.

This is a work of fiction. Names, characters, places, and incidents either are the product of the author's imagination or are used fictitiously. Any resemblance to actual persons, living or dead, events, or locales is entirely coincidental.

ISBN 978-1-952928-00-0
ISBN 978-1-952928-01-7 (ebook)

Publisher's Cataloging-in-Publication Data

Names: Johnson, Carole Lehr, author.
Title: Permelia cottage / Carole Lehr Johnson.
Description: Pollock, LA: Ink Map Press, 2020. | Illus. ; 35 b&w photos.| Summary: Can an old English cottage bring renewed faith and healing to several broken hearts?
Identifiers: LCCN 2020909705 | ISBN 9781952928000 (paperback) | ISBN 9781952928017 (ebook)
Subjects: LCSH: Cottages—England—Fiction. | Faith—Fiction. | Friendship—Fiction. | Man-woman relationships—Fiction. | Mothers and sons—Fiction. | Yorkshire (England)—Fiction. | BISAC: FICTION / Christian / Contemporary. | FICTION / Family Life / General. | FICTION / Multiple Timelines.
Classification: LCC PS3610 O36 P4 2021 | DDC 813 J64--dc22
LC record available at https://lccn.loc.gov/2020909705

Printed in the United States of America
2020—First Edition

Printed in the United States of America
2020—First Edition

10 9 8 7 6 5 4 3 2 1

To My Lord and Savior, Jesus Christ, who is guiding my writing, making it better with each story He gives me.

Books by Carole Lehr Johnson

Permelia Cottage

A Place in Time

His Scottish Destiny

(co-authored with Tammy Kirby)

Chapter One

Louisiana, U.S.A.
March 2016

One decision can change everything. That was Susannah Wilkinson's thought as the cool breeze touched her face. The sweet fragrance of gardenias lingered on the wind as she spoke with the young mother of a fifteen-year-old girl. The girl's gaze shifted downward, forehead wrinkling. Her mother stood her ground, a forefinger pointed toward the clinic as she emphasized why her daughter needed an abortion.

"You don't have to make a decision right now," Susannah pleaded, staring into the mother's eyes. "Please take time to read over this literature before you decide." Her gaze returned to the teenager, then to her mother. "Once you do this, there's no turning back. It's life-changing."

The mother shook her head, leaning away from Susannah. Her hazel eyes reflected uncertainty. "I don't . . . I . . . *we* think this is the time to do it—while she isn't very far along. You see what I mean?"

Susannah sent up a silent prayer for wisdom. The woman stared at her, head tilted.

"I realize . . . but a child is a child no matter how far along your daughter is." One lone tear fought for release, and she blinked to keep it at bay.

The woman raised her pale eyes to meet Susannah's. "May I ask you a question?"

Susannah cleared her throat. "Certainly."

The growing crowd near them pulled her attention for a moment. She refocused on the question.

"Why are you so concerned about abortion?"

A sharp pain shot through Susannah. She drew in a quick breath as she clenched her purse strap. "Because I had to make this decision once."

The mother's eyes widened. Her lips parted in surprise as she brought a hand to her chest. She smoothed her daughter's dark hair. A trembling smile softened her lips. "Well, perhaps we should talk a little more."

Susannah moved closer and whispered, "May I pray with you?" The woman nodded. Susannah motioned to a bench several yards away, partially hidden behind a large oak tree.

Loud noise from the robust crowd reached them, but Susannah ignored it. Protesters shouted and blocked people from entering the clinic. They prayed, had a brief discussion and said their goodbyes.

Susannah walked the two blocks to her car to gather more material. She fumbled with her keys and almost dropped them on the pavement. When she clicked the lock, she swung the door open and slouched into the driver's seat. With a ragged breath, her hands trembled as she ran them through her hair and then massaged her temples as sirens wailed in the distance.

The trauma of seeing someone come close to an abortion twisted her insides and tugged at her heart. Eyes closing, she collected her thoughts before she left the security of her vehicle. She walked back to the clinic as police cars arrived, lights flashing. Several people lingered on the sidewalk, and a white-haired woman stood to the side with her hands pressed to her face while tears darkened her purple blouse. A rock hurled through the air and struck a streetlight overhead raining shattered glass over the woman.

Susannah thrust past a few bystanders and reached out as the woman stumbled. Thick white smoke engulfed the surrounding area. She grabbed her arm and led her from the noxious cloud.

Once they escaped, Susannah coughed. "Are you okay, ma'am?" Susannah held her arm, and she winced at her touch. People pushed past them and scattered in all directions. She led her to a nearby bench and gently brushed small pieces of glass from her hair.

The woman gasped for air and clung to Susannah for support.

"May I see your arm?" The woman nodded. Susannah

pushed up her sleeve and noted a large red spot, the precursor to a bruise. "I think you'll be sore for a few days, but you should be fine." She reassured her with a nod.

"Thank you, dearie." Her aged eyes squeezed shut. "Those people who were arrested tried to keep girls from going into the clinic. Can you imagine? It was loud, and the voices so angry. You'd think folks would realize it's easier to catch more flies with honey than vinegar?"

Had the circumstances been less dire, Susannah would've laughed at the analogy.

"Yes, ma'am, you're right. I guess when we're passionate about something we get carried away."

"Honey, I suppose that's true." She shook her head, tears gleaming on her wrinkled cheeks.

❧

Yes, one decision can change everything.

Susannah Wilkinson rushed from the Timlee Clinic mêlée to the restaurant, certain she'd find Diann already there. Conversations hummed as she settled against the back of her chair and contemplated the events of the day.

As always, when stressful things happened, Susannah thought of her son—the one person she loved more than life itself.

Their estrangement tore at her heart. She felt her lips curve as she remembered the early years when he would run to her with open arms and happy laughter. She swiped a tear from her cheek as their last painful meeting absorbed the good memories.

The gift was cradled in her arms as she entered his room. "Ryan, I have a going away present for you." She held out the wrapped package tied with a blue ribbon. He snatched it from her and mumbled 'thanks,' before he tossed it into his suitcase.

She avoided his eyes. "Aren't you going to open it?"

Ryan released an impatient sigh, grabbed the package, and yanked the ribbon free. Slender fingers shook as he ripped the paper, releasing an object to slide across the tile floor, making no move to retrieve it. He thumbed through the leather-bound journal that bore his name in gold letters then he returned it to his bag.

Susannah stooped to rescue the discarded pocket cross. Creases formed in her palm as she gripped it with force. She held out her hand, palm up. Her voice broke. "Keep this is in your pocket and every time you see it, remember I'm praying for you."

Silence met her words. His stony countenance grieved her heart. Time lingered as Susannah bit her tongue to stop the tears.

His blue eyes sparked. "I don't need your religion!" He pivoted, shoulders rigid, and slung clothes onto the bed.

His hurtful words echoed in her mind. The coppery tang of blood was a reminder to release her injured tongue. She left the room on wooden legs, the cross clutched in her fist.

The door slammed, rattling the pictures against the wall. One fell with a crash. When the silver-framed family portrait shattered, she picked it up with gentle movements, staring at the happy little boy that sat on her lap.

Memories of that special day released the dam, and tears of regret flowed.

⊂ঃ৪০

"Sue?" The quiet voice interrupted her thoughts.

Susannah's gaze shifted from the tablecloth to her best friend's face, her forehead creased.

Diann slid into the empty seat and touched Susannah's shoulder. "Are you okay?"

"Sorry, I'm fine. Just lost in thought." She forced the down-turned corners of her mouth up.

Diann glanced at her friend's fisted hand. "What did you want to talk about?"

Susannah shrugged and twirled the stem of her water glass as she watched the lemon float in circles.

"Well, I have news. But let me tell you what happened at the clinic a while ago." She gave Diann a lengthy, informative narration of her encounter with the woman and her daughter, the crowd, and the elderly lady hit with the rock. She toyed with her glass, wiped the moisture from her palms onto her napkin, and repeated the process several times.

Diann drew in a deep breath and let it out in a huff. "What's wrong with you?"

Susannah tilted her chin. "Excuse me?"

"You've been rambling."

Susannah slumped in defeat. "There is something I want to tell you—something you may not like."

"So, spit it out. We've been friends far too long to play games."

She leaned forward. "You're right. I asked to meet for lunch so I could tell you my news." She reached for her water glass to repeat the ritual.

"If you start that routine again, I'll take your water away from you." Diann's guttural voice didn't match the grin she wore.

"Okay, okay." Susannah pushed her shoulders back and stared into Diann's curious eyes. "You've always encouraged me to move on, follow my dreams. Now, I am." Lifting the glass to her lips, she took a long sip, and blurted out, "I'm moving to England."

Diann's face paled. "What? I didn't mean *move*, Sue. Move on. Let the past go. Have you lost your mind?"

"This dream has been with me for so long. I believe it's the right thing to do. I've always wanted to live in an English cottage. Why not now?"

"What about your son? He'll be having children in a few years . . . perhaps. You'll want to be near your grandchildren, won't you? I wouldn't be able to handle not seeing my grandchildren for months on end." Diann's eyes glistened as she rummaged in her purse. Susannah retrieved a tissue from her own bag. Her hand shook as she accepted it. "Are you sure you're not using this to run away from your estrangement with Ryan?"

Susannah averted her gaze and scanned the Victorian Tea Room, their favorite place to meet. Wood-trimmed chairs upholstered in eggplant chintz, tables with linen cloths, brass candlesticks, and fresh flowers in crystal vases. A Victorian sofa in rich brocade sat by a faux fireplace in a corner. Here, time froze. They loved this room because of its British flavor.

Diann had to understand her dream.

"I suppose there may be truth in what you said about Ryan." She pressed her lips together, her gaze scanned the creamy yellow walls, windows adorned with lace curtains bordered in heavy brocade panels. "But, with the money Aaron left me, I'll be able to fly home anytime I choose. Besides, Ryan has his own life and doesn't need me around. He's self-sufficient with a successful career."

Diann crossed her arms. "Are you listening to yourself?" Tepid sarcasm laced her voice. She sniffled and reached for the tissue. "This is a big deal. You'll be over four thousand miles away."

"I realize that, but I have to do this. It's my dream. When Aaron abandoned us, I thought I'd never hear from him again. To think he had a life insurance policy—and left it to me. The guilt must have eaten at him." His face appeared in her mind's eye, the face she first fell in love with, not the face of the man who screamed at her to do something her convictions could never allow.

"Well, it should have. I don't understand what got into him." She exhaled with a huff. "So, what exact plans have you made? I mean, are you going right away?"

"That's part two of why I asked you to lunch today. I want to go soon and spend about a month to explore, research real estate, and sightsee. I'll do preliminary research online first, as a starting point, but I . . ."

The server appeared with their order and brought their conversation to a halt.

Between bites Diann stated matter-of-factly, "You don't

need my help to plan the details. You're the travel writer, and I've never been to Britain."

"This is the thing . . ." Susannah grasped the napkin on her lap. "I need you to go with me." Leaning back in her chair, she bit the inside of her cheek.

Diann's fork suspended inches from her lips. "I . . . I'm not sure what to say. This is a surprise."

"I hoped you'd say yes."

"Wayne may not agree," she said, though Susannah saw a glimmer of interest in her eyes. "I've never been away from him for that long. What about my kids and grandkids? An entire month without seeing them?" She rubbed the back of her neck with vigor.

"Stop right there, don't try to convince yourself it's a bad idea. You and I both know you'd love to go. I'm not asking you to leave tomorrow. We'll plan this out." She met Diann's anxious gaze and waited.

Diann folded and refolded her napkin. "Deep down I'm thrilled at an adventure like this, but . . ."

"Don't decide now. Go home and discuss it with Wayne. Tell me soon, so I can make other arrangements if you can't go."

She tapped her fingertips at the base of her throat. "You would take someone else?"

"Perhaps." Susannah smoothed the wrinkles out of the tablecloth.

Diann lifted her chin and pushed her shoulders back. "If you're taking someone, it's most certainly going to be me. I'll convince Wayne."

Susannah grinned and pulled a small package out of her bag and slid it across the table.

Diann's head tilted to one side, eyes narrowing. "What's this?"

"A thank you gift."

Diann raised an eyebrow. "You knew I'd say yes?"

"That flash of determination in your eyes just confirmed how well I know you."

When ripped away, the rose floral paper revealed a decorated box. Diann gently removed the lid to disclose a long gold chain with an ornate carved oval pendant with *Live like you mean it* engraved in the center.

England
May 2016

Susannah believed springtime in England was one of the most peaceful places on earth.

The fresh, varied shades of green colored the English landscape as the small tour bus wound its way through the countryside. Each turn revealed rounded hills dotted with sheep, cows, horses, or fields laden with crops. The idyllic landscape captivated her. She possessed a sense of belonging.

Finances had prohibited extensive travel in the past, but her recent windfall had changed that. Was she mad? She was considering a move to rural England. Was this really a fact-finding mission, or maybe just to get it out of her system? She had prayed. All seemed to fall into place. It could be a wasted trip with nothing priced within her means. At least she'd have a vacation with her dearest friend if it didn't work out the way she envisioned.

The bus tires crunched on gravel as they stopped in the car park of a quaint little village called Neville. Susannah and Diann followed the group into a local pub. Marcy, their guide, stepped between them and linked arms. "Come on, dears, you sit with me."

"Thank you, Marcy. That's kind of you." Susannah glanced over her head at Diann's scowl that translated into her displeasure that her personal space was about to be invaded. She was aware of all of Diann's idiosyncrasies—and vice versa.

Marcy guided them to a corner table with the view of a courtyard edged in ornamental grass around the perimeter. Flower beds teemed with the first stages of vibrant, colorful blooms. A low stone wall enclosed the garden and added the perfect touch.

Susannah's steady gaze wandered over the profusion of color. Purple phlox encircled a granite birdbath. A perpetual stream of water spilled from a lion's head fountain into a stone dish. She could get used to this.

Marcy's perky voice broke through the fog. "Susannah, are you all right, dear?"

Diann responded. "Don't mind her. She tends to wool-gather when she's in her favorite place in the world."

Susannah jumped in. "Sorry. I was admiring the garden." She poked Diann in the ribs with her elbow. "And she's right. I daydream a bit."

"Well, the garden is lovely. Neville is my favorite stop on the tour." Marcy's smile broadened. "It's a marvelous place."

Susannah empathized with the admiration in Marcy's eyes. Neville's enchantment called to her almost spiritually.

After they all enjoyed a variety of scones, sandwiches, and two pots of tea, Susannah walked outside with the group and breathed in the fresh air as they followed the stone path to the car park. Susannah closed her eyes and inhaled the sharp smell of mown grass.

She took out her camera. "You two go on ahead. I want to take a few more pictures of the pub."

A split path led to the side of the brownstone building. She admired the thatched roof and leaded windows and took a few pictures. Beside the courtyard garden, an elderly gentleman leaned against the gate watching her. On impulse, she strolled over. "Good afternoon. It's a beautiful day, isn't it?"

He removed the pipe from his mouth, beamed and replied in a strong British accent, "That it is . . . that it is. How're you today?" He wasn't a tall man, lean and sturdily built.

"Fine, thank you." She scanned the garden's color. "It's so delightful."

"It's been my favorite spot in Neville since I was a lad."

"So, you've lived here a while?" Susannah admired his thick gray waves.

"Yes, ma'am. All my life. This pub—" He used his pipe to point at the building. "—was built many years before I was born, and I'm ninety-seven next week."

"You don't look it." Susannah took in his straight back.

"Thank you. Don't act it either." His blue eyes twinkled with mischief. "At least everyone around here says. I still tend my gardn' and the one here at the pub."

"You do a fantastic job. I admired it throughout our afternoon tea. Would it be all right if I took a few pictures inside the garden?"

"That'd be no problem at all." He held the gate open to allow her to step across the stone threshold.

"By the by, the name's Hodge." He tipped his hat.

"Nice to meet you. I'm Susannah." She snapped a close-up of the fountain and stood back to appreciate it.

"Caught your fancy?" He had stepped from the gate to stand beside her. "It's original."

"How old is this place?"

He straightened. "My family built it in 1702."

Susannah rose from photographing a cluster of white phlox, surprised. "It's yours?"

"Yes, tried to keep it as it was, except for modern plumbin'. The entire lot looks as it did over 300 years ago."

It touched Susannah to imagine the love and devotion of one family to keep a historic place like this for so long. She said as much.

Hodge's grey eyes sparkled with pride. "Most don't appreciate it, but I can tell you regard commitment. I may be a sentimental fool, but it seems your interest is more than a tour stop."

"That's perceptive of you. I love history especially Britain's. My family came from here, and they passed little of the information down. I have an aunt who traced our genealogy, and I value it, but I want to learn about my ancestors on a more personal level—by visiting where they lived." She held his gaze. "And how you must be proud of the devotion of your family to this place. You're a part of it, and I long to be a part of where my ancestors lived."

"I understand that." Hodge grew silent for a few moments. With a croak in his voice, he continued, "Susannah, you're a special lady. I'd love to share our history with you, but you must be gettin' on that bus." He pointed with his pipe. "May I have your address? I'll be glad to send you every spot of information on my place. And Neville."

On impulse, Susannah gave him a gentle hug. "Hodge, thank you . . . I mean that with sincerity. You're so kind." She pulled a business card from her purse and gave it to him. He glanced at it, and with gnarled fingers tucked it into the pocket of his tweed vest.

"You best be gettin' on that bus before it leaves."

Susannah started toward the bus and turned back. "Hodge, say cheese."

He gave her a broad grin and waved as she snapped the picture.

◌₃₈◌

A few days later, after the tour wound through other villages with their castles, cottages, pubs, and gardens, Susannah and Diann returned to Neville. They settled into the Horden Inn. Susannah perched on the edge of her bed and scanned a brochure about the village.

"It says Neville also has tea shops, two churches, and a castle."

"Oh, I can hear your brain-wheels turning." Diann placed her shirts in a dresser drawer. "The obsession must be fed." She raised her eyebrows in mock surprise.

Susannah tossed a pillow at her, then rummaged through her bag for the realtor listings. "I like this village. There were a couple of cottages I found here in my research. This place spoke far more than any of the others. And it is one of the villages where some of my ancestors lived."

"Hey, you may be related to Hodge." Diann winked.

"Could be. I need to ask him more about his family."

Diann sighed and paused her unpacking. "Why don't we go for a walk? It doesn't get dark till late, and I'm restless. We may see some cottages from your list."

"You're always restless—got more energy than your four-year-old grandson."

"Ha . . . I wish. Grab your purse, and let's take it outside, sister!"

The cool early evening air was invigorating. Susannah pulled her light jacket closed and inhaled a familiar scent that she couldn't place. "I'm not sure what that aroma is, but I like it."

"That's another thing—your nose is too sensitive. What's that all about?" Diann gave her friend a tight-lipped grin.

"Sense of smell can trigger memories powerfully. Maybe it's an ancestral pull to this place."

"I never thought of it that way, but I suppose it's true. If I smell biscuits baking, I always think of my grandmother. She made the most wonderful biscuits." Diann tilted her head back and closed her eyes. "I can almost see and smell them right now. Browned to perfection, fluffy circles of joy."

Susannah's delighted laugh brought Diann back from her past.

"Such a nice memory." She chuckled as they walked on in companionable silence.

As they strolled along the main street, Susannah studied the brochure. That internal tug toward Neville wrenched at her again. The market cross remained at the square's center as it had since the thirteenth century. At the end of the street, St. Gregory's Church beckoned, parts of it dating back to 1085. A defensive fortified tower, built in 1330, rose above the lower stone structure. Late afternoon sun glinted off the grey edifice that cast it in an amber-hue. It stood proud as it had once protected the village from marauding Scots, the eight ancient bells waited to warn citizens. Susannah could very nearly hear the past sounds of this history-filled village.

They stopped in front of the enclosed churchyard, its gravestones tilted sorrowfully, etchings worn away by time and weather.

"I don't want to walk in there right before dark," Diann's voice wavered.

"What? Are you serious? You're not afraid, are you?" Susannah teased.

"Of course not. I'm not fond of cemeteries at any time of day . . . or night." Diann drew a deep breath. "It's so sad to see all those lives gone, not knowing where they ended up." She shoved her hands deep into her pockets and stepped away from the cemetery.

Susannah drew her gaze from her friend, entranced by the antiquity of the stones. "I wonder if any of my ancestors are buried here? It's too bad that most of the engravings have worn off on the oldest stones." Her voice was solemn. She traced the top of the churchyard's closed gate with an outstretched finger. The yellow facade of the museum across the street darkened in evening shadow. "Hate that the museum is closed."

"Yes, sad." Diann gave her a gentle shove.

Susannah realized her friend's sense of morbidity. She picked up her pace, leaving Diann to follow.

"Hey, where are you off to? I thought we would explore." She added, "Except the cemetery, of course."

"We are." She held up a map. Susannah pointed to the street they were on. "If we go this way and turn right by the pharmacy, and down a short way and take another right, there's a cottage for sale. I couldn't tell much from the photos. But you never know . . ." Her voice trailed off as she studied the map.

Diann reached for the map, and Susannah released it. They stopped at the corner and spotted The Wynd posted on the building across the street. "We're on the right track," Diann gave a wave. "We turn here."

Susannah simpered. "Aye, aye, Captain."

After a short walk, they reached a paved one-lane road. A house's exterior wall curved to follow the turn. It was a medley of older grey stones at the base and newer red bricks stacked to the roof. A few feet further, a white gate led to an alley of sorts. The sign on the gate read— Beware of the Ferrets. Diann and Susannah glanced at one another and burst out laughing.

A sandstone wall topped with moss lined the left side of the road, and on the other side were trees. Beyond a deep curve, the cottage stood to their left. A white-washed gate hung loosely on its hinges.

"Hmm . . . it's seen better days." Diann stood with fists on her hips, lips pursed.

Susannah squeezed between the gate and wall and slipped on a moss-covered stone. She grasped Diann's shoulder for support.

"I'm not sure this is what you were looking for, Sue. It's dilapidated."

They gaped at the shabby thatched cottage. The panes stared, dark and lifeless. Plaster crumbled amidst dark green ivy that clawed its way to the roof. What was left of the garden held more weeds than flowers. A few struggling blooms peeked out like small bright insects climbing barren stalks.

Diann hung back for a moment and moved to the front window and peered through the dirt-encrusted glass. "The inside doesn't appear bad, but it could use a coat of paint. I wonder if the structure is solid."

"It doesn't matter." Susannah stood rooted to the spot and absorbed the derelict sight.

"Yes, I suppose you're right. It's too dilapidated to consider."

"I mean, it doesn't matter." Susannah pulled the realtor listing from her pocket, glanced at the cottage, and envisioned it as it could be. The tug inside her tightened, and joy swelled. "This is where I belong."

Chapter Two

Neville, North Yorkshire, England
2019

The cottage grew shabbier each day. The panes hung, cracked and lifeless, desire to live again in its windows like eyes in search of someone to revive its former splendor. Faded plaster revealed underlying stones of a previous life, deep green ivy weaving in, out, and up to the thatched roof. Exceptional artisanship from years long past held it together.

Each day, April Conyers paused on the path to stare longingly at the cottage as memories of when it was inhabited returned to her mind. She regretted those last days of secondary school education, before her short stint at Uni. At that time, she'd been painfully shy. The lovely, yet tired-looking woman, had moved into the cottage. She'd be gardening in her yard when April walked by. April made a point to walk past the cottage whenever possible, to view the progress of the cottage restoration. The woman had an American accent, her voice was sweet and kind, and there was a glint in her eyes when she greeted April with a "good morning" or "good afternoon."

One day the woman asked April if she'd like to sit in her garden and share tea and biscuits. Timidly, she'd declined. The woman was friendly but never invited her again. Oh, how she wished she'd said yes. Months later, she became brave and walked with purpose to the cottage to invite herself for tea, but no one came when she knocked. She tried again and again, noticing weeds as they crept into once immaculate flowerbeds. Then she was away to Uni.

Upon her return, many months later, April approached the cottage and saw a young man leave. He locked the door behind him. Soon after, the cottage became more derelict. No one lived there since. Each time April passed by her heart felt its sadness.

Now, two years later, April strode on her way from work and paused. A man stood in front of the cottage, arms across his chest, brows furrowed.

With a surge of boldness, April stepped toward him. The closer she got, the more she noticed the slump in his shoulders—shoulders that appeared beaten with the weight of grief. Hesitant to intrude on a private moment, she pushed on.

"Hello," she said in a small, cheerful voice.

Startled, he turned with eyes wide. His voice taut, he said, "Hi. Sorry. I wasn't aware that anyone was there." He presented a halfhearted smile, voice clipped in irritation.

His accent held her attention. "I didn't mean to surprise you. I have seen no one taking an interest in this cottage for some time."

His brow wrinkled. "You live around here?"

"Yes, and . . ." She wet her lips. "I've passed here almost every day, and the sweet lady who lived here even invited me for tea once, though I was too shy to accept." She hesitated. "But that was a long time ago. When I dropped by again, she was gone. Sometime later, I saw a man come out of the cottage. I never saw her again."

An awkward silence grew. His blue eyes stared at her—vacant. She waited for him to speak.

❦

Ryan's mind flew into his painful past and almost made him shudder. He saw the woman who had once lived in the cottage, yet she was younger, trying to raise a small son alone in the U.S.

"I'm sorry to intrude. I should be going. It was nice to meet you . . ."

"Sorry. My name's Ryan." Tentative, he reached out his hand. "I'm not myself right now."

She gripped his hand in hers. "I'm April."

The warmth of her hand engulfed his, a tingle of energy shot through his palm.

"Would you like to go for a cup of tea? There's a nice shop around the corner." April croaked, and cleared her throat.

Ryan glanced at his wristwatch. "Sure. I have time before my train."

April walked by his side as she pointed out directions as they strolled, nervously chatting. Footsteps shuffled around them. People were at the end of their day—heading home from work, tourists chatting with excitement after a day of sightseeing. Various aromas from the pubs and tearooms blended in the air.

"Well, here we are." She stopped in front of an old structure that must have dated back at least five hundred years. The timber-framed building had a plaster, facade.

"I hope you like this place. It has a lot of character and history. It's one of my favorites."

"This is the sort of place my mom would've liked. Everything had to be about character or have a feel to it." He pulled his gaze from hers.

"It's definitely got that. It's also a bakery. I meet friends here and sometimes come alone as a sanctuary of sorts."

The yellow sign above the door read, High Tea, in bold blue letters. The bell jingled as they walked through. White iron tables and chairs placed haphazardly in the petite room bordered the bakery with no divider between the two spaces. Arrangements with fresh daisies peeked from the center of each table. Traditional lace curtains adorned the large bow windows. Display cases were in view of the tables, and wonderful aromas filtered through the room from the unseen kitchen.

Once seated, April commented on Ryan's earlier mention of his mother. "Your mum sounds like someone I would've enjoyed visiting with." The server came over to their table before Ryan could respond. After April greeted her, the girl gave them each a menu. She smiled at Ryan and turned toward April. "How's the bookshop?"

"Splendid. I think I unpacked a dozen boxes of new books today. I could murder a cuppa to get me through the rest of the day." Without a glance at the menu, she told her, "Earl Grey and a cinnamon scone, please."

"Extra clotted cream and strawberry jam?" She raised her eyebrows.

"Oh, yes. You're a dear," April entwined her fingers on the table in front of her as the server turned to Ryan.

"And for you, sir?"

Ryan had a hard time moving his attention from April. How old was she ... about twenty-five? Her long, auburn hair hung straight with wispy bangs. She appeared to be just over five feet and of average build. Her face radiated kindness and a sincerity that he found uplifting, with a smile that lit round hazel eyes set in ivory skin.

He glanced at his menu. "Um, I guess the same."

"Good choice, love." The server winked at him.

April shook her head. "Watch out. She's a bit of a flirt."

Ryan bit his lip and hoped his cheeks weren't red. He changed the subject. "You must come here often if she knows your order."

"I do. Their scones are the best this side of the county. Award-winning. I'd eat them every day if I could," Her lips curved upward. "Do you like scones?"

"Can't remember ever having tried them, but . . ." He didn't complete the sentence. He'd started to say scones were a favorite of his mom's.

April gave him a blank stare. "Pardon me?"

"The scones. I can't remember ever having tried them." He repeated as he regarded the table. Well-manicured fingers fidgeted with the tablecloth.

"Well, you're in for a tasty bit."

Ryan asked about the cottage, which they discussed until their order arrived.

After a thank you to the server, April bowed her head and said a short prayer. Slathering clotted cream and strawberry jam on her scone, she added sugar to her tea. Ryan watched her, then dropped his gaze to his untouched plate.

"I'm sorry. I should've asked if you'd like to say the blessing."

"No need to apologize." He wasn't comfortable with the question. The subject of religion brought back painful memories. And—what was he doing here with a stranger? Yet she appeared to be nice, and after seeing the cottage again it brought on an uncommon desire for companionship. A flash of sunlight drew his gaze out the window to the view past April's shoulder. How many times had his mom walked this way and peered into the windows of the shops along the street—to come to this tearoom and enjoy her tea and scones? He fought to gain composure, his voice hoarse and unrecognizable. "No, it's fine. I'm not one to say grace." The window held his gaze.

He knew he seemed distant as he watched her from his peripheral vision. April tilted her head. But he had accepted her invitation for tea. Perhaps he was tired from travel. He mimicked April and prepared his scone as he'd seen her do, except he put too much cream and a blob shot out the side onto the teapot and tablecloth.

Their laughter ended the awkwardness. Simultaneously, they blotted the stain with their napkins, their fingers brushing, as the server arrived to clean the mishap.

April shifted in her seat and looked away. "Is this your first visit to the U.K.?"

Ryan leaned back, a smile on his lips. "This is very good." His cup clicked as he returned it to the saucer. "To answer your question, no, it's my second time. Two years ago, I was the one you saw leaving the cottage. My mother was the woman who owned it." He swallowed the lump in his throat.

Her eyes wide, she shifted her position. "That was you?"

"Guilty." Lips pressed tight, he shrugged and curled his long fingers around the teacup.

Checking his watch, he released a groan. "Guess I've missed my train." He added, "But I've enjoyed the company."

April's chin dropped to her chest. "I'm sorry. Where was your train to?"

"To London, to . . ." He paused. "I've business to attend to there, then I fly home day after tomorrow."

The server returned to see if they needed anything. "I'd like to pay please." Ryan gave her his credit card.

April reached out and touched his arm. "Please allow me. I'm the one who invited you."

"No, no. It's the least I can do. You've been more than kind. Besides, perhaps this can be repayment for not having tea with my mom. She would've enjoyed meeting you."

"If I may ask, will your mum return soon?"

"No ..." Ryan cleared his throat and looked out the window again. "No, she won't be back. I'm here to put it up for sale. That's why I'll be in London."

She put a hand to her mouth. "I'm so sorry for your loss, Ryan. I've just realized. How awful."

He didn't respond but dipped his chin into a half nod.

"And you're here to sell her cottage?"

"That's the plan. It's not needed any longer." He cradled the cup as he stared into it. "Do you know anyone who may be interested?"

"Yes." She wet her lips. "I mean—I'd love to buy it, but I suppose I should ask the price first." Her swallow was audible. "Also, I suppose I need to see what condition it's in on the inside, what with the cost of fixes and all." She muttered as her shoulders hunched.

"I can tell you what the realtor said was a fair price. As is."

"What do you mean by 'as is'?"

One corner of his mouth lifted. "It means with no repairs made. You buy it; you fix it. I would take care of it myself and get a better price, but I can't stay here long enough to oversee the renovations, so I'll let it go as is."

"I love fixing things up and have helped my mum do cosmetic bits to my parents' flat." April beamed. "I could hire out the internal stuff, like plumbing and electrical work." She played with the ring she wore on her right hand, a small silver band in the shape of a Celtic knot. Ryan had seen a ring like that somewhere before.

"You could get an estimate before you go any further and decide if the cost of the house, coupled with surface repairs, would work for you."

"Yes, that's brilliant. Won't you have to stay longer though? It may take a few days to get an estimate, and a loan could take a while."

He formed a steeple with his fingers and tilted his head back. "Why don't I take the next train to London and settle things with the realtor. I'll come back tomorrow and get a hotel room. There is a hotel here, right?"

"A very charming inn." April glanced at her watch. "The next train to London is in about two hours. We could walk over to the Horden Inn and see if they have a vacancy."

"Perfect."

The server returned with his card. "Thank you, sir."

Ryan nodded and placed his napkin on the table. They stood and moved to leave. Ryan made a motion for her to precede him. "After you."

She watched him with appreciation as he held the door open for her.

❦

The walk was short, so April ambled to prolong it. Not much was said until Ryan asked about the market cross, and she explained her town's history. The inn loomed ahead, three-storied with multiple chimneys rising from the age-worn roof. A carved wooden crimson sign hung over the door—Horden

Inn.

Rubbing the back of his neck, Ryan inquired, "Are there any other inns?"

"Yes, and there are also a couple of B&Bs." Uncertain why he asked, she offered, "It's rather nice. You could peek at a room if you'd like. Mr. Talbot wouldn't mind."

"This is fine. Simply curious." He shoved a hand into his pocket and rocked on his heels before he reached for the heavy oak door. Ryan held it open for April. Their shoes echoed lightly on the faded, red slate floor. Dark wood-paneled walls hung with painted plates and charcoal artwork, enclosing the narrow room. Ryan followed her to the front desk. She tapped a silver bell on the counter. An immense brick fireplace arranged with flickering candles of staggered height emitted a soft glow into the dim room.

Ryan took in the aged room. "Feels like we've stepped into the past."

The sound of shuffling feet behind the desk brought their focus back.

"This is Mr. Henry Talbot, the inn's proprietor. Mr. Talbot, this is Ryan . . . ? Sorry, but I don't know your surname."

The portly, ruddy man behind the counter emerged carrying a half-eaten apple. He nodded rather than speak around the piece of apple in his mouth.

"Nice to meet you, Mr. Talbot. I'm Ryan Wilkinson. I'm interested in a room if you have one."

He chewed and swallowed. "My pleasure, Mr. Wilkinson. I have a room available. How long will you be with us?" He took another bite from the apple, smaller this time.

"I'm not sure. I suppose I could book for a week and see how it goes."

"Splendid." The bump in his cheek bobbed around as he spoke.

"Okay, put me down for the week." He presented his credit card.

"Thank you, Mr. Wilkinson. Here's your confirmation and key."

Ryan studied the large brass key that appeared as old as the inn. "There's been a misunderstanding. I'll be here tomorrow."

April noticed a flash of frustration in Ryan's eyes as he looked at the key and tightened his grip, his knuckles white. He relaxed, stared at Mr. Talbot and slid the key across the counter.

"So sorry, sir. My apologies." He rearranged the reservation and offered Ryan a confirmation. No mention was made that Ryan had not said when he'd be checking in. "We'll see you tomorrow." He reached for the apple core.

Ryan and April stepped outside. "I guess I need to get to the station. Would you point me in the right direction?"

"I'll do better. It's on my way home. I'll walk with you if you don't mind."

"Not at all." They walked in companionable silence for a few minutes. "About the cottage—would meeting at Horden Inn at six o'clock tomorrow be okay?"

"That should be fine. It's Polly's turn to work Saturday."

"Where do you work?"

April led him though an alley shortcut. "At a bookshop called Books-on-the-Green."

"Very nice. And let me guess. It's near the town green."

"Precisely."

"How long have you worked there?"

"We opened it about two years ago." April watched her feet, and then pulled her gaze to the shops they passed before she glanced at Ryan. His face had taken on a surprised expression.

"You're the owner?"

"Co-owner." April loosely clasped her hands behind her back, her purse bumped into her hip as she walked. "It was a dream of mine. I've always felt a great kinship for books. One can't feel alone or bored while surrounded by good books."

"I can understand that. Though, I must admit I'm not an avid reader. My mom always had our house crammed with books. She'd read to me before bedtime." He let out a sigh and grew pensive.

April didn't press him yet wondered what had happened to his mother. He spoke of her wistfully—not as if they had a recent relationship. She strode beside him in silence, leaving him to his thoughts.

She stopped outside the rail station and turned to him. "Well, Ryan Wilkinson, it has been a pleasure. I look forward to tomorrow."

"Until tomorrow." Ryan stepped toward the ticket office. He turned toward her and reached into his pocket and pulled out a key. "I almost forgot. Here's the key to the cottage. I thought you might want to tour it."

"Are you certain?" The gesture touched April. He nodded

as she accepted the key. "I'd like that very much." He pressed the key into her palm.

Ryan walked toward the ticket counter. April grasped the key, anticipation welling inside her. She would at last see inside the cottage. And to think it might belong to her. She peeped over her shoulder and stole a glimpse of Ryan heading for the train. She turned toward home.

⊗

Ryan boarded the train as his thoughts slipped to April and his mother. He needed to get back to New York. The office couldn't function without him—or so he believed. If he stayed another week in England, they'd think he lost his mind. Was there something special about April, or was it her vague connection with his mom? The two seemed to have a lot in common. Is that why he was staying? Was he trying to make amends vicariously?

Ryan shook his head. He must get a grip. The snack cart rolled by, and he stopped it to purchase a bottle of water. The bills crumpled as he stuffed them into his wallet, and he froze. His fingers fumbled until he found the newspaper article, but the printout of the blog post wasn't there. Nothing. It was gone.

Chapter Three

Neville, North Yorkshire, England
2016

The day was bright, bringing a golden glow to the morning. Susannah leaned back on her heels to appraise the work she'd done to remove weeds from the stone path to the old cottage. Her gaze wandered to the freshly potted plants that stood at attention in ochre-hued clay urns by the door. The windows shone from a thorough scrub she'd given them the day before.

The sound of the gate squeaking brought her attention to a middle-aged woman entering her garden carrying a large blue basket.

Susannah scurried to stand and help her with the burden. The breezy fall day whipped their hair as they greeted one another.

The woman leaned forward and extended a hand, "Good day." She held out the basket to allow Susannah to assist her. "Welcome to Neville. I'm Letice Short."

"Good morning. How sweet of you to stop by. I would shake, but they're dusty from gardening. I'm Susannah Wilkinson. Do come in." She led her through the door and shoved empty boxes aside with her foot. "Please excuse the mess."

"No worries. I quite understand." Letice stepped over the threshold into the lounge. "I won't keep you from your chores." Her gazed surveyed the room with interest. "This is a quite proper cottage. I've never been inside, though I've admired it for years."

"Thank you. Would you like a cup of tea? I'm about to put a pot on. I'm overdue for a break."

Letice gave an energetic nod and followed as Susannah led the way to the kitchen. "Please have a seat." She pulled out a chair at the kitchen table and turned to wash her hands. Over her shoulder she watched her guest. "Have you lived in Neville long?"

"My family moved here when my dad retired from the armed services. He was still quite young at the time. His family, and my mum's, came from Neville and once he got his pension, they returned to the place where they grew up. Since I'm the youngest, I'm the only one of my siblings that was born here. A lovely village it is." She sniffed the air. "Do I smell something baking?"

The timer dinged. "Teacakes. My grandmother's recipe. Been in the family over 150 years." She removed the baking sheet and placed it on a brass trivet. "Just a moment, and they'll be cool enough to eat . . ." She returned to the table and lifted the towel over the basket and peeked inside. "...along with these beautiful scones."

Letice cleared her throat. "How did you come to move to Neville? Do you have any acquaintances here?"

"No, but I fell in love with Neville on a tour stop at the pub. I have ancestors from here. And I . . ." Susannah busied herself gathering the items for their tea. She turned to Letice. "I've always wanted to live in an old English cottage. For me it's anything British—castles, cottages, manor homes, tea and scones."

Letice's smile broadened. "Oh, that brings to mind a slogan my dad would say from the war, 'Tea Revives the World.'" She shook her head with a laugh and continued, "He also loved his scones. When I was but a girl, I vowed to create the best scones ever. That's when I began making raspberry scones. Tried to please him with bits to have with his tea. So, I decided I should bring some to the new occupant of this pretty cottage."

"How splendid. I've prayed about meeting new people here, and God sent you." The teakettle sang out. After she prepared the teapot, she slipped into the chair across from Letice to chat while the tea steeped.

She tapped her toes nervously. "Would you like to come to church with me?"

Susannah's lips curved. "You've no idea how great that sounds. I'd love to. It'll be so nice to have someone to sit with."

Letice squared her shoulders. "I was so afraid you may not be receptive. God prodded me to come here. We're supposed to go where He sends us, even if we're rejected. The rejection part is difficult to swallow though."

They sipped tea, ate scones and teacakes, and got acquainted by sharing their memories. She told Susannah about the history of Neville, and they found they shared a fondness of baking.

Susannah took a bite of a raspberry scone. "Mm, this is unbelievable. You should market these." Her blush warmed Susannah's heart.

"Thank you." Letice reached for her third teacake. "These are delicious. By the by, what ministries have you been involved in?"

Hesitant, Susannah smoothed the sleeve of her blouse, her mind strayed to the painful day at the abortion clinic when the police took away the aggressive protesters. "I counseled women, for the most part young girls, against abortion." She took a teacake and continued between bites. "My main focus was to help my closest friend, Diann, with her job as director of a homeless shelter. I helped serve meals, sort clothes, and distribute items to the homeless."

Letice offered a questioning gaze. "You may be interested in a project that the church is about to begin. We hope to convert an abandoned factory into housing for homeless families."

"Sounds hopeful. How far along is the project?" Susannah twisted in her chair.

"Well, our first goal is to gain support from a wealthy

businessman who grew up here. He has an extensive background with philanthropic work, so we believe it'll be a concern for him. The trouble is, he's a busy man and hard to get in touch with. We'll not give up though."

"He doesn't live here any longer?"

"When he left for university, he came back to visit family from time to time. His parents passed a few years ago. He's an only child, but he returns a couple times a year to stay at his parents' house—a two-story stone house passed down for centuries. Did a complete restoration. It's quite beautiful."

"I bet. Though that's sad. He has no more family, no wife or children?"

"He's divorced. No children. But it's no matter, it hasn't changed Colin. He's still the nicest chap around."

"It can be tough to get a project of that size off the ground since most of the committee members have full-time jobs and families to take care of. I'd like to help. That is, if the others will have me." She lifted the teapot. "More tea?"

"No, thanks." Letice brightened. "Your help would be brilliant. I'll mention it to our group. They are great people to work with . . . well, except—oh, never mind." She held her tongue and studied her tea.

Susannah didn't prod her to elaborate. "Do you already have the factory?"

"We've made an offer on it and are awaiting a response."

Susannah nodded. "And you think Colin will speed it along with his, I assume, connections?"

"Yes, indeed," she said with the raise of an eyebrow. "Colin's about fifty, and dishy I might add." She patted her hair and gave a cheeky smirk. "Since you're not married, I thought I'd toss that in."

Susannah laughed, her tea rippling like tiny waves in her cup. She already knew she liked Letice and hoped to be friends.

"Anyway, Colin went to school with a couple of our members. They're all younger than me." Letice snorted. "Well, more than a little, but who's counting?"

"I see what you mean. It seems the older I get, the younger people appear."

"I understand how you feel. Age has a way of doing that to one, doesn't it?"

"Yes." Susannah took the last bite of her scone. "Letice, these are the best scones I think I've ever had."

"Thank you, love. My gran's recipe. Three hundred years old." Letice winked. "But, of course, I tweaked them for my dad."

Letice pulled out her cell phone and checked the time. "I suppose I should shove off. I've had a splendid time. And the teacakes are scrumptious."

Susannah held up the basket. "It was so kind of you to welcome me."

"A delight. And you keep the lot." Letice nodded toward the rest of the scones. "Bring the basket to church Sunday if you'd like. St. Gregory's—a few blocks over." She pointed in the general direction of the church. "And I'd love to have you over for Sunday roast."

"That sounds too good to pass up."

"It's decided then, and I'll save a place next to me at

service." Letice moved toward the door and turned back. "I almost forgot. We're having a bit of a do next week, or maybe it's this week. Oh, my. My memory is rubbish." She tapped her chin with a forefinger. "Tell you what, I could give you a ring."

"Sure." Susannah jotted down her cell number and presented the paper to her. "What is a bit of a do?"

"Sorry, love," She gave a dismissive wave. "A party of the committee, more of a meeting with food." She continued toward the door. "We need little excuse to eat at our gatherings. Although it's just a few tidbits, appetizers of a sort. And we're always open to guests."

"I see. May I bring a dish?"

"Brilliant. And you can see how you take to our crazy lot. Cheers."

Susannah waved a goodbye and watched Letice disappear into the crisp morning air. She'd made the right choice, indeed. She belonged here.

CB80

Susannah juggled an armload of shopping bags onto the train platform. Why on earth had she bought so much in Northallerton? She was used to having a car and tossing it all in the trunk. The week had been spent organizing the cottage. Yesterday, she'd had a pleasant roast lunch after church with Letice and her husband, Peter. Tonight, she was to attend the committee gathering and must return home to unload her burden before she had to be at the church.

The walk down High Street toward her cottage brought her in front of a bakery and tearoom, *High Tea*. The warmth, and the strong scent of cinnamon pulled her in. A break with a nice cup of tea after a full day of shopping sounded like heaven. She piled her bags under the nearest table, stepped to the glass counter and examined the pastries. A tall blonde girl greeted her kindly. "May I assist you?"

"I'd like a cinnamon scone and a cup of Earl Grey, please."

"Grand. Would you like clotted cream as well?"

"Of course." Susannah nodded. "And strawberry jam." She added.

The cash register ring coincided with the doorbell. "That'll be three pounds fifty." Susannah passed her a five-pound note. "Back soon."

Another girl appeared at the counter to help the new customer. "How may I assist you, sir?"

"I called in a takeaway for two dozen cinnamon scones for Mr. Heard." A deep, smoky British voice seized Susannah's attention.

"Yes, sir." The girl scurried to the back.

Susannah turned discretely and glanced at the man as she made her way to her table His gaze was on her. Before she looked away, she noted his lightly tanned complexion and brown wavy hair curling over the top of his collar. A feeble smile was all she could manage under his scrutiny as she slipped into her seat, her server arriving with tea.

"I'm sorry, but we're out of cinnamon scones. Would you like another?"

A girl at the counter passed two white boxes to him. "Here's your order, sir."

"Thank you. Have a smashing night." The tall man turned to leave.

"What would you like to exchange for the cinnamon scone?" Susannah's server waited for a response.

The man paused at Susannah's table and peered down at her. "Excuse me, I couldn't help but overhear your request. It seems I've taken the last of the cinnamon scones." He opened one box. "Please take whatever you'd like. I'm certain they won't be missed."

"I'll choose another, but thank you." She analyzed her tea, not able to maintain eye contact with the stranger—his light blue gaze was too intent.

"I insist." He seized a napkin and used it to remove a scone from the box and placed it on the edge of her saucer. Her gaze met his to refuse the offer, but he interrupted. "Would you like another?" His mouth curved into a disarming smile.

She stammered, "Oh, no . . . I . . ."

He persisted. "I'd feel much better if you'd accept."

Susannah held her breath and nodded with what she knew had to be an idiotic grin.

The man placed another scone on the opposite side of the saucer. "I must say, for the price of two scones that smile was well worth it." He closed the box. "Have a marvelous evening." His long legs took him from the bakery. The bell jingled as the door closed behind him.

Neither Susannah nor the girl had moved, their stares followed the man. Susannah smiled up at the girl and shrugged. "And who said chivalry was dead?"

The girl grinned. "Indeed." She lifted her eyebrows. "Be back with your clotted cream, jam—and a plate for your scones."

Susannah drank her tea and savored every bite of the scones, the man's face fixed in her mind's eye. My, but he was nice to look at—and that voice. She shook off the memory and hoisted the bags and returned home with enough time to drop her packages and head to the gathering.

The dusk air turned cooler as Susannah entered High Street toward the church. She tugged her jacket closer. Though not yet dark, it seemed odd walking alone in a new place. The stroll from the cottage was but a few short blocks, and taking it at a brisk pace, Susannah arrived in roughly five minutes.

The stone church stood at the edge of Neville, watching over it as it had for centuries like a sentinel. It had changed over time—grown, reduced to rubble in parts, rebuilt again and again. The newer building on the grounds of the property held the community center where meetings, celebrations, and the like were held by locals.

She stood at the door as she hugged a tin of teacakes to her chest. A deep breath gave her a boost of courage to enter. With deliberation, she settled into a seat at the back of the room, hoping to blend in until Letice found her.

Susannah grew conspicuous, not knowing anyone other than Letice. Eyes down, she rummaged in her purse until she saw a pair of sensible brown loafers appear at the base of her chair.

"Hallo, I don't believe we've been properly introduced."

She looked into the face of a smiling, perky woman who looked as if a little older than Susannah, with bright red hair cut short surrounding a round sweet face.

"I'm Amanda Singleton, the secretary of this lot," she said with a contagious smile.

Susannah extended a hand and was met with a firm grip. "It's a pleasure to meet you."

"Pleasure's mine, dearie. So glad you could join us. Letice told me all about you owning the old cottage. Smashing place."

That was the second time in the span of an hour that she'd heard the word 'smashing'. Previously from the cinnamon-scone man. "I like it and hope to make a lot of improvements. Nothing to change the character, of course. Simply restoring."

Amanda sat sideways in the chair in front of Susannah and faced her, arm dangled over the back of the chair. "Wonderful. Too many people think they have to make everything old seem like new."

"Yes. The character of a historic building needs to remain the same—not made to look like it was built this century."

"Bravo! A like mind."

"Amanda. Where's Amanda?" A firm voice echoed through the room.

She stood and waved. "Over here." She peered down at Susannah. "Duty calls. See ya."

Amanda called the meeting to order as Letice slipped into the chair beside Susannah. She whispered, "I see you met Amanda. She's a prize."

"Welcome all," Amanda announced while everyone was being seated. "First, I'd like to say we have not gotten word back from Colin. But don't lose heart."

A male voice called out, "Don't think he's interested in

helpin' a bunch of dossers and—" Another voice interrupted. "Oh, hush Virgil. Colin's a standup chap."

"Alrighty. Let's not get miffed over nothing," Amanda chimed, settling the din.

The creaking door drew everyone's attention to the back of the room. "Sorry to be late, all. Had a last-minute phone emergency." The man filled the doorway with his broad shoulders and height.

Letice caught Susannah's arm and in an excited whisper, she said, "Colin."

Susannah willed her jaw not to drop as the man stepped into the room. The man with the cinnamon scones.

Chapter Four

Neville, North Yorkshire, England
2019

April strolled the short path to the cottage, hoping she'd be making the trip many times in the future. As she unlocked the door, she trembled. Once over the threshold, the faint sniff of lavender captured her. The modest lounge area lay before her, and she scanned it, but no evidence of the lavender presented itself.

The yellow stone fireplace had a whitewashed mantel with an ornate iron garden gate hung above. The honey-colored stones reminded April of a trip she'd taken to Bath years ago—

many of the buildings there were made of the same material. Facing the street, the large leaded window embraced a built-in seat. Drop cloths covered the furniture like languid ghosts. Beyond an archway that led to the kitchen, April saw the back door to the rear garden.

She pushed the door on her right. It gave a squeak that filled the silence before revealing an office. A dust-coated drop cloth covered the desk facing the window facing the street, its vantage point divulging the front garden. April removed the desk chair cover to find it upholstered in pink and cream toile. As she lowered herself into the chair, she leaned back into its plush comfort.

Bookshelves built on each side of the large bow window drew her attention. They were crammed to capacity with books and bric-à-brac—miniatures of the Eiffel Tower, Big Ben, the Statue of Liberty—souvenirs from travels, she assumed. She pushed herself up and started as something brushed her foot. Fearful of what she'd find—a spider was one of her greatest fears—she glanced down to find a crumpled paper. Gently, she retrieved it and smoothed out the wrinkles. It appeared to be a printout from a blog post.

WOMAN EXTRADITED FROM ENGLAND ON MULTIPLE CHARGES

I'm questioning the validity of the charges made against a local woman who was the subject of an arrest report posted in the City News. The newspaper had buried the story in the bottom corner of page 15. The headline was misleading. In actuality, they arrested the woman because on multiple charges no first-time offender rights apply. It's one strike, and you're out. No lighter sentence. I've attached the arrest report below. Note the vagueness of the charges against this woman. What's the true story here?

The text ended there with no report attached. The paper was torn. Who was this woman?

April placed the paper on top of the desk and stared at it for a time, pondering the possibilities. She shrugged and headed to the kitchen where she saw an old but well-maintained Aga. After a survey of the room, she saw a white-washed drop-leaf table with a vase of dead flowers, heads drooped miserably. The dirt-encrusted window of the back door looked onto the rear garden, enclosed by a stone wall.

Beyond the wall and through the trees, the view resembled a beautiful pastoral watercolor with a field of vibrant yellow canola flowers. A wide stream was a silver ribbon meandering across the landscape, sun glinting off the water between the trees. The scene brought back fond memories of summers with her grandparents. Days of running through fields, avoiding new plants. Her grandfather had been so particular about his plants. April turned back to the room.

The door to her left opened into a small washroom. White distressed cabinets lined the French-yellow walls.

In the kitchen, April noticed the back door had lace panels pushed to each side of the glass, covered with dust that blocked the design. Odd how they had been right in front of her a moment ago, and she'd paid them no attention. The gorgeous landscape captivated her.

April took note again of the lounge's covered furniture—an

overstuffed armchair, a small sofa with a square table between them, a coffee table, and a rocker.

She walked back to the office and opened the door across from it to reveal a loo with plastered off-white walls, a claw-foot tub, and yellow cupboard.

Down the short hall, she stepped into a tiny room. Sun streamed in from the window, dust motes dancing in the air. A small antique settee nestled against a wall. An oval table with more dead flowers in a vase and a rose floral tea service seemed ready for guests at any moment.

Floor to ceiling shelves stuffed with boxes filled the closet, each labeled with the name of a city or country. With care, she touched each box as she read the names aloud. Travel had always been a dream of hers.

She dragged herself from the boxes. The temptation to open one was far too strong. The last room was down the hall—the bedroom. It contained a four-poster bed. Bronze Victorian lamps atop nightstands stood guard on each side of the bed. A corner possessed a burgundy wing-back chair accompanied by a floor lamp and square table. The chest of drawers and a tall, framed mirror on a stand completed the furnishings of the room.

She returned to the kitchen and peeked into the back garden again, over the wall to the hillside. Yes, the garden was meager, but the view more than made up for it.

"I love this place." April sighed. "Lord, if it's meant for me, it'll be in my price range." The lavender scent wafted to her again. She lifted her head and sniffed the air like a puppy onto a new smell. She walked as close to the wall as she could, inching her way around the perimeter of the room.

The fragrance grew stronger near the fireplace. She knelt and peered inside and spotted a bundle of dried lavender tied with a paper ribbon. April imagined that the smell would permeate the room throughout the summer. When the cool nights of autumn came, the lavender under the first fire of the season would perfume the entire house. April wanted to be the one who lit that fire.

附

A blinding storm greeted Ryan as he stepped from the train platform in Neville. He pulled his raincoat tighter and hugged his bag to his chest. As he gripped the umbrella, he sprinted for the curb to a waiting taxi. "Horden Inn, please."

"Yes, sir."

The inn was a few short minutes from the station, but the taxi ride saved Ryan from being soaked to the skin. He paid the driver, gave a generous tip, and another sprint carried him into the inn's lobby. He'd arrived with thirty minutes to spare before meeting April for their six o'clock appointment. He propped his wet umbrella next to the coat rack.

"Hallo, Mr. Wilkinson," chimed Henry Talbot as he pushed his spectacles onto the bridge of his large nose. "Nasty day to be out and about."

"You got that right." Ryan placed his bag on the stone floor and shed his coat.

"Here's your key for number 37." Mr. Talbot pointed to the stairs. "Sorry, no lifts here. Up the stairs, three floors, second room on the right. Great view of the village and the countryside beyond."

"Sounds good. I'm meeting someone here at six. Do you

serve full meals in the evening?"

"'Fraid not. But since the weather is so horrid, I could get the missus to throw somethin' together for ya and your lady friend." He chuckled.

"She's a business associate," Ryan said, his voice gruff. "Thanks for the offer. I'll let you know."

He snapped open the newspaper and answered, "You're most welcome."

"I'll be down at six." Ryan picked up his bag and climbed the many stairs to his room without effort.

The room was masculine, in a Victorian-style like the lobby—paneled walls, a mahogany four-poster bed, and a hunting scene tapestry above it. He placed his bag on the stone hearth. Electric logs glowed from the mock fireplace. He changed his clothes and made his way downstairs. Thick Persian carpet muted the creaks of each step.

With five minutes to spare, he stepped into the inn's lounge and was greeted by a perky server with a long blonde ponytail.

"Hallo, sir. I'm Petronella." She greeted him with a wide toothy grin and motioned for him to be seated. "'ow may I 'elp you?"

Ryan greeted her and asked for coffee and a small appetizer of her recommendation.

"How 'bout mini Cornish pasties?" The grin reappeared.

"What's a pasty?"

"Like a tart but filled with meat and potatoes."

"That sounds good, but just a small portion as I'm not certain if we'll be going to dinner later. Where I'm from we have something very similar." Memories inundated him. "It's what my grandmother called a meat pie."

"Yeah, it's kinda like that. I bet they stole the idea from Cornwall." Petronella cackled. "I'll be back in two shakes of a duck's tail." She waddled away, her blonde ponytail swinging from side to side.

The room wasn't large, just enough space to house five wood-stained tables and mis-matched chairs of varying sizes and styles. The area was cozy, warm, a place meant for relaxing.

Ryan faced the lounge's entrance and within minutes was rewarded when April walked in wearing a yellow raincoat and black rubber boots—or wellies as they called them.

"Oh, this weather. I thought I'd have to swim here. It's lashing out there, and my brolly wouldn't work. I'm sorry, but I must be a sight all drenched from head to wellies." She laughed and smoothed her dark hair.

He stood at her approach. She was a mess—damp spots on her jeans and drops of rain spattered on her cheeks. Yet he found her appearance pleasing, and her smile infectious. He matched it with one of his own and helped her off with the coat.

"Thank you ever so much." He took the coat to the lobby coat rack. She sat and pressed the wrinkles from her red and blue plaid shirt. Ryan noticed a small gold cross dangled from her neck.

"Well, now that's done. Hello, Ryan. How are you?"

"At the moment, fine, though I was also drenched when I arrived." He tugged on his shirt cuffs. "Nothing a quick change couldn't repair—and, don't worry, you look nice." He glanced at his watch to avoid her eyes. *Did I just say that?*

"Thank you." April took extra care unfolding her napkin. Petronella's timely arrival met with Ryan's silent gratitude. "Here you go, dears." She placed a gold teapot and a yellow cup and saucer in front of April. Sugar and milk followed. "I knew what you'd like, love, as soon as I saw you come in."

April thanked her and turned to Ryan. "Won't you try the tea?"

"Maybe later. Hot coffee sounds too good right now."

"Pasties out in a sec."

Ryan nodded, and the ponytail bounced away again. "I hope you don't mind. I ordered an appetizer. Mr. Talbot said they don't serve a full menu here, but 'the missus could throw something together'." A corner of his mouth twitched.

"If you prefer a meal, there's a tavern two blocks over. Talbot's Tavern. Mr. Talbot's grandfather still owns and runs it."

"His grandfather?" Ryan's spoon hovered over his coffee like a bird about to take a dive. Mr. Talbot had to be at least fifty. "How old is he?"

"Almost a hundred and spry as a spring chick." She sipped her tea, her eyes sparkling with amusement. "I've known Mr. Hodge Talbot all my life. He's one-off. No one like him, and . . ."

Ryan spooned sugar into his coffee and added milk. April's upbeat attitude was contagious. He could feel his tension ease, the sensation triggering a thought from long ago. She reminded him of his mom, so calm and collected—like nothing could shake her, though as a teenager that trait had caused him a lot of anger and left him with lingering questions.

His mother always seemed so perfect and put-together. But if she was so perfect, why did his dad leave? The question had eaten at him, but now a different emotion gnawed at his insides—regret.

April was speaking, and he hadn't heard what she'd said. ". . . so, Mr. Hodge told them they could just leave."

Ryan laughed with her, but his heart wasn't there, and he hated himself for it. Silence lengthened, and he could taste his embarrassment. Was she aware he hadn't been attentive? Petronella's timing was impeccable again. She presented the pasties between them with ceremony and gave a wide grin. "There ye be." She left before either of them could speak.

April bowed her head. "Thank you, Lord, for this food and for the company of my new friend, Ryan. And please ease the pain of losing his mother. Amen."

Ryan's jaw clenched. He fidgeted in his seat, and mumbled, "Excuse me a moment," and fled the room.

CS&SO

April jerked her head up as Ryan stepped through the doorway. She listened to his fast-paced, muffled footsteps on the carpeted stairs, leaving her with the pasties. She squeezed her eyes shut and Ian—a chap she'd once dated—filled her memory.

The relationship was as brief as her stint at Uni. He'd been a short-tempered guy, always upset over small things, and rushed out like Ryan had done. He hadn't liked her bookish way of life—her habit of mentioning literary characters in their conversations. She'd tried to break the pattern, but books were her life. That's when she'd decided men weren't worth the stress—at least if it meant she had to change who she was.

Chapter Five

Neville, North Yorkshire, England
2016

Susannah couldn't drag her gaze from Colin Heard as Amanda called him to the front of the room. The meeting reconvened. With his presence, they put extra care into the explanation of the plan that caught Susannah up to date on the project's details. She had to admit that it did interest her.

Colin seemed to share that interest, and he promised to get back to the group about the extent of his involvement.

After the meeting concluded, Letice glowed as she nudged Susannah in the ribs. "See, I told you he'd come through."

Susannah patted Letice on the shoulder. "You sure did."

"And what do you think about it all?"

Her attempt to avoid following Colin's movements around the room as he greeted others, fell short. He was an impressive figure. "I'd like to help." She brought her gaze back to Letice.

"Oh, grand." Letice gave Susannah a hug. "I sensed you would." She laughed and led her across the room. "Now, let's get to the food. I'm starved."

Susannah followed her to the refreshment table. Colin approached, and their eyes met and held before she broke the contact. She touched her cheek and felt the heat there. Did he remember her from the bakery?

Before Colin could address her, Letice jumped in, "Why, Colin, thank you so much for being here—and for your generous offer. It's splendid of you."

Colin's green eyes crinkled at the corners. Susannah found it made him even more attractive. "I'm more than happy to help. This place holds such fond memories for me. I hope all local children have the chance to say that one day."

Letice turned to her. "Colin, let me introduce our newest resident, Susannah Wilkinson."

Her stomach fluttered as she forced an extended hand. "It's a pleasure to meet you, Mr. Heard."

"The pleasure's mine. Please call me Colin."

His countenance was as warm as his hand when he grasped hers with a gentle, firm hold. He held it a few seconds longer than was customary.

"It seems Susannah and I already met this afternoon."

The use of her first name didn't go unnoticed. An errant wave of brown hair slid to his temple.

"I trust the cinnamon scones were to your liking."

Susannah watched Letice's eyes widen.

"Yes, very much." Her forgotten cookie tin gripped tight against her chest.

"I'm glad you enjoyed them." He smiled and held her gaze.

She stammered, "I . . . I suppose I should take these to the dessert table."

He opened his mouth to say more, but a honeyed voice from across the room interrupted and pulled his attention elsewhere.

"Colin, dear!"

The door slammed with a bang. All eyes turned to face a voluptuous brunette glide across the room, wearing a turquoise dress laced with sequins, straight to Colin. "I haven't seen you in ages, darling. Where have you been?" She pulled him to her and kissed his cheek. Her hand lingered on his forearm as her eyes consumed him.

"Oh, here and there. The usual." He stepped back a pace, but she pulled closer.

The woman nodded at Letice, ignored Susannah, and tightened her lips a moment before stretching into a smile not reflected in her eyes. She greeted Letice and introduced herself to Susannah. "I'm Vita Morris. And this devil and I—" she slapped Colin's arm with affection "—go all the way back to primary school." She stage-whispered, "He's been secretly mad for me ever since. Haven't you, love?"

He ignored the question and cleared his throat.

Susannah responded with a forced smile, "Hello. Nice to meet you."

"An American. How nice." She flashed perfect teeth at them again and Susannah noted her grip on him tightened.

"You are quite the character, Vita." His gaze danced around the room, one eye twitching.

Susannah couldn't tell if he was interested in this woman or merely humored her. What did it matter to her? She'd just met the man.

Vita looped her arm through his and steered him toward the food. "Let's do have some refreshment and catch up. I'm quite peckish."

Colin glanced over his shoulder to the women and said, "Pardon me," as he was led away.

Letice scowled. "Vita Morris . . . that woman sinks her claws into whatever, or whomever, she wants." She met Susannah's gaze, and softened her features. "Oh, never mind me. Let's have food. Shall we?"

"Indeed." Susannah forced the corners of her mouth upward, even though something about Vita with Colin made her blood simmer.

⚜

"Good day, ladies. Welcome to Horden Castle. As soon as everyone has queued up, we'll get started. My name is Annie, and I'll be your tour guide for today."

Susannah and Letice chatted while they waited for the tour to start. After several minutes, Annie excused herself to discover what the holdup was. She returned with haste. "Sorry to keep you. It seems the other ladies want a private tour for their club. Since you were here first, you get your own private tour." She shrugged. "Well, not exactly a queue with just the two of you." Her face brightened.

They wound their way through the castle with typical tourist eyes, examining every detail, poring over information of past occupants.

Annie stood back to let them take in the room they now viewed. Letice pointed out a panel they'd missed on a far wall that spoke of yet another person who had lived at the castle. Susannah laughed. "If my friend Diann were here, she'd say, 'I'm sure they were ancestors of Susannah's.' She loves to joke about my many English and Scottish forbears."

The thought of her dear friend and the antics of their cottage-scouting trip brought a broad grin to her face that she couldn't hide—she knew she wore a goofy smile—Diann had remarked on it countless times. She shrugged. "Though, I'm sure thousands of other people could make a similar claim."

"I wouldn't dismiss that so fast." Annie glanced around them. "It's marvelous that you can walk these halls where your ancestors once lived." With affection, she stroked the doorframe as if petting a cat, her expression wistful. "How many times your ancestors walked through this door—on their way to seek someone, run an errand, or stroll in the gardens."

Susannah broke into her thoughts. "Annie, are there any books in the gift shop that list the timeline and people who lived here?"

"Yes. There are several."

Susannah always had a sense of belonging when she visited the homes of her ancestors, but Annie's revelation brought a new excitement to her heart and mind. She was walking the halls they walked, peering across the hills and valleys they viewed, and it gave her chills. She couldn't explain her love for this country. There may be truth to genetic memory, though not past lives, or reincarnation, because she didn't believe in that sort of thing. However, genetics are factual.

Letice gently shook her arm. "Susannah, are you listening? Do you want to browse the shop or sit in the garden?"

"Sorry. The shop. I want to get one of the books Annie told us about."

The tour now over, Annie led them to the shop and told them she had to go take the next tour. "I've enjoyed the two of you. Please come back sometime."

"Now that I live in Neville, I'll be sure and make regular visits to my family home."

"I haven't been here in many years and had forgotten how well maintained it is—seems much better than I remember." Letice paused. "Who's taken over management?"

Annie answered, "Colin Heard." She released an appreciative sigh.

"Colin? Oh, my, we just saw him at a meeting, and he didn't mention that." Letice teased. "Annie, aren't you a little young for him?"

"Oh, well, yes," she stammered. "But he is rather dishy." Her face flushed. "No harm in admiring him from afar."

Letice gasped, her gaze on another part of the garden. "Oh, no. There he is . . . I hope he didn't hear us."

Susannah turned and found where Letice stared. "Oh, girl." She laughed. "How high-school of you."

Letice pulled her gaze from Colin. "What?"

"Oh, never mind. Merely teasing." Their subject held Susannah's regard. Even though she'd met the man at the meeting, and previously in the tearoom, she felt a peculiar connection.

Colin Heard had a presence about him, and he wasn't movie-star gorgeous but not unattractive either. It was the way he walked, the movement of his hands when he spoke, the way he tilted his head slightly while he listened—the timbre of his voice. The man he spoke with held his attention. He wasn't distracted by his surroundings but devoted his complete awareness to what this man, the gardener, had to say. Mr. Heard was as attentive to him as if he were a business colleague, which spoke volumes of his integrity.

Letice slanted her head to one side, eyes narrowed. "Your expression tells me that you do think he's attractive."

Susannah could hear Diann's voice again, something she'd said in the past. 'I haven't seen you look at a man in decades—well at least not more than a fleeting glance.' Diann's smiling face came to mind. Her dear friend had helped her through many hard times in the past twenty years.

Susannah pulled her concentration back to the present and watched Colin approach and speak to Annie, a few yards away.

"Good afternoon, Annie. How goes the tour guide business?" His smile was warm and relaxed.

"Hello, Mr. Heard." Annie's voice faltered as she blushed.

"The tours are going splendidly. I'm on my way to start another now."

"Well, I won't keep you. Have a good day." He turned to Letice and Susannah. "Good afternoon, Letice, Susannah. I hope you enjoyed the tour."

Their voices rose as one. "Yes."

"So glad. Wish I had time to chat, but I've a conference. Have a good afternoon." He strode toward the castle grounds exit.

Letice gave Susannah a curious expression. "Let's have lunch, shall we?"

☙

High Tea was a buzz of activity when Letice and Susannah arrived. They chose a table by the large window facing the street. Susannah set her heavy shopping bag down with a thud.

"You must've bought enough books at the castle to start your own library." Letice grinned. "Although, I suppose through the years I may have collected as many."

"I understand. I'm addicted to books—among other things. Like purses."

Letice cackled. "I quite get that."

They studied their menus while, by turns, they watched buyers at the open-air market outside the window. Two women browsed long, colorful scarves. The younger of the two chatted with animation about the choices while the older woman grinned and listened as she made her own selections.

Susannah sighed, and returned to her menu as the server

approached with a greeting. She took their orders and glided away.

They settled back into their chairs, and Letice began the conversation with a question. "So, tell me what brought you to Neville?"

Taken aback, Susannah read between the lines of the question. Time to ease into a closer friendship. "It's a long story I'm sure you don't want to hear. Suffice it to say that I have had a long-held interest in anything involving the U.K. It began when my aunt did genealogy back in the 70s and found all of our English and Scottish ancestry. Ever since, I've been hooked. A true Anglophile."

Letice grimaced. "You're likely more knowledgeable about this country than I am. Sad, right?"

Susannah gave a knowing smile. "I realized a long time ago that most of us know less about our own surroundings than other parts of the world we're interested in. Makes little sense though."

Their food arrived, and they dug in. Letice held her fork half-way to her mouth. "Back to your long story."

"Sorry, yes. After my son left for college, I was on my own since I'd been divorced for years, so I focused on my life as a single person. Selfish, I realize, but I dove more into ministry than I had when Ryan was young. It's a bitter-sweet thing, but he became so independent when he went to college and didn't need me any longer. He got an excellent job in New York and moved on with his life and career." Her gaze slid back to the market outside the tearoom, eyes moist with unshed tears. She noticed the two women who now strolled down the street in cheerful conversation, their purchased scarves around their necks, a mother and daughter on holiday, she supposed.

"I'm sorry I urged you to share an obviously painful memory." She toyed with her teacup.

"It's okay. I'm fine." She assured Letice and took a deep breath. "On my fiftieth birthday I had an epiphany. What was I waiting for? Diann and I came to England on a scouting mission to view cottages for sale that I'd found online. We'd looked at a few in various villages, but once I came to Neville, home to some of my ancestors, I realized this was the place. Talbot's Tavern and meeting Mr. Hodge Talbot was my defining moment."

"Oh, Hodge is a lovely man. I can see how you'd be taken with him."

"Yes, he is. We should have lunch at Talbot's next time." They ate in companionable silence for a while. "Now, it's your turn. Tell me more about yourself. How did you come to live in Neville?"

"It's rather dull. I told you how my parents settled here after my dad left the services. He was in France during the war. I was born here, and here I am still."

"There's something to be said for living in one place your whole life. My father was in the military, and we moved a lot. Even after he retired. He changed jobs as often as I change purses."

Letice chuckled. "I can't say I've ever experienced that way of life. Mine's a quiet one."

"It was painful at times to leave friends, a school you'd just gotten accustomed to and all." Susannah sipped her now tepid tea. "Seriously, other than getting married and now having grandchildren, what are your interests? Your passions?" She studied Letice's face and glimpsed mixed emotions.

"I love to bake. Bonkers, I know." Letice shrugged. "Most would find that a bore."

"What's wrong with that? I take pleasure in it myself."

"You don't understand. I love to bake and would all day if I could. My husband says I'm daft. I nicked my grandmother's recipe for the raspberry scones—and tweaked it."

Susannah straightened and toyed with her necklace. "Why don't you start a tearoom? Your raspberry scones are amazing." She leaned in and whispered, "They're even better than the wonderful scones here."

Letice beamed. "You're too kind."

"No, I'm not being kind. I'm being honest. Have you ever thought about it? Seriously?"

With force, she said, "Yes, I have. But it's only a dream. My husband is so protective. He'd be heartbroken if it failed, and then there's the dosh—sorry, the money."

"If you're serious, I'm sure you could work it out. I'd be glad to be your support group of one. I'm sure Amanda would join us."

Susannah lost herself in thought. She'd had no support from her husband, and now her son, and yet she'd finally made her dream become a reality—with God's help. "Letice, my dream came true when I moved to England. I never thought I'd have the courage to do it, but God made it happen. And He can make your dream come true as well."

Chapter Six

Neville, North Yorkshire, England
2019

"Idiot," Ryan muttered to himself. Forcing back tears, he stumbled to the bed and buried his head in a pillow. The painful scene rolled over him like a huge tumbling boulder, the memory as vivid as if it'd been yesterday. He'd been in his office and was elated at the capture of a very prominent new client. His aunt Diann called and nearly screamed into the phone, gasping between sobs.

"Ryan, I cannot believe what's happened . . ." She drew in a deep breath. ". . . to your mother."

"What's wrong. Has she been in an accident?" He stood, began pacing around his desk, fear gripping him more than he could ever remember.

Diann's deep inhale was audible. "She's been extradited from the U.K.—arrested, brought home, and put in jail."

Ryan's heart beat furiously against his chest. "What?"

"Wayne saw it in the newspaper. I'll send you a copy, but you can probably pull it up online. She . . . she's in prison, Ryan. Has been for a while. I didn't know." Her weeping grew louder, more intense. "I didn't know."

It was Ryan's turn to pull in a deep breath as he paused to stare out his office window at Central Park. He ran a shaky hand through his hair as he hung his head remembering a recent phone call he'd received from his mother. She'd left a message, but he'd deleted it without listening. He hadn't wanted to hear anything about her prayers nor anything about faith.

"Please calm down, and we'll take care of this. I'll research online and be in touch. I . . . we'll help her. We'll take care of this. Okay?" His voice broke at the strain. The silence festered—he thought the call had been dropped. Until he finally heard her unsteady breathing.

"All right, Ryan. Please keep me posted. I'm praying." She sniffled into the phone. "Bye, sweetie. I love you." The phone clicked.

Tears now slipped down his face, self-hatred expanding into his very core. He had to get a grip and go back downstairs to April. Why had her praying over their meal triggered that particular memory? What would she think of him? He'd never faced his sorrow like this—not even as a child. His father told him that men don't cry, so he'd always shoved his emotions down deep. Once more he'd do so.

He pushed himself from the soft comfort of the bed and ambled to the bathroom where he splashed his face with cold water and gasped at the contact. As he rubbed the towel over his face, he took in his reflection in the mirror and asked himself if he could lie to her.

His excuse would be that he'd forgotten to make an important phone call and rushed off without regard. Would she be able to see through it? Maybe this once. There was no way she could be aware of the truth about his mother.

It was bizarre how he always thought of her as mother when it concerned something unpleasant and mom when it was a fond memory. Sometimes it was difficult to separate the two.

೮೩୨୦

April sipped her tea as Petronella bounced to the table. "What's up, love? Where'd that cutie run off to?"

April shoved her shoulders back. "He said he had to take care of something he'd forgotten. He'll be right back."

"Chin up, love. Men can be so unpredictable. And they call us emotional."

April twisted her napkin. "I wouldn't know, Petronella. I've had little experience with men. Are they that difficult to understand?"

"Ha! You don't know the half of it." She turned and swaggered away.

April watched as Ryan entered the room. She stiffened her posture as their eyes met. She hadn't touched the pasties.

He slid into his seat. "I'm so sorry. I forgot to make an important call and shouldn't have left so abruptly. Again, I apologize." Ryan suspended the teapot spout over April's cup, his eyebrows raised as he looked at her.

April nodded. She read pain in his eyes. After a long pause, she said in a low voice, "You shouldn't apologize. I should."

He ran his hands through his hair. "I don't understand."

"I shouldn't have mentioned your mother's passing. I'm insensitive and ought to have realized how painful it must be."

Ryan wriggled in his seat as he lowered his gaze to the table.

"No. I . . . I had to make that call." He averted his eyes as he reached for a pasty.

She brought her teacup to her lips with a nervous twitch.

Ryan fractured the silence, now cheerful. "Well, let's try these pasties and talk about the cottage."

As they nibbled, the conversation merged to a more relaxed rhythm as they spoke of the cottage, village sights, and local history. April was careful not to mention his mum. "There's a castle nearby that you may want to have a look-see, if you're interested."

"Do you go often?" Ryan spoke with a pasty poised in front of his lips.

"No, not since I was in school. It's in excellent condition though. A descendant of the original owners brought it back into the family many years ago—Douglas I believe—or was it Butler? Or possibly Weatherly? It was built around 1300. All those names are within that ancestry. It's so hard to sort them out to the time they belong in." She leaned back in her seat. "My memory isn't great regarding dates or names, yet that doesn't lessen my interest or enthusiasm." She shrugged. "A local resident recently bought it. He restored it to what it would've been like centuries before and has tours. Well, his staff does. His business is based in London."

"You know . . . my middle name is Weatherly. It was my mom's maiden name." His expression petulant.

April blinked. "Perhaps your ancestors lived at Horden Castle."

"I remember my mom tried to interest me in our family genealogy. After a while, she yielded and never asked me again. If this place has a special family connection, I'm sure that's a reason she moved here."

"So, you aren't aware of why she chose Neville?"

"Would you care for anything else?" Petronella interrupted before Ryan could reply. "Perhaps more tea and coffee to finish your pasties?"

"I'm fine."

April shook her head and smiled at Petronella.

"All righty. Here's your bill. I'll be back in a flash."

"She's a gem, our Petronella." April grinned. "Her family is somehow connected to the Horden Castle ancestors as well."

"So, you're saying it may relate me to a woman named Petronella?" Ryan gave her a teasing grin.

"I suppose so." April took another pasty and bit into it.

"Do you find any resemblance?" He shifted his head to

show her his profile. April watched as the corners of Ryan's mouth struggled not to curve upward. She laughed, and he joined her. When Petronella re-appeared, Ryan handed her his credit card, and she bounced away again. This time she left without a word, returned in a few minutes, and placed the bill in front of Ryan, a fist on her ample hip.

After reviewing it, he asked where he was supposed to add in the tip. Petronella rolled her eyes. "You, Yanks, worry too much about tippin.' Just sign it and have a nice evenin' with my cousin. She's a love." She was gone with the bill before either of them could respond.

Ryan's eyebrows peaked. "She's your cousin?"

"'Fraid so. I didn't mean that in a bad way. She's very nice. We're distant relatives, and she likes to joke about it." Clutching her bag, she asked, "Are you ready to go?"

Ryan stood by the table and waited for April to lead the way. As they gathered their raincoats and umbrellas, Mr. Talbot spoke from behind his newspaper, "Won't be needin' those." He went back to his newspaper. Ryan helped April into her raincoat and shrugged his on.

The sun painted gold streaks across the cloudless sky as they stepped onto the sidewalk. Slashes of pink and lavender glowed within the sunset. April stood still, taking in the scene. "Magnificent."

Ryan sent her a questioning glance. "Will we be able to view it from the tavern?"

"It's a ten-minute walk. It'll be nearly gone by then," she said, her voice tinged with regret, her eyes sparkling. "We could stop at the green and watch." She added, "If you'd like."

"And a green would be . . . ?"

"A village green is a small park or spot of grass for children to play, have a picnic, or relax. Most villages have one. Ours has benches and a gazebo. It's rather nice."

"Is it on the way to the tavern?"

"There." April pointed to a large grass-covered square a block in the distance.

"Okay." Ryan slowed his pace to match hers.

April appreciated his slower gait as she pointed out a few historic buildings and paused at the green and pointed to a nearby bench. "This one faces the sunset."

Ryan nodded and waited for her to sit and settled beside her. Thin scattered clouds gathered and mingled with varied shades of blue, gold and yellow as the sun slid from sight.

"I'm so amazed at God's creativity," April said, her tone reverent. "No painter could ever put that on a canvas." She glanced at Ryan when he didn't respond.

Ryan kept his gaze on the darkening horizon and rose. "Are you ready for dinner?"

"Yes, please." April grew silent on the walk to the tavern. Ryan hadn't been comfortable with her mention of God or his mother, and she wondered why.

CB☙

Ryan stretched his shoulders to lessen the tension caused by the subject of God—his mother's favorite topic. Was April trying to push her faith on him too? She reminded him of his mother, but he hadn't been uncomfortable about it until now. He ran fingers through his dark hair. April wasn't his mother.

He glanced at her, her expression pleasant, undisturbed by the silence. She stopped in front of a two-storied building. "This is Talbot's Tavern."

"Looks old." Ryan took in the red brick structure, his gaze roaming the facade.

"It should." She glanced at him with raised eyebrows. "It was built in the mid-seventeenth century."

His laugh was light. "Definitely an antique."

"Yes, but I don't think about it much. I suppose growing up here I've taken things for granted. Not very appreciative, is it?"

The notion stirred something inside Ryan—not appreciating something or someone until it was too late.

Ryan considered April, knowing his face reflected his now solemn mood. Upon entering the tavern, April addressed an elderly man with thinning gray hair dressed in sturdy work pants, a white button-down, and tweed vest. He bent over a book with colorful pictures of roosters, his forehead creased in deep thought. "Hello, Mr. Talbot." April clapped his shoulder.

Nonplussed by the interruption, he greeted her, "Why, hello there, pretty young girl. It's nice to see ya." He noticed Ryan. "And who is this fine-lookin' fella?"

Ryan felt heat rise to his face. "Ryan Wilkinson, sir. Nice to meet you."

Hodge Talbot gripped Ryan's hand with a strength belying his age. "You too, you too." His appraising eyes travelled over the much-younger man.

"Mr. Talbot, it's good to see you. But I'm far from being a

young girl anymore."

"At my age, it seems but yesterday you were in the pram." The wrinkles around his eyes deepened as his smile grew, eyes sparkling with mischief. "I'm teasing."

April placed a kiss on Hodge's cheek. "I know." Turning to Ryan, she continued, "He's quite the jokester. Have a good evening, sir."

"Don't be strangers now." He nodded and held his place in the book.

From their table, the view was of a courtyard with long grass flowing in the breeze and flowerbeds in full bloom. Their brilliance stood out against the stone wall enclosing the garden even as dusk settled into night, and a wall-mounted fountain gurgled from deep in shadow.

Tiny lights dotted the darkening space, their soft glow illuminating the area enough to appreciate the garden in its entirety and offer the illusion of a fairyland. As they waited for service, April stared out at the scene, and in her gaze, Ryan saw both admiration and a child-like wonder. "I love this spot—night or day. Mr. Hodge does such a fine job. You must see it during the day. Although, the lights do bring a certain ambience of intrigue and romance." She coughed sharply, her face reddened, and she fidgeted with the edge of the tablecloth.

Ryan glanced at the courtyard. There was something familiar about it. April spoke, her voice low, but he didn't catch it. Get control of your thoughts and pay attention, he chided himself. He looked at her. "Yes, I'd like to see it during the daytime." It struck him. His mother had written a travel article about this place. He'd seen it in a magazine while in a client's lobby.

The server placed the menus on the table, and Ryan glanced up to see a tall man around his age with his gaze fixed intently on April.

"Good evening, April. How've you been?" the man said, his grey eyes only for her, which somehow unnerved Ryan, though he didn't want to admit it.

She brought her gaze up, seemingly taken aback by the man. "Hi, Tristan." Introducing Ryan to Tristan Durham, he shook the man's hand, matching the strong grasp with his own, the hint of challenge in his eyes not getting past Ryan. Who was this man to April?

Tristan turned his attention back to April. "Thought you'd be out with Polly tonight."

April pushed a strand of hair behind her ear. "Ryan and I have business to discuss and decided to do it over dinner."

Ryan watched their exchange but didn't see the same interest in April's eyes that he saw in the man's.

Tristan only gave a curt nod. "What would you like to drink?"

April asked for water with lemon, then studied the menu as if she'd never been there before. Ryan ordered iced tea.

"Right." Tristan turned on his heel and sped off, his shoes squeaking on the tile. He returned with the drinks before Ryan had read past the appetizers. "Have you decided yet?"

"We need a few more minutes." Ryan heard the curt tone in his voice, and April peered over her menu at him with a curious expression. He lowered his voice and peered back at her. "Sorry, I didn't mean to be rude, but your friend is a tad pushy."

"I guess that's my fault." She sighed. "I try to be nice to everyone, but I think he may have misread my friendliness as more—" She cleared her throat "—well, as more than friendship. We went to school together, and he's a stand-up chap and all, but it's just not like that between us."

Ryan met her eyes. "I see." He raised one brow and added with a smirk, "I suppose we'd better decide before your fellow comes back."

April's mouth fell open, though she quickly closed it, the corners of her mouth tugged upward as she threw him a humorous expression. "Yes, I think you're right. I'll have the fish curry."

"Have you tried the roast?"

"Yes. It's rather tasty. Tender roast, sliced thin, with your choice of steaming vegetables."

"That's a glowing endorsement." He gave a lopsided grin. "Maybe you should write the menu." His cheek tingled from all the smiling and banter. He hadn't enjoyed himself this much in a long time. There was something about this girl. He felt lighter, less burdened, around her, but he had to clear his head and stay focused on the purpose of their dinner.

Tristan suddenly appeared. "So, you'll have the fish curry?" April's smile faltered, and Ryan wished to ease her discomfort somehow. She nodded, eyes downcast.

"I'll have the roast with broccoli and potatoes." Ryan fixed Tristan with a stare, holding contact longer than necessary.

Tristan didn't back down. "Coming right up," he said and left with a scowl.

April's voice was quiet. "How do you do that?"

"Do what?" Ryan took a sip of tea.

"I've never seen Tristan like that. Docile. He always seems in full control of every situation—at least when I've been around him."

"I think he's threatened by another man. Since he doesn't know me or our connection, he believes he's competing with me."

She straightened in her seat. "Hmm . . . I guess that means he suspects he has a chance with me. Am I sending him mixed signals and not realizing it?" She bit her lip.

"From what you've said, and the short time I've spent with you, I find nothing that would show you've given him the wrong impression."

"You seem sure of yourself and reading others. Does this have something to do with your profession, or are you just a good judge of character?"

"Maybe a bit of both." Ryan massaged the back of his neck. "I meet with a lot of clients. It helps to read body language to make a judgment call on their reaction when I deliver a proposal."

"Perhaps you can tell me what I can do to dissuade Tristan." She tapped a finger on her chin. "I'm clearly in need of some help."

"In my experience, sometimes a direct approach is best. You may need to have a one-on-one conversation with him and tell him the truth."

Her face paled. "You mean, tell him straight out I'm not interested?"

"I take it you're uncomfortable with confrontation?"

She gave him a sheepish look. "I'd hate to hurt anyone's feelings."

"I don't mean to tell you what to do, but if you want a suggestion . . ."

April interrupted. "Please."

Ryan continued, "—stop by here during a slow time of day. Ask him for a quick chat. Tell him you think he's a great guy, and you appreciate his friendship, but you're getting the impression he may want more than friendship. If you've misunderstood, there's no problem, but if you haven't, you can set him straight. If you talk while he's at work, it'll provide a forced time limit, so it won't become a marathon discussion. A break only lasts so long." Ryan shrugged. "Confrontation is best to get over with quickly, so you can move forward."

Ryan noticed April's attention stray from him to the table. In the silence that lay between them, the surrounding conversations buzzed, servers bustled back and forth, and dishes clanked.

Finally, April peered up just as Tristan arrived with their food. "Here you go, milady." He beamed and placed the plate in front of her. He said nothing while serving Ryan and glanced at April. "Need anything else?"

"No. This looks wonderful." April closed her eyes and inhaled, savoring the aromas of the scrumptious food.

Ryan noticed Tristan shift his weight from one foot to another as if he wanted to say something. A thought popped into Ryan's mind, an offer of distraction for April. "Do you remember if a Mrs. Wilkinson ever came here? She was about fifty and slender with shoulder-length brown hair and glasses. She had a cottage over on Bramley Lane."

Tristan's eyes held surprise at Ryan's cordial manner. "What was her first name?"

"Susannah."

His eyes widened. "Yes, she insisted I call her that, which is why your surname was familiar." His eyes narrowed. "Why do you ask?"

"She's my mother," Ryan said in a low voice.

"I've not seen her for some time. Miss her coming in. A kind lady. Where is she?"

Ryan didn't respond, so April answered, "She passed away, Tristan."

He lowered his head and focused on his utensils, straightening the napkin on his lap, not allowing his eyes to betray him. He should've never mentioned his mother. How would they ever understand what happened to her?

Chapter Seven

Neville, North Yorkshire, England
2019

April couldn't read the expression on Ryan's face as he surveyed the table. She eased her gaze to meet Tristan's. "Ryan is here to sell her cottage, and I'm trying to buy it."

"Yes, that's why we're meeting—to discuss the details." Ryan brought his eyes to meet theirs.

"I see." Tristan's shoulders relaxed. "Congratulations, April."

"Don't congratulate me yet. There's still a lot to do. I may not be able to afford it."

"I'm sure this gentleman will cut you a deal." Tristan gave Ryan a probing stare, raising an eyebrow.

"Yes, I will. I don't have a lot of time to be away from work, so I need to make the sale as quick as possible."

The look in Tristan's dark eyes was triumphant. His shoulders slid back, more confidence exuding from his strong build. "Let me refresh your drink, Ryan." He grabbed the glass and was gone in a split second, his rubber-soled shoes squeaking.

"Well, guess it's on again since Tristan thinks I'm no threat to his claim." Ryan chuckled.

"This is painful," April snapped. "I am going to have that talk with him."

"Sorry . . . couldn't help myself. His improved posture spoke volumes. You saw it too?"

April brought a finger to her lips. "Hush, here he comes."

Ryan put forth his best fake smile. "Thanks, Tristan. This tea is good. I didn't think you Brits knew how to make good iced tea, only hot."

"Oh, we Brits adapt. Now, we specialize in hot and cold tea. Enjoy your meal." He strutted away back toward the kitchen.

Ryan shrugged. "Guess I've won him over since I'm no longer competition."

"Yes, so you've said." April put her fork down and looked at him.

"Please don't be upset. Nothing I could do would stop him from pursuing you. I'll be gone in a week. Even if I pretended we were on a date, after I leave, he'll be right back at it. You've got to have that talk with him sooner than later." He picked up his fork and tucked into the roast.

"You're right. I don't need to let this bother me. Soon I'll have a talk with him—like you said."

Ryan nodded and continued to eat. They ate for several minutes until Ryan broke into April's thoughts. "You haven't mentioned whether you looked at the house or not."

She swallowed. "I did go by but am unable to have a contractor stop by until later in the week. He's to call and set an exact time."

Her gaze fell on the flowers that adorned their table. She brought her gaze to his. "I can't lie. I once read that when you want to purchase something you should be nonchalant about it in order to keep the price down. Possibly even point out flaws or act as if having second thoughts." She paused and took another sip of water. "I can't do that." She felt excitement rising. "I'm in love with that cottage."

"I'm glad to hear it." Ryan's eyes glinted with amusement.

"Unless your price is too high for my budget, or the contractor finds some expensive patch-ups that need to be done, I'm hooked. Everything about the place speaks to me."

April chattered on for several minutes while Ryan nodded often.

"All we have to do now is get that repair estimate. Do you have the name of this fellow? Maybe I could contact him tomorrow, and we could meet."

Tristan appeared. "Do you need anything before my shift ends?"

April shook her head, and Ryan asked for the bill. Tristan returned with speed, accepted payment, and bid them goodnight.

"Okay. Now that he's out of the way, you can relax." Ryan's eyes twinkled over the top of his tea.

"Yes, I suppose so." She took her last bite. "That was delicious as always."

She placed her napkin on the table. "So, Ryan, give the news, good or bad . . . your price?"

His cheek twitched. "That depends on what the contractor says. I can't very well sell a house at a higher price if there are extensive renovations to be made. Why don't you tell me what your budget is?"

April gazed into the distance. She chewed on her lower lip as she pulled out a pen and piece of paper from her purse. Studying the paper for a moment, she looked into Ryan's eyes.

She rapidly jotted a figure and pushed the paper across the table. "This is the absolute highest I could go. I was hoping for a little less so I could do some minor adjustments—not to mention possible restorations."

Ryan glanced at the numbers and settled his attention out the window at the garden. Without looking at her, he said, "That's feasible."

April's gasp sounded more like a squeak, and Ryan turned to her. "Are you okay?"

She stammered. "I—I'm fine. It's a dream come true."

"Good." He rose, and April followed. He gently cupped her elbow and escorted her out. She was taken aback by the gesture but said nothing. Once outside, he released her, and they walked in silence toward the Horden Inn.

"Do you live far? I can walk you home."

"No—about a ten-minute walk. You don't have to do that. I walk this all the time by myself."

"Nonsense. Go on." He took her arm again and started walking. "Hope this is the right direction."

"Actually, it's not." She cocked her head to one side.

"I guess we'd better turn around." They made an about-face.

They chatted about Tristan and the wonderful meal they'd shared until they arrived at her door. She thanked Ryan and bid him good evening after making plans to meet him the next day for lunch. He would call the contractor, Roland Jenks, and make an appointment to meet him at the cottage as soon as possible.

⋙⋘

April jerked the door open, almost falling as she tried to stop the door from crashing against the wall.

"Mum, Mum!" she shouted and heard only running water. She rushed to the loo and knocked with vigor. "Mum, are you in the shower?"

"Yes, dear, is everything all right?"

"Couldn't be better. I have wonderful news." She shouted to the door.

She rocked back and forth, foot to foot, like an excited child and remembered the time she'd found an ornate Victorian perfume bottle in a charity shop. Not having quite enough money, she'd looked at her mum with doe eyes that always got what she wanted, pleading for the remainder she needed for the purchase.

She'd carried the bottle with care throughout the store as she would a fragile bird and admired the way the colors changed in the light's reflection on the iridescent glass—translucent hues of purples, pinks, and blues. The gold oval stopper was carved with swirling designs, and, upon closer inspection, she identified them as tiny angels in flight. She was smitten.

From that day forward, she was determined to collect antique perfume bottles like that one from charity shops, markets, or trunk sales—never new.

April's voice rose. "Mum, are you listening?"

"Yes, ducky." Her mother's silvery voice replied from the other side of the door. "Can this wait until I leave the loo? Your father will be home in a moment. You can share your news with both of us."

"Oh, all right. I suppose." But April felt she would explode at any moment.

By the time her mother was out and dressed, her father walked through the door. "Where are my lovelies?" his soft-spoken voice sang out.

April emerged from her bedroom like a springing kitten. "Da!"

"Halloo, love." He gave her a bear hug.

"I have wonderful news for you and Mum."

Her mother entered the room. "Good evening, Mr. Conyers. Pleasant to see you." She kissed his cheek.

"You also, milady." He made a sweeping bow with one forearm tucked against his waist, the other held high behind him.

"You two are daft. If a passerby observed, they'd agree," April said with a giggle. They shot her a look and led her to her father's favorite armchair.

"Okay, what gives?" Mrs. Conyers crossed her arms. "You're up to something all right."

April wished to build suspense with a gradual retelling of how things came about, but it was too much for her, and the words tumbled out, "I'm buying the old cottage on Bramley Lane." Her voice squeaked with delight.

"What!" Her parents said in unison.

April's words spilled out in a torrent, explaining the events of the last few days. She'd kept it to herself. She was afraid if she talked about it too much, it wouldn't come true.

"And there you have it. I'm going to have my own home." Brimming with satisfaction, she gave them a questioning gaze.

Her mother appeared stunned. "What will we do without you?"

"It'll be hard to let her go, Agnes. But she *is* over twenty and plenty old enough to be on her own."

"Yes, yes. I suppose so." Her mother's gaze lowered.

"Mum, be happy for me, please. I can't wait to show you the place. It's wonderful."

"I am, dear." Her mother's face brightened. "Now, tell us about this nice young American chap."

April felt heat rise in her cheeks. "Oh, Mum. He's a nice fellow who lost his mum and is selling her property. It's painful for him. I get the impression he's selling for less than the place is worth to be done with it."

"Lucky for you." Her father held his arms tight across his chest.

April raised her eyebrows. "Da, that sounds dreadful."

"You know what I mean. It sounds as though this fellow has plenty of money and doesn't need the property. It's too far away for him to deal with, so he's ridding himself of it."

"Well, I suppose." April tucked a stray hair behind her ear.

Mrs. Conyers had slipped from the room without their noticing. She emerged from the kitchen carrying a tray with a bottle of sparkling juice, stemware, and a plate of biscuits. "Let's have a toast to April's new home."

"Oh, Mum, how nice." April patted her on the shoulder. "You're so thoughtful and Johnny-on-the-spot."

"To April and her cottage." Mr. Conyers held his glass out to meet theirs.

"What're you going to call her?" Her mother nibbled on a biscuit.

"I hadn't thought of that. Did it ever have a name?"

"We could check at the Land Registry office." Her father grabbed a pen and paper. "What's that address?"

"Number One Bramley Lane." April tilted her head back and sighed with drama. "Doesn't that sound romantic?"

☙

Mr. Conyers walked into the register's office moments after the woman unlocked the door.

"Good morning." His fine mood from the previous evening held.

The woman gave him a friendly nod. "Good morning to you

too, sir. How may I help you?"

"I require some background information on this address in Neville." He handed over the paper with the address.

She squinted to make out his writing. "All right, let's see." Her stout frame moved toward a lengthy row of gray metal file cabinets against the far wall. Muttering to herself while pointing to the label of each drawer, she paused at the bottom and lowered to her haunches to pull open the heavy drawer.

"Here we are." Her thumb dragged across the spine of the grey bound books and pulled one from the series and returned to the counter where Mr. Conyers waited with patience and expectation. She placed the book in front of him and turned the pages until she found what she was looking for.

Taking a ruler, she laid it on the page and moved it line-by-line until she found the address in question. "The cottage was built circa 1700."

He glanced over the document, eyes widening with excitement. "Is it possible to have a copy of that page?"

"Certainly, for 50p."

"Fine, fine. That's splendid."

The idea had come to mind the previous evening after he'd gone to bed and lay awake thinking about his little girl moving to her own place. He wanted to find the perfect celebration gift for her new home.

He exchanged coin for the paper and scanned the information once more. He'd hoped to find the date it was built, but, according to the paper, he'd found something even better. The cottage had a name.

Chapter Eight

Neville, North Yorkshire, England
2016

Susannah yanked on her pink work gloves and knelt before a small bed of daisies, and proceeded to pull the unwanted weeds, struggling with some as if their roots grew to China.

A small jingle drew her attention, followed by a timid meow as a beautiful dainty, white cat landed on top of the daisies she was trying to save. The cat looked at her with a sociable stare and repeated the meow with a bit more feeling.

"Hello there, little fellow. Aren't you a pretty thing?" With care, she reached a gloved hand toward its fluffy ears and asked, "May I pet you?" The cat leaned into her palm, brushing against the glove.

"Doesn't meet a stranger." A disembodied voice startled Susannah, almost sending her tumbling to the grass.

She turned to see a tiny grey-haired lady several feet behind her, smiling. "Didn't mean to scare you, dearie."

Susannah stood, removing her gloves, thinking how alike the cat was to her owner. "Good morning." Their hands met with a friendly shake, and she introduced herself.

"I'm Adelaide Claxton, your neighbor." She waved toward the cottage next door. My husband and I have been on holiday for a while and heard you'd moved in. How're you liking Neville?"

"Very well, thank you. This is a nice village. I've met many wonderful people."

The cat sailed into Mrs. Claxton's arms, and she caught the cat nimbly.

"What's her name?" Susannah rubbed the cat's ear, which brought a loud purr of contentment, the tiny bells jingling at each rub.

"She's Olivia, my baby. Never had any children, so cats have always been my babies. It breaks my heart when I lose one, but I go out and get another." She shook her head, long grey wisps of hair floating from side to side, her blue eyes sparkling. "I name all of them Olivia."

"Sounds charming." Susannah stopped petting the cat, noticing the bright pink collar around her neck.

"Suppose I should be gettin' back home to take care of the dust bin and such. Have a good day, dearie." She turned to leave.

"You too, Mrs. Claxton. Nice meeting you and Olivia."

The older woman waved and disappeared through the greenery covering the arbor. Susannah heard her speak to someone on the sidewalk and peeking past the arbor she noticed it was a girl, head ducked to her chest with a shyness that Susannah recognized in her younger self.

When the girl walked past, Susannah greeted her and received a reticent reply before she continued on her way. Susannah had seen her walk by before, and next time, she determined she'd ask her to stay for tea.

☙❧

Letice and Susannah strolled High Street, popping into a shop now and again. Letice kept Susannah company while she searched out bits and bobs for the cottage. An architectural piece she purchased would hang over the fireplace in the living room. A black, wrought-iron coat rack would stand sentry by the front door.

At the end of the village, Letice stopped and pointed across the street. "That's Colin's house."

A honey-colored stone house perched among old evergreens created a typical English country scene—an effective postcard.

"How lovely," Susannah told Letice, and, in fact, it was one of the loveliest homes she'd ever seen.

Though not massive, the golden-hued manor with large windows lent a pleasant simplicity to its façade.

A sleek black car pulled up at the corner and stopped, the

window lowering. A dark green clad arm slid onto the edge of the open window, and Colin's warm welcome greeted them. "Good afternoon, ladies."

"Speak of the devil." Letice grinned at him. "I was just pointing out your home to Susannah."

Susannah felt her face warm and couldn't meet his eyes at first.

"I'm in the midst of doing a bit of renovating and such." He glanced toward the house and back at them. "Bring the old girl up to date."

"Oh, what fun." Letice exclaimed and shot a glance at Susannah. "We're out shopping for bits and pieces for Susannah's delightful cottage. She has a keen eye."

"Really now?" Colin met Susannah's gaze, his dark eyes radiating with warmth and openness. "Would you care to join me for tea tomorrow and offer a few pointers?"

Susannah shifted her bags from one hand to the other. "I—I believe I'm tied up tomorrow," she said. "Maybe another time. Thanks, though."

Disappointment dashed across his face. "Alright. Another time. You two have a brilliant afternoon." With a nod, the window closed, and the car spun out of sight.

Letice scoffed. "Refusing tea with Colin Heard? Whoever heard of such poppycock."

Susannah set her jaw and grasped the handle of a bag a little tighter. "But I—I've something I must do."

Letice shook her head in disbelief. "I don't understand you, Susannah Wilkinson." One eyebrow rose. "I'd go anywhere that man asked in a flash, if I wasn't happily married for thirty-odd years. I mean, really?"

ᏓᏍᎣ

The small congregation poured out of the centuries-old church, its stone glistening in the early afternoon sun. Parts of the church dated back to the eleventh century, with a fifteenth-century tower.

Amanda called aside those involved in the renovation project of the homeless shelter, including Susannah, and asked if they could meet briefly at High Tea.

Once seated, each ordered a drink and settled in, the meeting was called to order. Amanda apologized, "Sorry to pull you from your Sunday roasts, but I have important news. First of all, Colin Heard rang me last night to say he plans to attend the next meeting, and he's totally on board with the project." Murmurs and nods of approval travelled around the table. Reclaiming everyone's attention, she continued, "Again, sorry, don't mean to dampen that good word, but I do have some disappointing news." She looked crestfallen. "Someone has purchased the old factory."

96

Chapter Nine

Neville, North Yorkshire, England
2019

The paper was filmy beneath April's fingers, like butterfly wings yet not as fragile. She adored the touch of old books—thinking of all the individuals who had held them through the decades. Electronic devices, cold chunks of technology, couldn't give her the same emotional connection. Real books didn't run out of energy, either.

The soft rattle of the bell signaled someone's entrance into the shop. Without glancing up from her stool, April greeted them. "Good afternoon, may I help you?" She turned toward her customer and straightened as she met Ryan's eyes.

"Hello. Fancy seeing you here." She clung to the tattered book at her chest like a shield.

"Hi. Thought I'd drop by to tell you the contractor wishes to meet us at the house today." He surveyed the room as he spoke. "Would you be able to meet after work?"

April put her book on the nearest shelf without looking and stood as it slipped to the floor. Ryan stooped, rescued the volume, and returned it to the shelf before April could move. "I take off at half-five, but Polly will be here soon. I could leave early. Why don't we meet there at five?"

"Sounds like a good thought. I'll call Mr. Jenks and tell him." Ryan turned to go as the bell sounded behind him. For the second time within minutes, a visitor surprised April.

"Da. What're you doing here?" April moved toward her father and gave him a hug.

"Hello, kitten." He shuffled a brown paper-wrapped package from one arm to the other. He glanced at Ryan but spoke to April. "I'll browse until you're finished with your business."

"Sir, that won't be necessary. We're finished." Ryan made one step toward the door, but April touched his shoulder to stop him.

"This is my father, Cecil Conyers. Da, this is Ryan Wilkinson."

"Pleased to meet you."

"Yes, yes." Mr. Conyers' eyebrows peaked. "You too, young man."

"Da, Ryan is the man selling the cottage."

"I see. Well, well. Pleasure to meet you. You've made my little girl quite happy, Mr. Wilkinson."

April's eyes widened. Her father gave her a half-smile and shrugged a shoulder in silent apology.

"Please call me Ryan."

"I'm glad you're here. I have a gift for my li ... daughter." He coughed, giving her the gift ornamented with a huge yellow bow at one corner.

"Da, this is enormous . . . and heavy." April struggled to get a grip on it. Ryan reached for one side of the package, so she could open it.

"Thank you," April offered, and tore the paper with care. She gasped as the rest fell to the floor. "Da, you didn't."

Ryan held the large plaque, so she could view the words on it at a better angle.

Permelia Cottage

Est. c1700

Joy filled April, her face growing warm with pleasure. She looked at her father, eyes misting. "Oh, Da." She hugged him. "But the cottage isn't mine yet."

Ryan jumped in. "It may as well be."

On impulse, April hugged Ryan before she realized what she was doing. He struggled to hold the sign. Her father grabbed it in time.

She withdrew from the hug as quick as it began, gazed at her feet, and stammered, "I'm sorry. I got carried away."

Ryan didn't meet her gaze but stared out the window. "No problem."

April met her father's watchful eye after the embarrassing display and hoped he hadn't read more into it than there was. She shrugged it off. "Da, this is wonderful, but why Permelia Cottage?"

"In my research, I discovered it's the cottage's original name. Seems the last owner—several years ago—came asking the same questions I did."

April saw Ryan's shoulders stiffen and relax. "What a wonderful gift"

"Why don't I take it with me since it's so heavy," Ryan added. "I'll put it in the cottage, and when we meet this evening, we'll ask Mr. Jenks about hanging it."

"Splendid." April and her father spoke at once. Mr. Conyers returned the sign to Ryan.

"Okay, I'll see you later." He looked at April, and turned to her father and offered his hand, which the man shook heartily. "Nice to meet you, sir."

"And you."

April piped in. "Thank you. I'll see you later."

Ryan tucked the sign under his arm and made his way to the door. The jingle indicated his departure and faded in the growing silence.

"So, tell me about Ryan." Mr. Conyers' eyes twinkled. "You certainly didn't tell us he was so handsome."

"Oh, Da. I told you and Mum everything." April salvaged the brown paper and made a show of folding it with meticulous precision.

He offered a sideways grin. "If you say so, pet. See you tonight." He stopped halfway to the door. "Guess you'll be late. Shall we save a plate?"

"I suppose so." She turned toward the counter and paused. "Da?"

He gripped the doorknob. "Yes?"

"How did you have the sign made so swift?"

"I know a chap, and he did a rush job for me." Hesitant, he added, "Perhaps Ryan will want to eat after you meet with Mr. Jenks. He could come with you." He presented her with a crooked smile, eased the door open, and left without waiting for her reply.

"Oh, Da," she said and laughed, happiness surrounding her the rest of the afternoon.

☙

The countryside sped past in blurs of green, yellow, and occasional glints of brilliance when the sun reflected on water. April had forgotten she needed to run a brief errand in Northallerton before meeting Ryan at the cottage and was behind schedule.

Images of the cottage sign, Ryan's cloaked reaction at the mention of his mother, and the hug, flashed in her mind. Why had she done that?

She'd been so delighted she'd have likely hugged a total stranger. Wouldn't she?

No, that simply wasn't true, and if she were honest with herself, her unusual behavior as of late stemmed from Ryan— or was it only from the camaraderie she felt for his mother? She didn't know him. Why was she dwelling on this? God, please ease my mind to be at peace and not over-analyze everything.

For distraction, April made a mental list of things to do—hire a dustman and someone to mow and pull weeds perhaps once a month. She could do most of the gardening. She would need cleaning supplies.

The train eased to a stop at Neville. Being lost in thought had made the twenty-minute train ride seem like five. The book lay open on her lap, bookmark still in place. She closed it with a snap and placed it in her pink chintz bag. As she stepped onto the station platform, she wondered how many times she'd made this walk after a trip on the train. Ten minutes to the cottage soon to be her home, five minutes to her parents'—her home for all her life. Oh, my, was she having second thoughts—surely not? She loved the cottage.

She remembered the paper she'd found. Her curiosity got the best of her, though it was most likely nothing.

When she approached, Ryan stood by the cottage gate in deep discussion with Roland Jenks, the contractor. She slowed her pace. She knew Roland—he was a nice man, and honest.

"Good afternoon, gents." Her voice cheery.

"Hallo', lass." Mr. Jenks laughed. He seemed to laugh at any and everything. It was his nature to be in a perpetual good mood.

Ryan was leaning against the wall surrounding her cottage. "Mr. Jenks and I were discussing a paint job for the exterior."

"That would be splendid. I suppose a list of repairs and such, with the cost, should be where to start. I'm uncertain I can afford the paint job yet. Do you have a basic tally?" She rubbed her jaw. Could she afford the house and the repairs as well? "I may have to wait on the cosmetic issues and repair the necessaries for now."

Ryan sounded confident. "The bank may give you a better loan if I spruce up the outside. I'll have Mr. Jenks paint it tomorrow before the bank appraiser comes out. Don't worry about the cost."

April's eyebrows rose, her lips pulling taut. "Ryan, you said you were selling it 'as is'—no repairs and such."

"Yes, I did, but Mr. Jenks gave me such a good deal, and I feel responsible for the lack of care. I don't want this to lower the value of the house and be the reason for the refusal of your loan."

April relaxed her lips as she understood his reasoning, yet the offer to pay for the repairs was unexpected at the least.

Mr. Jenks' smile grew wider by the second. She saw the glint in his eyes.

April bit the inside of her cheek and cleared her throat. "Well . . . thanks. I'm not sure what to say."

Mr. Jenks broke into their conversation. "We'll cover the plants 'round the 'ouse. They look a sight better since your gardener tidied things."

Gardener? April wheeled and took in the garden. The weeds were gone, shrubs trimmed, no longer blocking the windows. The encroaching grass between the flowerbeds was replaced with large flat stones and formed a beautiful winding path throughout the garden. Assorted pink and white flowers bloomed sporadically, freed from neglect and overgrowth of vines and weeds.

Even the whitewashed arbor over the gate peeked through since the ivy and the wisteria had been given a creative pruning. The sweet scent of lavender wafted in the air, reminding April of the dried lavender in the fireplace.

Ryan and Mr. Jenks were speaking, likely to her. "I'm sorry. I was admiring the garden. It's brilliant."

"Glad you like it. I had met with the landscaper the same day I first met you here. I had it all arranged that day. I was asking you what color you wanted the house painted."

"I haven't given it much thought, but I suppose a whitewashed finish." April considered the cottage. "I don't wish it to appear too modern. The cottage will be restored . . . to what she once was."

Mr. Jenks clutched a clipboard under his arm as he held the gate open for her. "Why don't we go 'round and discuss the repairs."

Ryan stood back and let April walk into the garden. She paused here and there focusing on various improvements while the men pointed out roof and window issues that needed attention. She nodded, not paying much attention to either of them.

Ryan opened the front door, allowing April to enter, leaving it ajar to let in more light. Mr. Jenks began a detailed inspection using small tools from his utility belt—inserting an odd-looking tool into an electrical socket, pressing a flat screwdriver against windowsills to check for wood rot and so on.

April walked alone into the office and took a seat in the desk chair. Her heart pounded as her gaze searched out the room's contents—all the books and travel memorabilia. The creaking of the door brought her head around with a jolt. Ryan stood in the doorway.

"There you are. Mr. Jenks has a list of repairs ready and is working on a rough estimate." His face held no humor, nor was he frowning. "Do you like this room?"

April cleared her dry throat. "Yes, yes, I do—very much." She softened her voice. "When will you pack and move the furniture?"

He parted his lips to answer, hesitant. He took a moment of quiet contemplation before he answered, "I'm not sure. I haven't considered that. Are you interested in any of it?"

She slid her fingers along one arm of the chair, feeling the soft chintz fabric. "It would be nice to not shop for furniture. I rather like it all. Your mum had such good taste. What about her personal things—books and bits?"

A crease formed on his forehead. Mr. Jenks called from the kitchen. "I think you'll be needin' a new fridge. They don't do well sittin' empty for so long a time."

Ryan leaned against the door frame, filling it with his height. "Sure, Mr. Jenks." He spoke to her again, his tone resolute. "If you're interested, you can keep it all. If there are any personal items, you can send them to me later if you don't mind." He stepped forward as he reached in his pocket to retrieve a business card and found a pen to scratch something on the back. "Here's my home address." His voice was curt as if reigning in emotion. He avoided her eyes. "I'll reimburse you for the shipping." He tossed the card onto the desk and left the room.

His tone and abrupt action astonished April, and she realized it must be the ache he experienced when he thought of going through his mother's belongings. She called to his retreating form, "That's fine. Let me know how much you want for it all."

Ryan paused in the hall and called over his shoulder, his voice terse. "I want nothing. It all comes with the house. You'll be doing me a favor by going through my mother's personal things and sending them later. Saves me the time and effort—it's a small price to pay." He banged the office door closed behind him.

April started at the bang of the door. Why was he angry? Perhaps it was his mother's private things that unsettled him. She took a deep cleansing breath and released the tight grip on her purse. Using the arms of the chair, she levered herself to her feet. The entire incident had left her shaky. She disliked confrontation of any kind.

Once inside the lounge, she heard voices coming from the kitchen. Mr. Jenks and Ryan were going out the door to the back garden. She hurried after them and stepped into the waning sunlight that covered the garden in an ethereal glow against a backdrop of the rolling hills.

April thrilled with the possibilities of the space—imagining tiny clear lights strung around the perimeter wall, the arbor over the side gate, and the small trees. She envisioned having teas and luncheons with her friends and Sunday dinners with her parents.

Mr. Jenks shattered her thoughts. "Well, here ya' go." He presented Ryan the paper with the list of repairs and costs. "Barrin' any unforeseen thing that may rear its ugly head while we're doin' our surgery." He cackled at his own joke, blue eyes dancing.

Ryan's smile was faint. "And how long to make this happen?" He glanced at the paper.

"Ryan, may I?" April reached for the list.

Hesitant, he relinquished the estimate.

"Are you able to start tomorrow?" he asked Mr. Jenks.

April perused the list while they spoke.

"If so—it'd be after lunch—if not, would have to be early the next mornin'. Shouldn't take more than a couple o' days— includin' the paintin'—what with a full crew and all."

"When do you need payment, Mr. Jenks?" The frown line between her eyes deepened. "I must go to the bank and include the repairs in my loan. It could take a few days."

Before Mr. Jenks could respond, Ryan looked at April. "Why don't I go with you to the bank. I'm sure something can be worked out."

Uncertain what that meant, she felt he was trying to delay the issue. Mr. Jenks must have sensed it also because he made no reply to April's question. He scratched his head, which ruffled his red hair, making him appear scruffy in a comical way.

They walked back inside, and Ryan asked Mr. Jenks, "How about going for a cup of coffee? We can discuss the repairs in more detail."

April wasn't sure why he'd made the invitation. To take things in a friendlier direction? She stiffened and tried to fight the growing skepticism within her.

Ryan shrugged. "April may have questions and thoughts on the repairs."

April sagged against the wall, trying to relax. She now was a part of the decision-making process of her new home.

Hers. The cottage would actually be hers.

"Yes, please, Mr. Jenks. Join us—some appetizers with that coffee, or tea?"

"Aye, I'd love to lass, but the missus is expectin' me at the usual time. Without givin' her proper notice, she'd 'ave my hide."

"Even though I'm a bachelor, I can see your point." Ryan laughed. "You have my phone number, so please call if you need anything. I'll drop by tomorrow evening to see if you can get started."

"Ta-ra. Nice meetin' ya, Ryan. An' good to see ya', April. You've grown into a fetching lass." Mr. Jenks turned his stout, muscular body, and walked toward his lorry. His strength defied his age of sixty.

April turned to Ryan. "You've done enough in tidying the cottage. I feel like a charity case." His complexion paled while her cheeks warmed.

"What do you mean?" His eyes narrowed. "I told you I'd already arranged the gardening before we met."

"Not the repairs. You told me you were selling it as-is." April's brusqueness matched his own as she slung her purse over her shoulder. The strap slipped, and the bag dropped to the ground. Contents spilled out. They both stooped to retrieve the items, one of which Ryan still held. April snatched it back so quick it caused Ryan to teeter on his haunches. She stuffed it back into her purse with the other items and rose.

They glared at one another for a moment before Ryan spoke, "Listen, I'm only trying to speed up the transaction. The bank will not loan money to someone who wants to buy a rat-trap."

April's eyes widened at his elevated voice. He lowered his voice to a near whisper. "I didn't mean to sound angry. I'm not mad." His shoulders sagged. "I need to get this done and return to New York."

April hadn't considered the urgency of his impending departure. Was his work that important, or was the cottage a painful reminder of his mum and he needed to separate himself from it?

Her voice softened, and her gaze flitted to the flower garden. "Ryan, I'm sorry. You need to go home. If you can accompany me to the bank in the morning, maybe we can move things along. Please forgive me for speaking so rashly."

"It's fine." His expression of irritation lessened, but his physical posture told a different story. His gaze was on the distant hills.

"Guess I best be going. Mum is holding dinner for me." April pulled the gate until the latch clicked. "Have a good evening."

Ryan stood still, hands in his pockets. "Is your bank here in Neville?"

She turned to face him, the gate separating them. "Yes, down the street from the bookshop. You can't miss it. See you there at nine?"

"Sure." His voice had lost its sharp edge. "See you."

Tears lurked beneath the surface as April walked home. She had to compose herself before she got to the flat. Her parents would grill her if they thought she was upset. One block over was a bakeshop that also sold ice cream. Her father was weak for ice cream and cake. That'd cheer things and take her mind off Ryan.

A while later, she took a deep breath before turning the key and then pushed the door open to the flat. "Good evening. Mum, Da. I have treats."

"'Allo, love. Treats, did you say?" Mr. Conyers glanced over his shoulder, eyes widening at the announcement of a treat, the telly no longer his sole focus.

Mrs. Conyers placed the book in her lap and looked at the writing on the side of the bag. "Extravagant aren't we, pet?"

"Oh, Mum. I don't do this often, and I wanted to do something nice for the two of you." April went to the kitchen. "I'll be right out."

Her mum called from the lounge. "But you haven't had dinner yet, love."

"I'm not hungry." She lifted her head and peering through the cut-out opening to the lounge area and watched her father reposition himself in his comfy chair in anticipation. Her mother, however, placed her book on the table between the two chairs, rose with a groan, and headed to the kitchen. April's stomach rolled.

"You're upset about something and trying to cover it. What's happened?" She retrieved three spoons and placed them in the bowls April had put on the counter.

"Mum, I'm fine." April refused to meet her gaze.

"I won't press you as long as you're all right." They worked in silence while one cut the sweet-smelling butter cake and the other scooped soft creamy vanilla ice cream into the bowls.

"I'll take Da's." She struggled to make her voice sound normal.

"Glad you're better, pet."

"Thanks, Mum . . . love you."

April said a silent prayer to forgive Ryan for his anger—and to ask God's forgiveness for her anger. She felt peace wash over her.

ᘇᘙ

April shifted her position on the bed, her phone at her ear after Polly answered her call. "Hope I'm not calling too late."

Polly cleared her throat. "No, no, I fell asleep in front of the telly."

"Wanted to tell you I'll be late in the morning. The bank opens at nine, and I'm meeting Ryan there to complete our business arrangements."

Polly let out an audible yawn. "So, it's Ryan now and not Mr. Wilkinson?"

"Oh, Polly." April dreaded the teasing.

But Polly stopped, "So, I'll see you when I see you. Good luck. Bye." The phone clicked.

April returned the phone to its cradle. She sighed and chose not to take Polly's behavior personally.

"Mum—Da. I'm off to bed." She grabbed a book from the side table, stretching her shoulders to ease out the kinks.

"Night to you, love," they said in unison.

April sighed as she slid between fresh, crisp sheets smelling of lavender. "Lord, thank you for all your blessings and for forgiving me for my anger with Ryan. Please guide me regarding this cottage purchase." She paused, "And bless Ryan. Amen."

She tried to read, but her thoughts switched from subject to subject like a runaway train, moving in and out of stations without pause—from Ryan to the bank and back again to Ryan. What was it about him?

Boys—men—were mysterious to her. She'd never even had a boyfriend, though most twenty-something girls would have gone through several by now.

Her short stay at university didn't produce even one. Friends that were guys, yes, but never a handholding, kissing chap. Was there something wrong with her? There had always been so many things to do that there never seemed to be enough time for boys.

Why did she keep saying *boys*? She should say *men*. Ryan was most assuredly not a boy. Oh, good grief. From where had that thought come?

Tristan's face formed in her mind's eye. Tristan was good-looking, though he was younger than her. Ryan had commented that age shouldn't matter. She guessed he had a few years on her at perhaps twenty-nine or thirty.

Also, Ryan had asked why it was okay for men to date younger women, but society said the reverse was unacceptable. He seemed irritated by the concept.

Did he have an older girlfriend? Maybe that's why he seemed so agitated. April drifted to sleep with the faces of both men displayed in her head, her book slipping to the floor.

Ϙϙ

It proved to be a superb, cool morning as April walked by Books-on-the-Green. She passed the shop as Polly was unlocking the door.

"Good morning. Did you go back to sleep on the sofa last night?"

She wasn't smiling. "Funny for so early in the day, aren't we, April?"

"Sorry," April said and kept walking. "You haven't had your coffee yet, have you?"

"No, Miss, I'm-always-chipper-from-first-light." Polly's sarcastic tone rang out behind her.

"Have a huge cup, and I'll be back in a jiff." April was halfway down the block. She had a few minutes to spare before the bank opened, so she stopped by Coffee, Tea, and Crumpets. She reached for the door as it lurched toward her.

"Excuse me," a man said in an unmistakable American accent. She glanced up to meet Ryan's smiling eyes as he held the door with his shoulder, a cup in one hand and a napkin-wrapped muffin in the other.

"Ryan."

"Morning." He pointed along the street toward the bank with his cup. "I was about to have a quick breakfast and keep an eye out for you."

"I had the same idea. I'll see you there." She thanked him and ambled inside, still shameful over their encounter the previous day.

113

A few minutes later, April exited with a cup of tea and two petite scones. Before she could locate a free table, Ryan called out to her. He sat underneath a blue-striped umbrella, facing the coffee shop door.

"Please join me." He motioned toward a chair at his table.

She placed her tea and scones on the table, looped her purse over one arm of the chair, and sat. "Thanks." She bowed her head and said a brief silent prayer, and took a bite of scone, an urge to break the stillness tugging at her. "It's a lovely morning, though nip."

April flashed up to find him studying her with care. Her chest tightened.

"I'm sorry I got short with you yesterday." He hunched over his cup as he stirred it. "I meant nothing by it."

April broke her scone into another bite-sized portion. She dared not take a second bite for fear of choking from the lump in her throat.

"I'm used to being in charge of projects, people, and negotiations . . . didn't mean to interject it into our business arrangements." He stopped, sipped his coffee, and waited for a reply.

Ryan bit into his muffin. As he was chewing, April looked into his eyes. "Ryan, it's me that must ask for your forgiveness."

He shot her a bewildered look. "For what?"

"For my anger, yesterday. I mirrored your anger, and that was wrong of me. I've asked God to forgive me, and He has— I need yours, too."

Ryan stilled in his seat. "What in the world are you talking about? I'm the one who's ashamed of my actions. I don't think I need to be forgiving you. You did nothing wrong."

"In God's eyes, I did, and I must have your forgiveness—if you're willing."

"If it means that much to you." He nodded.

"Thank you." She placed a piece of scone in her mouth and chewed with a closed-lipped smile.

He mimicked her and finished his muffin. They drank and chatted for a while when the click of a lock caught April's attention. "The bank is opening. Guess we need to get this going." April rose from her seat, and put their rubbish in the bin, and grabbed her purse.

Once in the bank and seated in front of Mr. Dunbar's desk, they exchanged greetings and introductions, and got to business. Mr. Dunbar estimated the loan based on the unknown condition of the cottage until he could get an appraiser to see the property. "April, here is the preliminary amount we are prepared to loan you without the appraisal." He pushed a piece of paper toward her.

April observed Ryan as he leaned back farther into his chair, avoiding the paper. She looked over the figures. "Mr. Dunbar, this is the cost of the cottage alone and nothing for the repairs."

Mr. Dunbar leaned back as well and rubbed his dimpled chin. "Yes, until we see the property, that's all we can do. I could have someone out there next week." With a heavy sigh, he said, "I'm sorry it can't be sooner."

Ryan's brows creased in concern, and April was crestfallen. "But Ryan has to get back to America and cannot wait that long." Her swallow was distinct.

"I'm sorry, but our appraiser is booked. If she has a cancellation, she may move you up in the queue."

Ryan touched April's arm as he looked at Mr. Dunbar. "May we speak privately for a minute?"

April's cheeks burned as she turned toward Ryan. Mr. Dunbar stood. "Why don't I go get us a cup of tea while you talk." He didn't wait for a response before leaving his office.

"Yes?" April rubbed her upper arms, suddenly cold.

"Please don't be angry, but I have an idea." His pause was brief. "You have approval for the loan on the house. Let me pay for the repairs." He lightly touched her hand to silence her disapproval and continued, "If the bank won't loan you the repair money after they do the appraisal, you can pay me back in installments. We'll even draw up papers if that would make you feel better."

April's muscles tightened, and she began to twist the delicate cross pendant of her necklace. "I suppose that would work." Her voice uneven. "But are you certain?"

"I trust you. I'm a good judge of character, remember?" He leaned toward her and rested a hand on one of his jean-clad knees, his gaze reassuring. "That's a big part of my job— knowing whom I can trust."

Mr. Dunbar came in with a tray containing three cups of tea, milk, and sugar. Ryan prepared April's tea the way he'd seen her do it, and then his own. Mr. Dunbar reached for his as Ryan shared the agreement he and April had made.

Ryan raised his cup to clink lightly with April's, his eyes smiling, his tone gentle. "Here's to the deal."

She paused, her mouth at the edge of the cup, his gaze lingering on hers, and his words came back to her about knowing whom to trust. And despite the fact she'd only known him a few days, something deep within April told her this was a man she could trust.

Chapter Ten

Neville, North Yorkshire, England
2019

Ryan entered through the gate in front of Permelia Cottage. He pulled in a deep breath as he perused the garden and its new plantings, neat, tidy, and now free of weeds. It gave the place a more lived-in and cared-for facade. He pushed the gate closed behind him as he heard the soft tinkle of bells. Before he could search out the source, something brushed against his leg. He looked down to find the whitest cat he'd ever seen.

"Well, hello there, fellow." He bent to the cat's level and

reached for the fluffy ears and rubbed with gentleness. The cat purred with pleasure. "Assuming," he continued, "you are a fellow." The cat hummed like a small motor. Ryan noticed the bright pink collar with tiny bells. "You must be a terror on birds to have warranted so many bells—not very ladylike."

As Ryan petted the now-enamored cat, light footsteps brought his gaze around to see an elderly woman approaching the cottage.

"I see you've found my Olivia." The cat's ears perked, and she sprang toward her, jumped over the gate, and straight into the lady's waiting arms.

The woman was of slight build, about five feet tall, with shoulder-length gray hair pulled back at the nape and held together with a silver barrette. She reached into an ample pocket on her blue-checked apron and pulled out a treat to feed to the cat.

"She's a naughty one—always roaming. I hope she didn't bother you."

"No, ma'am, not at all. She reminds me of a cat my mom and I had when I was a child."

"How lovely. Are you moving into the cottage?" Her eyes looked into his, hopeful, as she cradled the cat like an infant.

Ryan, surprised by the question, responded, "No, ma'am— I'm selling it for my mother."

"Oh my, she doesn't wish to return and live in Neville again?" She stared into the face of her cat as she rubbed her ears.

"It's not that . . . she . . . well, left it to me, and I live in the U.S." He let his attention wander over the garden as he looked away from her imploring stare.

"I'm so sorry. She was such a kind and thoughtful woman. She once cared for my Olivia a few days while I visited my sister in London. I've missed her. She left with no word. Was she suddenly taken ill and passed swiftly?"

Ryan struggled to speak, but no words would come.

She broke the silence. "Please accept my condolences. I shouldn't have intruded. It must be sorrowful for you." As an afterthought, she added, "She dearly loved this cottage. A day rarely passed without my seeing her tend a plant or flower in it. She had a special way with it—giving life to something so long neglected."

"Thank you." The quiet could have been dissected—lying there—hard and mournful.

"Well, I suppose I should get Olivia home." Spry, she turned and stepped away at a clipped pace.

Ryan hesitated, bolted through the gate before she could get away, and called out, "Ma'am."

Turning, Ryan noticed tears on her wrinkled cheeks. "Yes, son?" Her voice trembled.

"My name is Ryan." He extended his hand. "It's a pleasure to meet you. I'm glad my mother was happy here."

"She was, dear." She juggled the cat, holding her in one arm and grabbed his with the other. "I'm Adelaide Claxton, and it's my pleasure. You favor your mum." She smiled through the tears. "A beautiful lady, she was."

ભ8

After the pleasant conversation with Mrs. Claxton, Ryan sat

at the desk facing the street. The late morning sun shone through the large window, bathing him in a soft glow. Mom liked painting in the morning—said it was the most flattering light. He leaned back in the chair, his gaze roaming the room as his fingers gripped the arms. He pictured her in the window seat, a book in her lap and a cup of tea on the sill. He looked over the collection of framed photographs on her desk. Several were of him as a child, images of them together during happy times.

In the past, such recollections brought anger—now it had shifted to a gloomy aura surrounding the memories. The slam of a car door brought him out of his reverie. As he rolled the chair back, he heard paper tearing. Still seated, he bent and spotted the torn article. He must've dropped it on his previous visit. He reclaimed the paper and stared at it for a moment, crumpled and tossed it into the trash basket. "I should never have saved it to begin with," he muttered.

"Mr. Wilkinson!" A voice called from the open front door.

He took long strides from the office and met Mr. Jenks as he stood in the doorway.

"'Ow do? We're ready to get started right after we down a quick pasty." The genuine joy in the man's eyes coupled with the many laugh lines endeared him to Ryan. He had yet to see the man with so much as a cross look at anyone, and he seemed to love his job—one accomplished by the strength of his hands, sweat, and hard work. Though Ryan's job was nothing like it, did he truly like his job as much as this man did?

"Good morning, Mr. Jenks. It's good of you to come on such short notice." Before Ryan could ask when they would begin the repairs, a hammer pounded on the far side of the cottage.

"Had another job that cancelled." He tilted his head toward the pounding. "Guess my mates have eaten their pasties on the drive over. If you don't mind, I'll polish mine off in the back where the hammerin' ain't so loud." Mr. Jenks chuckled to himself as he walked through the cottage, Ryan following. They perched on the edge of the low stone wall surrounding the garden—legs dangling—and discussed the plan for the repairs.

"I hope you don't find any surprises while you're working." The crease between his brows deepened as his lips tightened.

Mr. Jenks chewed, deep in thought. "You never know with an ole place such as this—if someone made a real bodge of a job in the past?"

Ryan wasn't aware what bodge meant, but he grasped the concept and nodded. "Well, if you happen upon something not covered in the estimate, would you mind keeping it between us?"

Taking a big gulp from his thermos, Mr. Jenks' eyes sparkled over the rim. He screwed the cap back on. "Up to you—none of my business." He slid from the wall. "Best get to it, guv—should be done by tomorrow if we don't get a lashing." His eyes moved upward to the sky.

Once again, Ryan didn't understand but realized Mr. Jenks was talking about rain. He shook his head as Mr. Jenks set off to work and bent to retrieve something that had fallen from his pocket. Ryan dropped from his perch on the wall, a moment between he and April coming to mind. Her purse had spilt its contents, and he'd hastily helped her gather the items, including a small stuffed doll in a plastic bag.

When she'd seen the item in his hand, pain flashed across her face, and she'd snatched it from him. Ryan wondered why something so odd to be in a woman's purse lingered in his thoughts. It obviously had a purpose to be there. He shook his head again, but it was absolutely none of his business.

◌◦◌

April shoved the bookstore door open and squealed at the sight of Polly wobbling on the upper stile of a ladder. "Polly Marie! What're you doing on that ladder while you're alone in the shop?"

Polly's blonde, chin-length hair rippled as she descended. She froze on the third stile and twisted her head toward the still jangling bell. "I'm being extra careful."

April glared at her. "We had an agreement. You don't so much as touch ladders without me here. Remember your great fall last year when you got all pear-shaped. You whined about your sprained wrist for months." April shot her a teasing look. "I refuse to go through that again."

"Oh, all right, madam. I'm only trying to do my job and restock that high shelf."

"I'd like to keep my business partner in one piece. Okay?"

Polly took the remaining steps toward the floor and placed the books she'd been juggling on the nearby counter. "April, no offence, but ta-ra." She turned on her heel and exited to the storage room in a huff.

April would allow her friend to fume for a while—as was best for Polly when she was in one of her moods—and moved to the office behind the counter. April put her purse away, hung her sweater, and put on a kettle of water. She held a spoonful of sugar over a cup as a loud crash came from the storage room. Sugar flew into the air and fell like snowflakes. She dropped the spoon with a clang and bolted through the door.

"Are you all right?" She stopped dead in her tracks to see no sign of Polly except her shoes peeking out from under a huge pile of fallen boxes. "Polly!" she cried and reached for the box on top of her legs and prepared to lift something heavy when instead the box flew over her head toward the door. The box was empty. She reached for the next one—empty again. "Polly."

"I'm fine." The empty boxes muffled her sarcastic voice.

April continued tossing boxes. "You gave me a fright. What happened?"

Once the area was cleared, April had to stifle a laugh. Polly was laid out spread-eagle on her back, her expression a mixture of embarrassment, anger, and loss of dignity.

"Don't you dare laugh or say I-told-you-so." She lifted her hand to April for help.

As April reached for her, she said, "You were on a ladder, weren't you?"

Polly's eyebrows lowered and pinched together.

April grabbed Polly's hand. "Do you want to tell me what's got you so off-kilter today? I haven't seen you like this since you stopped seeing Jamison."

Polly's eyes shot darts at April as she pulled her to her feet.

"Is it a chap? You're seeing someone?" April began stacking boxes against the wall. Polly joined in but remained silent.

All boxes now organized, April asked, "How about a cup of tea—my treat?" She followed Polly as she led the way to the office-cum-kitchen.

Polly plopped into a chair at the small drop-leaf table. April swept up the sugar-snowflakes and prepared two cups of tea. The lid of the biscuit tin gave a metallic pop, and she tugged it away and placed a few biscuits onto their chipped Royal Doulton plate. April remembered the day she and Polly had purchased the plate in a charity shop in Salisbury. They had the same idea when they glimpsed it, both commenting on the beautiful blue floral design. It would be their bookshop biscuit plate. It was a happy day—shopping for their new business.

April eased a chair back and sat. "Want to tell me what's going on?" Sipping her tea, she eyed Polly with unease. They each nibbled a biscuit in silence.

Polly's voice rose just above a whisper. "It's Tristan." She studied the table.

"What about him?"

"Why don't you like him? He's like some attention-starved puppy following you around, and you give him the brushoff. He's no div?"

"What on earth are you talking about?" April crossed her arms over her chest. "I'm always nice to Tristan."

"Give over. You know he's interested in you—and he's a fine chap. I'd be over-the-moon to have a chap like him so attentive to me." Polly hung her head, her hair falling like a curtain to frame her face.

April grew still, munching her biscuit. Why did Polly care

so much about Tristan's feelings toward her? "Has he been here while I was out?" April studied her friend's reaction.

Polly twisted in her chair with discomfort—she took a long, slow drink of tea—avoiding the question.

April waited a moment. "Well?"

"Yes, he's been coming by almost every day and keeps missing you. If I didn't know better, I'd say you were hiding 'round the corner to be sure he'd left before you came to work." She slumped in her chair.

"Oh, Polly—I wouldn't do that. I like Tristan but as a friend. I suppose I'll have to tell him and be done with it."

Polly's eyes widened, and she straightened in her seat, eyes now bright. "You would do that?"

"I suppose I must. Don't you think?" She expelled a deep breath and poured another cup of tea.

Polly's shoulders relaxed. "It's the honorable thing to do—not leading him on."

"Yes . . . I . . ." The sound of the bell over the door stopped April in mid-sentence.

"I'll get it April, finish your tea." Polly shuffled from the room.

What's going on with her? April's thoughts mulled over Polly's anger and overall attitude. Why did she care so much about her attention toward Tristan—or lack of it? She appeared to brighten when April told her she would talk to Tristan.

"Someone to see you." Polly's sing-song voice floated on the air. A little too cheerful to suit April's taste.

April forced herself up and out into the shop. As their eyes met, April groaned—guess there was no time like the present since Tristan stood in front of her with a winning smile.

Chapter Eleven

Neville, North Yorkshire, England
2017

The sound of a gavel against the table resonated throughout the modest dining area of the church in Neville. "Let's call this meeting to order, please." Amanda Singleton spoke above the numerous conversations as she took her place. Her kind face made eye contact with each of the seven people in the room, bobbing her flaming head to each one in silent greeting.

Letice asked, "May we please first discuss the disappointing news about the factory being sold?" She sank to her chair with a thump. "Rumor has it that it may be pulled down, but we don't wish to assume anything."

A deep familiar voice from the back of the room chimed in. "I wouldn't be anxious about that."

All eyes shifted to Colin as he strode to the front of the room and stood at Amanda's side. He wore a pair of tan slacks and a long-sleeved navy cotton shirt. The color highlighted his vivid green eyes.

"Please let me know when I may offer information about the building. I don't wish to disturb the order of your meeting." He nodded a greeting to Susannah and Letice as he settled himself in front of them.

Letice stood again. "I make a motion we let Colin speak."

A woman Susannah knew as the local librarian—glasses perched on the top of her head—seconded the motion, her silky voice barely discernible over the low hum of voices.

"Motion accepted by Carleen." Amanda fidgeted in her seat, leaning in toward him. "You have the floor, Colin."

Colin rose and returned to stand by Amanda. She peeked at him with admiration as he grinned at her. "Amanda, ladies and gentlemen, thank you for allowing me to be privy to your meeting, considering I am unable to attend often. The company I began some twenty years ago has been successful. It was not by my design, but God's. He enabled me to hire talented people, and they, too, are aware it was through His divine grace we have been so prosperous. We all realize that because of this success, we must give back to Him. Although I hold a seventy-five percent share in this company, I still consult with my board on how we should allocate our profits. Much of those profits go to charities around the world—with considerable funds remaining in this country."

He halted as he made eye contact with every person—his gaze lingering a millisecond longer when his eyes met Susannah's. "I'd like to ask if I may work with you closely on this project. It's my understanding that several of you have been at work in filling needs for the homeless in Neville. I've renovated my original home and will reside in Neville again—part-time. I must share my time between here and London, where my organization is based."

A brief round of applause broke out.

"Well, thanks for the reception. I appreciate that. Now I'll tell you about my company's recent acquisition," He leaned in toward Amanda and requested a cup of the water from the tray next to her. She complied with a nod, grinned at him warmly, and offered him a cup. He took a sip and proceeded. "C. Heard and Company has acquired the abandoned factory where the homeless are currently residing."

An awkward silence fell over the room. Susannah kept her focus on Colin. She sought to weigh his explanation, good or bad, as she continued studying him. He noted her questioning expression and bobbed his head in an imperceptible nod.

"Please don't be alarmed. When we purchased the building, we were aware of what was going on there. We do our homework before making such a massive investment. It took a while to close the deal as we were trying to get the best price possible. We acknowledge that it will require another huge investment to renovate enough to make it livable."

It took but a few seconds for this to register, and Colin opened his mouth to speak again but was interrupted by a rugged-looking man, who stood to be recognized. "So, you intend on turning it into some high-priced flats to make even more money than you already have? Is that your big plan? You think we'll stand for this? That we should overlook it since you're bringing more jobs and lodging to our community, but I say . . ."

Colin held his right palm out to halt the man. "Tom, will you please stop for a minute and hear me out? That is not our purpose at all. We mean to give something back to this village by building flats and charging rent based on the person's income. Please don't misunderstand . . . this is not free housing. They will have to sign an agreement to maintain their home. This is not—I repeat—not going to turn into a hovel, nor is it a luxury housing project for the wealthy. There will be stipulations attached to it."

Someone stood and asked, "How are they going to pay anything for it if they don't have jobs?"

"There'll be a board overseeing who's allowed to live there and how much they'll pay, which will be nothing until they have a job. We'd also like to offer training programs for those without skill sets. It's also my hope that someone here will chair the board with volunteers to aid them. We want people to learn how to take care of themselves by arranging education programs to help them get on their feet."

Too timid to stand, Susannah raised a trembling hand. Colin nodded for her to speak. "My friend, Diann, runs a shelter in the States and could give us some advice on a training program if the committee is interested. She's mentioned to me the different types of jobs they train for as well as someone to guide them in obtaining jobs. They also have volunteers who do the actual training for those in need.

I'd be happy to help in some capacity."

Colin's eyes sparkled. "Thank you, Susannah, that would be tremendous. Any volunteers would be welcomed."

A voice rose from the back of the room. "I'd be glad to help. This homeless scene has gotten out of hand. I remember when that factory closed twenty years ago. So many people lost jobs that most had to move from Neville to find employment. Some lost their homes that had been in their family for decades. So sad. The ones that couldn't move have struggled all that time, and the homeless people you see here are a result of that. I could teach computer classes. With so many jobs requiring computer knowledge, that should be of some assistance."

"Tammy, that's a marvelous idea. It's never too soon to start a lesson plan. Would you be willing to do that?"

"Yes. It's such a pleasure to be part of something bigger than ourselves." She bobbed her bright head in affirmation. Others around the room joined in with job training offers as the excitement grew.

"Thank you all."

Letice stood. "I'd like to make a motion for Susannah to head the training committee."

Susanna's eyes widened, and she shot her friend a glare. Letice whispered, "You're perfect for it."

Amanda agreed and asked Susannah if she would be willing to head it up. Susannah met Colin's eyes and saw the eagerness in them to go forward with the project. She couldn't say no, so she accepted, and the motion was voted on and passed.

Colin seated himself next to Amanda, who rose, head held high. "Well, Colin. You have made our meeting a success. There's no need to bring up previously scheduled topics as your news has negated them all. If there's no further business . . ."

Vita stood, and Amanda recognized her. "Colin, when would this improvement begin, and how long before these people may move in?" She held her gaze on him.

Colin relaxed into his chair. "We aim to set up next week. I expect that it will not take over three months. We're bringing in a large construction team, so it'll take as little time as possible."

Vita gave him a dazzling smile. "What do you propose we do with the families until that time?" She looked like the cat that swallowed the lizard with the tail protruding from its mouth.

"We decided to settle them at the Horden Inn." He waited for his remark to settle in. A tight silence followed.

Vita's countenance flushed. "Bravo, Colin."

Tom rose, not waiting for approval to express himself. "And who'll pay for that?"

Without hesitation, Colin answered. "My company."

Further points were raised about the recommended training programs, support, and sub-committee selections before they adjourned the meeting, and everybody headed for the refreshment table. Susannah hung back while Letice made a direct path to Colin.

Susannah struggled to not look in his direction. She ambled toward the drink table and poured lemonade.

Mindlessly, she singled out a chicken salad sandwich and found a seat. As Susannah took a nibble, Colin maneuvered himself into the place across from her, and Letice sat next to Susannah.

"Hello, Susannah." His eyes crinkled at the corners. "Thank you for heading the committee. We'll work well together to help those in need."

Struggling to chew, Susannah finished and sought to respond with a mere "Yes." Her answer sounded hollow, but it was too late to take it back—or to add enthusiasm.

He reached for his water and ran the tip of his finger around the rim of the glass and brought his gaze to meet Susannah's.

Letice broke in. "I think I'll have one of those sandwiches. Yummy." She turned to leave and sputtered under her breath as she pulled a face. "I must be microscopic."

Susannah caught her words and glanced as she watched her new friend go, almost falling into Amanda, who asked, "What did you say, dear?"

"Oh, nothing—talking to myself."

Amanda tilted her head toward Susannah and Colin, a question on her face. Susannah grew horrified that they'd mention something about Colin and her that he'd overhear. Susannah munched while conducting the observation, effectively ignoring Colin, and noted Vita step into their chat. Vita gave Susannah a seething stare, straightened her necklace, and strutted toward Colin. Susannah watched her approach and bump into Tom by accident.

"Sorry, love. Didn't mean to plow into you." She grabbed

Tom's arm to steady herself. His puffed-out chest revealed the ego-boost.

"No probs, love."

They strode together and sat by Colin. Tom slapped him on the back. "Hey, old chap. Didn't mean to call you out on that whole deal a bit ago. Bein' old chums, I knew you'd not take it wrong."

"No, Tom. I understood. You always jump to conclusions. Guess that's why you came to be a solicitor."

Susannah watched and listened to the exchange with utter confusion. Tom was a lawyer—and a long-time friend of Colin's? Perhaps she'd read him wrong after all. And what did it matter anyway?

An hour later, while walking home, her thoughts hadn't strayed far from the man who seemed to be of great interest to everyone, especially after the enormous contribution to the area's homeless. She pulled her sweater tight to ward off the crisp English evening. There was no way she would allow herself to become entangled with another man after what she'd lived through. It may begin well enough yet result in catastrophe. After Vita's presence created a spectacle of the unmistakable way she was after Colin, she refused to be associated in any drama.

Her relationship with Aaron had started out incredible but nevertheless ended in disaster. Now, her own child wouldn't even have much to do with her. No visits. Snatches of phone conversations on occasion. A gulf much wider than the Atlantic Ocean separated them.

A swift breeze lifted her hair and returned her to the Azores in the 1980s. The lush island of Terceira was charming, the Portuguese people hospitable and pleasant. The presence of the U.S. Air Force at Lajes Field was a comfort. That's where she'd met Aaron. He was serving a tour of duty as an Air Force pilot—all masculine, self-assured, and attractive. His charisma had fascinated and overwhelmed her shy demeanor. Thinking back now, she recognized he relished having authority over others—those he was certain he could conquer. Her blindness to his true nature brought her trouble, and she'd happily walked right into it.

She'd been relaxing in an outdoor café writing in her travel journal about the day spent at the Cinco Picos Volcanic Complex. She could still smell the sulfur and feel the sharp rough volcanic rock underfoot. Her pen raced across the pages. It had been a delightful day.

Oblivious to the surrounding activity, the gentle wind playing with her hair, she hadn't noticed the man sitting at a nearby table until the backfire of a motorcycle startled her into the present. Her head darted up to discover his silvery eyes upon her. He was in uniform, sipping on a bottle of some sort of Portuguese drink. He smiled, and she cautiously returned it and bent her head back to the journal.

She sensed his eyes on her and refused to look again. A few minutes passed before a pair of Air Force issued shoes appeared at her feet. His tone was velvety and rich. Thinking back now—smooth—much too smooth.

"Good afternoon. May I join you?" His smile was arresting, his eyes languid. She was swiftly sucked in.

Her stammer was obvious. "I . . . I'm not staying. I was about to take off." She grasped her backpack as he sat, uninvited.

"I didn't mean to startle you. It's just that I don't get to meet many American girls here. I caught your voice when you ordered and guessed you were from the South . . . Texas?" His grey eyes lanced her to the core.

Even the way he sipped his drink made her knees weak. "No, Louisiana." She managed to mutter the words.

"Oh, yeah, Texas's neighbor. I'm from Tennessee." He presented his hand. "Name's Aaron. What's yours?"

Well-manicured, sculpted—she had no choice but to accept. "Susannah." She now realized it was the way Satan stole into one's life, wrapped in an enticing package.

The rest was like sinking into a sweet, cool stream on a humid Louisiana day. At least it was until the honeymoon was over, and Aaron's authentic character presented itself with flashes of anger and words to match.

Susannah returned to the present and hurried toward the door of her cottage, the painful memories stabbing at her like a knife. No, she would not allow herself to be hurt by a man again.

Chapter Twelve

Neville, North Yorkshire, England
2019

"Morning, Tristan. How're you today?" April struggled to offer him a cordial reception.

"G'morning, April." Tristan's wide grin held affection. "Morning to you too, Polly."

Polly gave him a nod. "I've boxes to break down. Later, Tristan." As Polly brushed past April, she bumped into her and hissed, "Tell him now."

"Bye." April's voice dripped with sweetness. She turned back to Tristan. "What can I do for you?" She prayed it was a book request.

"You're a hard miss to find. I've popped in several times, and you've not been about." Tristan lounged against the counter, relaxed.

"Yes, well, I've been dealing with the purchase of the cottage, and it's taken me away from the shop." She straightened books that didn't need attention, moving them around absently.

"I understand. Has Ryan—Mr. Wilkinson—left the country?" Tristan's enthusiasm evident, he mimicked her actions by arranging other items on the counter.

"No, not yet. He'll be gone in a few days. He's overseeing the repairs on the cottage. In fact, I should get over there myself, soon." She trusted he'd take the hint. "Was there a book or something you needed?" Her heart hoped again.

"Well, no. I was . . . uh . . . hoping you'd have dinner with me this weekend. That is—if you're available." Tristan squared his shoulders as he fumbled a display of bookmarks.

April had never seen Tristan unsettled before. She felt sorry for him. No, she couldn't let this go on any longer.

"That's kind of you, but . . ."

The door groaned open, and the bell jangled. Tristan stood there with a doe-eyed expression. How could she concentrate?

Polly bolted from the back room, playing defense. She accosted the customer, over-compensating with extreme friendliness, and steered the woman away with record speed.

Flustered by the interruption and Tristan's forlorn appearance, April faltered, and hastily replied to his proposal.

"Dinner sounds great. There is something I want to speak to you about. Why don't we meet at Talbot's about seven on Saturday?"

"Sure." He gave her a tentative smile. "I guess that would be fine." Tristan's face was an open book. He'd not expected her unenthusiastic response.

April turned toward Polly and the customer. She called out over her shoulder, "See you on Saturday, Tristan. Cheers."

"Cheers," he said in return.

April met Polly's eyes over the customer's head. Her glare told April she couldn't wait to get her alone.

The next hour seemed a blessing for April and a curse for Polly. The bookstore welcomed a continual buzz of shoppers in and out, allowing no chance for the women to communicate except for work-related requests.

Once the shop was silent, other than the smooth classical music in the background, Polly made a direct path to April.

"Please, don't be upset." April's eyes pleaded. "I was about to explain everything to him when that girl came in. It was such a distraction I couldn't do it."

Polly paused, feet apart, fists on hips. Her lips had retreated into a taut straight line, hazel eyes hard.

April tried to subdue her own anger at Polly's posture.

"I told him there was something I wanted to talk to him about. It'll be much easier in a relaxed setting with no interruptions."

Finished with her explanation, she wondered why she experienced guilt.

A response from her was unnecessary—but her friend's contempt was clear—no words were needed.

ᏣᏁ

April walked the path she always took—to her parents' home. She wasn't conscious of her surroundings. She left Books-on-the-Green into the warm afternoon sun, her thoughts on Polly. Over the years, they'd had a fair amount of tense moments, especially when working out the particulars of their joint business, but an agreement of sorts always followed. Not this time.

They hadn't closed the shop on favorable terms, with Polly unresponsive to April's cheery parting to have a good evening.

Anger flaring, April kicked a pebble on the pavement. "She's the most stubborn, insufferable person." She shuddered. "How dare she interfere in my personal relationships?" April turned in time to see her image in the boutique window, her face contorted with fury. If she hadn't been so upset with herself, she would've laughed at the reflection.

"Oh, God. Please forgive me. I'm ashamed to be so bitter." She closed her eyes and halted on the pavement. Her typical response to severe stress was sleep. That was her escape. Perhaps a nap would be in order when she got home.

The sound of her name in an all too familiar voice made her eyes pop open. She angled her head. Too late. A pair of beady eyes found hers before she could resume her weary walk home.

"How do you do today?" A flat, whiny male voice rose behind her.

A deep guttural moan escaped April's throat. Mr. Pompous—not today. Self-reproach at her negative thoughts brought remorse for the second time within minutes.

"Good day, Mr. Borren. How're you?" She pushed her shoulders back and faced him—an attempt at civility.

"Fine, fine. I meant to drop by the shop and see if you have a copy of a book entitled 'Famulus Defined.' It's a rare book about . . ."

"Sorry, Mr. Borren. I've an appointment to keep. Please stop by tomorrow, and we'll work to locate your book. Have a pleasant evening." Her words trailed over her shoulder as she hurriedly walked away. In the store window, she saw the stunned expression on his fat, round face. No one had ever left one of his conversations before until he'd kept them at least half the hour.

"I can't believe I did that," April mumbled as she rushed along the sidewalk.

Lord forgive me, again, but I couldn't endure one of Mr. Pom . . . I mean, Mr. Borren's endless I-know-everything-about-everything—one-sided discussions.

She shrugged. "It wouldn't be so bad if he didn't sound so haughty." She thought about what she'd said to him. "Also, please forgive my little white-lie about the appointment. I mean—I told Ryan I was stopping by the cottage." There went her nap. Out of guilt, she turned and peeked to watch Mr. Borren's massive frame trudging in the opposite direction, his blue tweed newsboy cap angled atop his balding head.

A sharp pang of sympathy gripped her heart. He might be lonesome. His wife had died some years before. Though, if he'd let someone else have a say, he might not be alone.

Thoughts of Mr. Borren faded as she approached Permelia Cottage. Her sign hung proudly attached to the wall next to the gate.

"Looks brilliant—don't it, lass?" Mr. Jenks' grin ran ear-to-ear.

"Oh my. Yes, Mr. Jenks. You did a famous job of it."

"Mr. Wilkinson's in the cottage." He performed an about-face and proceeded with his rusty red toolbox toward the side of the cottage.

April stood gawking at the sign a moment longer, then walked the path to the front door. She went in and called out, "Ryan, are you about?" She traveled from room to room but found no trace of him.

As she moved through the kitchen and peeked out the window, she saw him sitting on top of the wall under the dappled shade of a tree. He appeared relaxed—at peace. She'd not noticed him with such a serene air in the brief time she'd known him. He'd always seemed so composed, so . . . together. Given that, April hesitated to trouble him. He caught sight of her through the window. She stepped back into the room as he slid from the wall and strode to the cottage.

A strange sensation overwhelmed her, watching his approach. Something deep in the pit of her stomach—an uncertain awareness. She immersed herself in surveying the cabinets—not looking his way when he opened the door.

"Have you been here long?" Ryan leaned against the inside of the door opening.

With her head almost inside the cabinet, she replied, "No,

not long—reviewing the storage capacity." She struggled to sound indifferent, but it came out dull. Her throat tightened.

Ryan closed the door, stepped to the table, and leaned against it. "Do you know Mrs. Claxton who lives down the street?"

She withdrew her head from the cabinet and closed the door, relieved to have a change of subject. "Yes, somewhat. She's a nice person. Why?"

"I met her today—and her cat. Seems she was acquainted with my mother. I think she mentioned that they attended the same church. She also asked me to tea before I leave." He seemed to contemplate the idea. Silent, he stared at his feet.

April observed him as he folded his arms across his chest—deep in thought.

"You should go."

He blinked his eyes. "What? Go where?"

"To tea at Mrs. Claxton's. You'd enjoy her company. She's a wonderful cook, and she loves to bake." Turning to the last cabinet, she opened the door and feigned interest. "Tea is at three."

 C3❦80

April and Ryan walked around the house and garden, complimenting Mr. Jenks on all he'd done. There was still no sign of rain, so they'd be through with the overhaul in good time. Mr. Jenks was saying, "... we should be done by mid-day tomorrow. We had one slight delay on a rotten window—held us back—no concern."

"Doesn't sound too bad." April glanced at Ryan with an

uneasy, heavy sensation, and looked back at Mr. Jenks.

Mr. Jenks jumped in. "It's a cheap fix," he said with confidence.

April relaxed.

"April, 'ave you shown Mr. Wilkinson our castle?" As he turned his head, April thought she caught a fleeting smile cross his lips.

"No, she hasn't. I'm glad you mentioned it," Ryan said. "Could we go in the morning, then come back here? Mr. Jenks should be finished."

Polly's face slid into her mind. "That sounds great ..." She bit her lip to check her forthcoming words. "But I need to check if Polly can be at the shop."

Mr. Jenks gave a knowing nod. "Is that lass at it again? She has a real moody streak in her—that one."

"When Polly is in a good mood, which is most of the time, she's wonderful. But when she's not . . ." April hesitated to be derogatory about her friend. ". . . she's a tad difficult."

"Huh." Mr. Jenks huffed. "That's bein' polite."

Ryan intervened with a playful glint in his eyes. "Why don't I come by the shop tomorrow morning, and we'll find out what kind of mood she's in?"

April wasn't sure that was such a good idea. But what could she say? Ryan was leaving on Sunday—and she was having dinner with Tristan on Saturday evening. This was her Saturday to watch the shop and the only day she could go with Ryan. "I suppose that'd be fine."

Mr. Jenks walked away and called out over his shoulder, "Best prepare yourself, just in case."

April sighed. If looks could kill, the glare Polly *had* shot April after Tristan left would've struck her dead right in the middle of the shop. What was up with her? Mr. Jenks had said Polly had a strong personality, but this was somehow different. What was going on?

Chapter Thirteen

Neville, North Yorkshire, England
2016

Colin's gaze skimmed the room in search of Susannah. Her enthusiasm in this project was strong, so, where was she?

Amanda's tone rose as she asked Virgil to make the treasurer's report for the committee. Once completed, Amanda resumed by moving that they elect members to occupy the special sub-committees regarding the factory.

"Glad we have all present today. Well, except Susannah. She sends her apologies. We need to address two issues. One being the overall renovation committee, which Colin will chair, as well as a committee for funding, fundraisers, etc. Also, we'll need a committee for designing the floor plans for each flat, as well as for the cosmetic design of each one—like color scheme, décor, and furnishings. Do I hear any nominations or volunteers?"

Deep in thought about Susannah, the sound of his name called him back to the meeting. He stared at his pen and noted that he'd been idly writing her name. He shook his head. Ridiculous. What was he—a juvenile with an infatuation? He barely knew the woman. He scratched out his scrawling, and with a snap clipped the pen to the pad.

Vita stated, "I'd like to organize the indoor design scheme—floor plans for each flat and so on."

Several members nodded. Virgil stood. "I'll make that motion for Vita." His leer was blatant, which she accepted with a smile, nodding in Virgil's direction. "Thank you, Virgil."

"Okay, now we have someone to chair a committee we had not considered." Amanda's gaze darted around the room. "I'm sorry I didn't think of that."

Colin asked to speak.

Amanda's sigh held relief. "Yes, Colin."

"While I do believe Vita would do a fine job with the task, I must remind the committee that it falls under the structural renovation of the property. I think there should be one committee that manages the flat floor plans and another regarding cosmetic, décor and furnishings.

Vita popped out of her seat like a jack-in-the-box. "Well, thank you, Colin, for your vote of trust. That means I'd better meet with you as soon as this meeting is over so we can get set up.” With allure, she slipped into her seat, crossed her legs, and glanced at Virgil.

Amanda cleared her throat. “Let’s get on with other committee appointments. Maybe three per committee. We’ve just enough people to do that.”

The remainder of the meeting progressed without incident considering the tension that Vita had created by her spectacle. As soon as Amanda adjourned, Colin walked straight to Letice and attempted to keep his voice casual. “Where’s Susannah this evening? I hope she’s well.”

Something glinted in Letice’s eyes, and then it was gone in a flash. “She’s well. She had another engagement this evening.”

Colin offered a gentle smile. “Good. She seems to be a wonderful asset to this committee and the community.”

That sparkle in her eyes returned as she nodded and said, “I completely agree, Colin. I’m glad to see you do too. Susannah is a very special person.”

ೞ⊗ೞ

Susannah searched the crowd at Talbot’s Tavern for a free table. Hodge came forward, an apologetic expression on his face. “Sorry, ladies, we’re busy for a Thursday night.”

Letice pointed a long slender finger at a table that had not been cleared. “May we claim that nice table by the window? We don’t mind waiting for it to be cleaned, do we girls?” Susannah and Amanda nodded.

“Certainly, my dears. One moment and I’ll have it cleaned in a jiffy.”

Once Hodge had seated them, a slap on his back brought his attention away from them to Colin Heard behind him. The men addressed one another. Colin nodded and greeted each woman by name, saving Susannah for last. He fixed his gaze on her, and she twisted the linen napkin on her lap.

He laid a hand on Hodge's shoulder. "I can see you all are managing well. Is Hodge entertaining you, or is this an exclusive party?"

Letice chimed in, "You're welcome to join us if you like." She pulled out the vacant chair next to her, across from Susannah.

He took a seat while Hodge handed out menus. "I'll send Effie over to wait on you. Tristan is off tonight and will be sad to miss out on teasin' you girls." He showed them his sunniest smile and strolled away.

Colin's gaze settled on Susannah. "I'll not interfere with your hen night out but a moment. I wanted to ask if after our meeting on Saturday, I could take you all to the factory? I'd also appreciate your support with designing floor plan layouts." He paused. "That is—if you're interested. Susannah, since you're heading the training committee, and that won't start until after the residents move in, I thought this would be a good way to keep you involved. The construction crew has finished with all the load-bearing walls, so you'll have to design around them, of course."

Letice beamed her approval. "I'm sure Susannah would." She threw him a pointed expression. "I thought Vita was to chair that committee."

"No, indeed, I believe she agreed to organize the indoor décor scheme—design and color, and such. It's been a few days since the last meeting, so perhaps my memory isn't sound." He smiled, his sparkling eyes meeting Susannah's. "We missed you at the meeting on Saturday."

She straightened in her chair and remained silent.

Letice's fingernails tapped out a tune on the table. "So, Susannah, are you game?"

Susannah blinked a few times before she reluctantly agreed.

"Grand." Colin said. "I hoped you'd be eager to grant some vision." He leaned forward and in a low voice repeated, "You were missed at the meeting."

Susannah's face grew warm as she caught herself looking into his eyes, unable to respond, her mouth dry. She reached for her water and took a sip to buy a moment. "I—I had a tight deadline for a magazine article. That was all."

He gave her a nod, eyes flashing. "I see. I'm sure your article is smashing. I'd love to read one sometime."

To Susannah's relief, Effie arrived to take their orders, asking twice as she wrote, scratched through what she'd written, and tried again. When she turned to Colin, he informed her he already had a table and was waiting for someone. She flushed and turned to take their orders to the kitchen.

"Well, ladies, I've taken enough of your time. It was nice seeing you all. I'll meet you on Saturday."

"Well, well, well . . ." Letice said, her eyes on Colin as he walked to a table across the room. "Wonder who he's meeting?"

"Do you suspect it's a woman, Letty?" Amanda asked with

wide eyes.

Susannah stared at her crumpled napkin, focused on smoothing it. The man made her too nervous. How would she survive this committee? She sighed and brought her attention back to the lively banter.

"Perhaps, but we shouldn't meddle. Give him his privacy." She gave a stern expression to Amanda and snickered. "Though, if he wanted discretion he should have ventured from this nosy village for dinner."

Amanda laughed and gave her a keen look in return.

"Letice, what did you order?" Susannah asked, changing the subject.

Letice gave Susannah's arm a playful slap and whispered, "Susannah, don't play coy—he's dishy. Admit it."

Susannah grimaced. "And when have I ever called a man dishy?"

Letice laughed—loud enough for the neighboring table to turn and stare. Her cheeks flushed. "Okay, I'll behave." Though, she made a half-turn to peer at Colin's still empty table. "Amanda, tell me when his dinner companion arrives. Will you? You've a better vantage point."

Amanda sighed in resignation. "Not meddling, aye?"

"Stop it, you two," Susannah said in a hushed voice and shifted in her seat. "He may be on a date, and it's none of our business."

Amanda's eyes widened. "Oh, my."

Susannah, powerless to stop herself, twisted to glance at Colin's table as he pulled a chair out for none other than Vita. She felt her face heat as she turned back to meet Letice's eyes filled with compassion.

"I told you he wasn't interested in me," Susannah said in a soft voice. "There's your answer."

Susannah rose, tears stinging her eyes. She was being ridiculous. It didn't matter who he had dinner with. "Excuse me," she muttered and strode to the ladies' room, her path taking her past Colin and Vita. She focused on Hodge, who stood nearby. Through her peripheral vision, she saw Colin glance her way, but she ignored him.

❦

Susannah's abrupt departure and the tears welling in her eyes did not go unnoticed by Amanda nor Letice. They exchanged looks, unsure what to do.

"What is Colin doing with Vita?" Amanda's eyes bulged. "They're like chalk and cheese."

"Something's amiss here. Colin would never fall for her. I don't care how gorgeous she is." Letice's brow wrinkled. "I'm worried about Susannah. I knew she was interested in him—and I could've sworn he was too. But I could have it all wrong."

"I've known Colin for years, and I can tell you right now he did take a strong interest in Susannah. If Vita got wind of it though, and I'm certain she did at the meeting the other day, she's working in the background to put an end to it." Amanda sighed. "That sounds harsh, and Vita is a kind person in many respects, but when it comes to Colin—if she can't have him—she'll make sure no one else will either."

Letice nodded. "It seems the way of it. I had no idea they knew each other so well."

"Oh, they go 'way back' as Vita once put it." Amanda

155

narrowed her eyes. "I think they even walked out a bit in school. And, perhaps, whatever might have once been there between them is now rekindling."

⚜

Susannah stared at her reflection in the mirror in the ladies' room. She'd stopped the tears before they fell, yet she still felt so downhearted. Was she interested in Colin but too afraid to admit it? "Oh, you silly old fossil." she muttered to her reflection. Naturally, a woman came out of a stall as she'd said it.

"You alright, dearie?" The small white-haired woman asked with genuine concern.

"Oh, yes, ma'am. Just having a bit of a heart-to-heart with myself."

The woman patted her shoulder. "Don't be ashamed of speaking to yourself. I do it all the time. Sometimes, we're our own worst enemy—as the saying goes. We shouldn't be too hard on ourselves. Talk it over with friends, and they can help you sort it out." She hesitated before opening the door to leave. "Have a nice evening."

"You too." Susannah gave her an appreciative smile, remembering her own grandmother.

Turning back to her image, she said, "Well, you heard the lady. Talk it over with friends. And so what if Colin isn't interested in you? You weren't searching for a man anyway."

On her return, Susannah was once again forced to go by their table, and kept her eyes focused on Amanda and Letice—and the unhappy expressions aimed her way.

Susannah slid the chair back with a scraping sound and

sat. "Look, girls. I don't want your pity. I can see by your faces you think I'm crushed to see Colin and Vita together." She took a sip of water, "But I'm not. I told you both that he wasn't interested in me." She glanced at her food. "Now, for heaven's sake, can we ignore them and just eat?"

"You're right." Amanda's tone was repentant. "We let our speculations get away from us."

"Well, not me." Letice tilted her head and gave her a smirk. "I still think he's interested in you, and that he's no more infatuated with Vita than a cat would be in chasing an elephant."

Susannah burst out laughing. "That's quite the mental picture."

Letice scoffed. "I'm serious. They do not belong together, and I don't think Colin is at all taken with her." She lifted her chin a notch. "She has him here under some false pretense you can be certain."

Amanda shot a sideways glance at Letice. "You sound pretty sure of yourself. Got any ideas what that could be?"

Before Letice could answer, Susannah butted in. "May we please change the subject? I'm growing weary of the topic. And this delicious food is getting cold."

"Oh, all right." Letice gave in. "But you haven't heard the last of it. I'm good at summing people up, and I tell you, Colin is interested in you. There." She was emphatic as she crossed her arms over her chest. "I'll say no more—for now."

Their meal commenced with cheerful conversation, Effie checking on them from time to time, before delivering dessert, almost dropping a plate in Letice's lap. When Effie left, they exchanged plates until they each had what they'd ordered.

Letice leaned in. "She's a sweet girl, but having a tough time getting the hang of this job."

"Let's be sure and leave her a nice tip to encourage her," Susannah said between bites.

"Tipping in the U.K. is generally not customary," Letice said.

"So, I've heard, but in this case, I think we should. It certainly isn't more ridiculous than a cat chasing an elephant," Susannah said with a sly smile as Letice nearly choked on her next bite. The laughter that followed offered a welcome distraction to the pair that sat not far behind her. She'd almost convinced herself that what Colin Heard did wasn't affecting her at all. She'd vowed that there'd be no more men in her life—ever.

Chapter Fourteen

Neville, North Yorkshire, England
2019

For the first time in longer than he could remember, Ryan didn't hit the snooze on his alarm. He slipped from his bed and ambled to the window to check the weather. The sky was gray with dots of blue peeping through, struggling to make an appearance. The brochure he'd found in the lobby was on the nightstand, so he gave the first paragraph a brief once-over.

For more than seven hundred years, the stone keep castle sat perched on the hill overlooking the verdant valleys and forests near the village of Neville. Horden Castle and its grounds now encompass three hundred acres, including a five-acre lake and extensive, well-kept gardens.

"Oh. A day of touring in the rain." Ryan groaned as he headed for the shower, and half an hour later, with umbrella in hand, he met April at the entrance to the castle's grounds. The crenelated castle stood on the hill like a guard awaiting its next attack from unseen forces. The clouds had started to break, and bits of blue sky shone through, sunlight shooting beams in the gaps. Maybe, he wouldn't need his umbrella after all.

April smiled and glanced appreciatively at the castle ahead. "Shall we?"

Ryan nodded and followed her up the road leading to the castle bridge. The stream of water rushed over rocks that had smoothed through the centuries. "I'm glad Polly happily agreed to watch the shop for you."

April smiled. "Yes, she's in a generous mood today."

Ryan shielded the sun from his eyes as he looked ahead. "How old is this castle?"

"The original section was built about the middle of the thirteenth century. Each owner made additions." April brought her camera out and snapped a quick shot of Ryan.

"It's an impressive sight—like a fortress and palace all in one." He turned to her and said, "Let me know how the picture turns out."

April gave a sheepish grin. "Sorry." She cleared her throat. "I think it began as a fortress and was gradually added onto until it became a residence more than a defensive structure. Although I'm sure defense was a major factor in its location, and the fact that it was built on a hill overseeing the surrounding area. Being able to see your enemy coming was a prime reason for a hilltop location in those days."

Ryan gave her a muffled laugh. "You could be the Horden Castle tour guide."

"I've been here a lot." April shrugged. "And I love local history."

"It shows." He rubbed the back of his neck and they walked on, stepping through the only entrance to the castle via the bridge and a fortified gate.

April resumed tour guide mode. "This would've been built of wood during the time it was used for fortification."

The wide expanse of lawn lay in front of the castle, open for the gathering of people, events, or livestock. April stood to the side of the entrance, staring trance-like at the castle. Ryan watched her instead, noticing the awe in her eyes. She turned to him.

"It's a lovely castle. Don't you think?" She didn't wait for an answer. "I try to put myself in this place as it was in the early years—during the lifeblood of the times. The clothes, atmosphere, lifestyle, and the way people behaved then. I've read a lot of books on its history. It's quite fascinating, and sometimes frightening." She wrapped her arms around herself. "I'd love to go back in time—but only for a short while. Considering the medical and political practices of the time, I wouldn't want to stay long." She raised her eyebrows. "I mean bloodletting, right?"

Ryan laughed. "You make it sound so realistic—almost like you've experienced it."

"Oh, it's just my love of reading. I get so engrossed in whatever book I'm involved in. There are some medieval writings that offer a clear picture of what went on. Like dying from the common cold and how less than half of all children saw their fifth birthday." He saw her eyes mist before she turned away toward the castle again.

"Guess we need to be glad for the time we live in, even if it has its own troubles."

"Yes, we need to be thankful, don't we?"

Ryan changed the subject. "Where do we start?"

"We buy tickets at the gift shop for the tour. We can stop by the shop again if you want to buy a memento of the castle unless you want to buy something now."

"No, I'm good. Let's do the tour."

They bought tickets and made their way to the entrance of the main hall where the tour would begin. The massive wood doors were embellished with iron strips and stud. Ryan ran his hand over the thick wood and wondered at the weight of such a door. They stepped inside, and the tour guide waved to them from across the room. It became apparent that it was a slow day since they were the only participants.

"Good morning. My name is Eleanor, and I'll be your guide this morning. Looks like the clouds have kept some people at bay—if only they would have come ahead as the day is going to play out to be a smashing one." The peppy girl turned on her heel. "Right this way, please."

Eleanor led them from the main hall after explaining its historic value to the castle and the events held there. To their right, they walked a lengthy passageway toward the banquet hall. Eleanor told them about some of the royal celebrations held during the numerous reigns. Each king, or queen, had their own, sometimes odd, personal preferences as to how they celebrated a given occasion, which Eleanor explained usually centered on their fondness of meat—roasted lamb, capons, chicken, venison, rabbit, and even swan.

Ryan's mouth slackened. "You've got to be joking . . . eating a swan?"

"Yes, and that's the usual response I get . . . along with roasted lark." Eleanor made a face, and Ryan shook his head.

"I must admit, history has never been one of my favorite subjects, but the royal lifestyle in that time was rather enthralling. I'm sure if you weren't royalty, you must have had a pretty rough life." Ryan surprised himself at his interest, remembering some of his mother's comments on history.

"Royalty had all the conveniences—for their time. Yet, they did have a middle class of sorts. The majority of the population was living in poverty. The monasteries did look after the poor until Henry VIII took all the wealth from them. He allowed the poor to beg—once they bought a license from the state. But that's a long story. Let's continue our tour."

Walking toward an arched doorway, she added, "Here's a small, and I do mean small, enclosed courtyard. As you can see, there's a very narrow opening in the marble patio in the center. During excavations, coins from different eras were found. We believe this was once a fountain or coy pond, and people would toss their coins in to make a wish."

The courtyard was no larger than a fifteen-foot square yet held a certain quality. Situated in the center of the castle on the lowest floor the only light came from above. Now midmorning, the courtyard was in partial shadow radiating an eerie appearance.

Eleanor stood paused inside the door, silent. Ryan and April let their eyes roam over the square enclosure. The entire floor was covered in squares of marble with petite flower beds in each corner and one surrounding the now missing fountain, which had been replaced with a stone birdbath. The sparse plantings included lavender, poppies, and daisies. The scent of the profusely blooming lavender surrounding the birdbath enveloped Ryan, reminding him instantly of his mother as if she were at his shoulder.

"If you're ready, we'll head to the chapel." Eleanor stepped into the corridor.

They followed, and Ryan walked beside April. "This is an amazing place. It's hard to believe I actually had ancestors who walked these halls so many years ago. It's kind of a strange sensation." Embarrassment crept into his voice as if he'd revealed something of himself that he hadn't meant to share.

April didn't appear to notice. "Yes, but it's also very fascinating—knowing of that connection from the past. Someday, when I have time, I want to research my own genealogy. It's such a time-consuming task. I hear it can be addictive once you get started."

"Yeah, my mother said my aunt was into it for more than thirty years. That's how she was able to learn so much—and she started long before the invention of the Internet."

"Amazing. She must've been enamored with it since that would've taken a lot of phone calls, writing letters, and taking trips."

"By the time my mother came along, and then the Internet, her aunt taught her all she'd learned, which got my mother hooked for sure."

"Are you hooked now?" April teased him.

"Well, I wouldn't go that far, but I am interested. My aunt and mother have done so much work. I'd like to visit more places they found in their research."

Eleanor said, "Here we are. This chapel was built with the original part of the castle, not one of the later additions. Notice the wooden oak beams," she pointed overhead, "are still in excellent condition because they were protected from the elements."

The small chapel was lined with pews made from what looked like the same oak as the beams. There were rows of seven pews on each side of the middle aisle leading toward the gilded altar. Above and behind the altar a massive stained-glass window was divided into three sections. Each section depicted different Biblical scenes in bright, vibrant colors—the birth of Christ, the crucifixion, and the ascension.

"This is one of the finest stained-glass creations left from medieval England," Eleanor told them. "It's unbelievable how it survived all the battles, wars, and destruction for centuries."

April's tone was sincere. "I do believe God does protect some things for future generations to show us how He's worked throughout time—and to encourage us that His will does prevail during any calamity."

Ryan shifted from one foot to another. The peaceful silence in the chapel was palpable. April sat in a pew and bowed her head. Eleanor walked to the front of the room and looked at the beautiful glass. Ryan, uncertain what to do, looked around and admired the detail of the carved wooden pews.

The end of each pew held different intricate carvings—a shepherd with his sheep, a man slaying a giant, the parting of the Red Sea, a rod of wood budding flowers and almonds, water pouring from a rock. All were skillfully done, and time had not altered the vividness of the designs.

Continuing his perusal of the chapel, he noticed the detail of the wood wainscoting on the walls. It rose up the wall to about ten feet and painted a dull white.

"I see you admiring the wainscoting. It was added in around the fifteenth century by one of the kings. We don't have any wainscoting left from the thirteenth century, although it's mentioned in many of the surviving manuscripts."

April was still seated, looking around the room, taking in the architecture. She was at ease, her face relaxed.

Eleanor strode to a door in the corner. She pointed to a huge tapestry on the wall, but it did not depict another scene from the Bible as Ryan would have imagined. Instead, there were two knights standing over a long narrow table. In the middle of the table stood a gold goblet, which glowed. The two knights had their swords drawn as if in defense of the goblet.

"This tapestry depicts two of King Arthur's knights guarding the Holy Grail. The detailed stitching is magnificent. It must have taken years to complete. The devotion to the project was quite immense."

April said, "We have a book at the shop that's devoted strictly to the study of ancient tapestries. It goes into great detail about the types of stitching they used, the length of time it took, and the types of fabrics they used. It also discusses the reasons the subject matter for the tapestries was chosen since stitchery was more than a pastime."

She stepped closer to the tapestry. "They warmed rooms against the cold stone and added a decorative touch, usually reflecting some heroic or historic moments in the lord of the manor's life or of the country."

Ryan glanced at Eleanor, but her face was difficult to read. Either she was in awe of April's knowledge, or she was a bit miffed at someone hijacking her job.

"Eleanor, I'm so sorry. I didn't mean to interrupt your tour. I'm so captivated with the history of this castle and its contents."

"You don't have to apologize. I enjoy your interest. And you're job security as many times as you've been here. I've never heard all of that about tapestries in such detail. It must be a fascinating read. I may have to get a copy."

"Sure. I'll put it aside for you."

Ryan placed his hands on his hips. "Well, ladies, as fascinating as this discussion is about needlework, where are we off to next?"

Eleanor smiled at him. "We'll move on to the bedchambers." Leaving the chapel, they took a short walk down a wide hall and up a set of winding stairs of worn stone.

"They must've had small feet." Ryan motioned for April to step ahead of him as they followed their guide. He placed a foot gingerly on each narrow step as he climbed.

"Yes, they did. You'll see some of their shoes on display at the end of the tour. They were of smaller stature as well." Eleanor glanced over her shoulder at Ryan. "You would've towered over them."

"So, I take it there weren't many men more than six feet tall seven hundred years ago?"

"No. Although King Edward was known to be six feet two inches tall. He was looked upon as very intimidating."

April pointed to the low doorway ahead. "Ryan, you'll want to watch your head. The openings here aren't quite as high as they are downstairs."

"Thanks for the warning. I don't want to spend my last two days in England in the hospital."

"Have you been on holiday?" Eleanor asked as they made their way to the second floor.

"No—I've been here on business."

"That's right. April mentioned she was buying a cottage from you." Her face showed recognition. "Oh ... you must be Susannah's son."

Ryan's gaze had been out the window at the countryside, but at her words he swung around to face her. "You knew my mother?"

"Yes, she was a frequent visitor to the castle. Some of her ancestors lived here at one time. Something about her twenty-third great grandmother having married the owner of the castle."

"The gift shop has a book on the history of the castle and its owners," April told Ryan.

"Yes, that's right." Eleanor's interest piqued. "We could take a look and see who that ancestor was."

"I'm not that much into genealogy. It was my mother's forte."

Eleanor nodded and moved toward the first bedchamber. "This is the bower, used by the lady of the castle. Her private apartment. The furnishings are replicas from the era when the castle was in its heyday—roughly the thirteenth and fourteenth centuries."

A huge posted bed with stitched fabric hangings from its four corners was adorned with faux furs and pillows. Several ornate chests were scattered around the room. Eleanor pointed out they were used to store garments. A few benches and stools were strategically placed in groups to encourage seating for visiting, some of which were placed by the window for doing needlework near the light. Again, as in other rooms, more tapestries hung from the walls.

"The lady of the castle was taken care of by her ladies-in-waiting as well as entertaining other women with music, doing embroidery, or reading." Eleanor finished her dissertation by taking a deep breath. "You're welcome to take a few minutes to walk about the room. No sitting please." She gave a nod. "I need to step out into the corridor and make a quick call. Won't be a bit."

"She sure knows her stuff and so do you." Ryan gave April a grin and walked to look out the window. The thick bottle-green glass lent a hazy view of the country landscape. He felt he'd stepped back in time seven hundred years, peering out to see if a rider would appear over the hill to warn the castle's occupants of impending danger. He turned to see April standing on the opposite side of the bed, and due to its height, he could only see her from the waist up. Her white peasant blouse gave the appearance she could've been dressed in a long flowing gown from that century, ready to attend her lady. The sound of a cell phone's ring in the hall brought both of them to face the open door.

Eleanor pocketed her phone. "Sorry, chaps. A queue has formed, so we need to move on." They continued the tour at a brisker pace. Eleanor apologized. "Sorry to rush. I was so appreciating a slower-paced tour with time to discuss more of the history. April and I have had many a discussion over tea about this place."

"And will probably have several more." April gently shoved Eleanor on the shoulder and stopped as she stared ahead into the garden. "Isn't that Colin Heard?"

Eleanor's attitude transitioned as she turned toward the man April pointed out. "Yes, I do believe it is. This is a rare event. I wonder what he's doing here?"

"Well, he does own the place—or at least his corporation does. He may be taking a personal interest in how it's being kept."

Ryan strained his eyes to get a better look, but the man was too far away. He raised an eyebrow and pulled a face. "Why don't we walk that way and you two can ask him why he's here? Besides, it seems you may want a closer view."

Both women turned to him and gave an identical expression of children with a hand stuck in the cookie jar. April started to speak, but he held up a hand. "No need to explain. He's obviously rich, well-dressed, and a real catch."

They both glared at him. He'd said too much. "Guess that sounded a bit chauvinistic . . . sorry. That's not exactly what I meant—I mean—he must be somewhat of a local celebrity, and most people would want to get a closer look . . . so let's go." He shrugged and led the way.

As they drew closer, Ryan noticed that the description he had assumed about the man was spot on—except that he didn't appear to be very old to have amassed such a fortune. He appeared to be no more than in his late forties.

The man leaned casually against a low stone wall enclosing a small garden along the side entrance. He spoke with a stout, grey-haired man holding a shovel, who smiled at something he'd said. As they shook hands in farewell, the crunch of gravel brought their attention to the approaching trio.

Colin Heard strode toward them. "Hello, Eleanor. How goes the tour business?" His white, perfect teeth flashed from a broad, sincere grin.

Eleanor beamed in admiration. "Couldn't be better, Mr. Heard . . . how are you?"

"Fine. And you, April? I see you're still our best customer."

April laughed nervously. "I'm doing well. I'm not sure about being your best customer, but I certainly do love coming here."

Not waiting for an introduction, Ryan presented his hand and said, "Good afternoon, I'm Ryan Wilkinson. It's a pleasure to meet you, Mr. Heard."

"A pleasure to meet you. How are you acquainted with these lovely ladies?"

"I've been in Neville for about a week on business. April and I are working on a real estate deal, and I met Eleanor today. She's an excellent guide."

Eleanor's face reddened.

"Yes, I've heard good reports about her. Wish I had ten more like her."

Ryan smiled mischievously. "You could always hire April."

Mr. Heard turned toward April. "Oh?"

April's chin dipped. "No, he's joking."

"No, seriously. She knows as much about this castle as Eleanor."

Eleanor agreed. "He's right. April's been here enough and has all the books published about Horden Castle. She'd make a brilliant guide."

"If you're interested, April, fill out the proper paperwork at the office, and I'll put in a good word for you with the boss." Mr. Heard winked at April, she blushed and thanked him. The man paused and peered curiously at Ryan. His face grew serious. "Did you say your name was Wilkinson? You wouldn't by chance be related to Susannah Wilkinson?"

"Yes, I'm her son. I'm here to sell the cottage, which April is buying."

He cleared his throat, "I see."

Ryan rubbed his forehead. "Did you know my mother?"

"Yes, we worked on a church committee together some years ago regarding housing for needy families in the area." A fleeting look of pain crossed his face as he averted his eyes. "I was wondering what had happened to her."

April cleared her throat. "Mrs. Wilkinson passed away."

Colin's face paled, and he met Ryan's gaze. "Mr. Wilkinson, I'm very sorry to hear that. Please accept my condolences.

Other than the local church, did your mother favor any charities? I'd like to leave a memorial in her name."

"The local church would be fine," Ryan said in a low voice. "Thank you." Hesitating, Ryan pulled a business card from his pocket and gave it to Mr. Heard. "If you don't mind, give me your card, and should I come up with another charity, I'll contact you."

Taking the card from Ryan, he produced a black leather cardholder from his pocket. With a gentle tremor in his fingers, he placed Ryan's card in the front and pulled one of his out and offered it in return.

"Your mother and I became friends when she lived here. We had a lot in common. She, well, she was a special woman, and I—" He winced and looked away, then at his watch. "I need to get to a meeting. If you'll excuse me. It was great to see you, ladies—and nice to meet you, Ryan. Have a fine day." He gave them a thoughtful glance and sprinted away.

Ryan watched him go and ran their exchange through his mind. What exactly had his mother meant to this man?

C3&80

April and Ryan walked leisurely along the tree-shaded driveway from Horden Castle. The day had developed into a fine spring-like afternoon. The sound of a motor sporadically drummed out the chirping birds and a distant barking dog. They continued in silence along the cobblestone.

April was unsure if Ryan had noticed Mr. Heard's reaction to the news of his mother's death. She'd only met him a few times, but he'd always remembered her name. He was a very thoughtful man and seemed to be a sincere person. His expression revealed how deeply the news of Mrs. Wilkinson's death had affected him. Was it the loss of a friend or something more? Maybe that's why Ryan was so quiet, perhaps digesting the encounter.

Ryan ended the silence. "Thanks for the tour, April. It was a great history lesson—especially since I had ancestors who lived here at one time."

A calico cat streaked across their path with a dog close behind, bringing the conversation and their steps to a halt. They watched the pair run into a small meadow. The cat lowered himself into the grass, hidden from the dog's sight as it came bounding into the field, head swinging side to side in search of its quarry. Suddenly, the cat jumped straight up and pounced on the dog's back.

April drew in a breath and held it, fearing the cat would be bitten in half by the huge retriever. She swung toward Ryan in silent appeal for a rescuer.

Ryan watched her and read the look. "It wouldn't be wise to intervene." He shrugged. A sharp bark brought their attention back to the spectacle playing out in the grass.

The scene changed—the dog rolled over onto his back. The cat pounced and positioned himself onto the dog's chest. The dog licked the cat in the face. The cat stood perfectly still to allow the attention and lay on his chest while the dog's tail wagged rapidly.

Ryan's laugh started as a chuckle, ballooning into hearty laughter. Relieved she wasn't to witness any animal violence, April joined in. The animals heard the commotion and ran to meet the strangers, this time the cat followed the dog who rubbed against Ryan's legs. April bent and petted the cat's ears as it purred appreciatively. Ryan's laughter receded as he stroked the dog's head. "Aren't you aware that cats are the enemy?"

She looked up at Ryan. "Hey, don't tell him that. It may give him ideas."

The incident had altered Ryan's mood. He was cheerful, and April used the opportunity to pursue what had been going through her mind minutes before the dog-cat chase.

"Your mum never mentioned Mr. Heard?" She focused on the cat until he started to rise. If he'd heard, he didn't comment. He stood and dusted dog hair from his hands. Why had she asked? It was none of her business.

"Do you want to grab a late lunch . . . or an early dinner?" he asked her unexpectedly.

April realized she was hungry. Her breakfast of tea and blueberry scones had long since deserted her. "Certainly." Realization struck. "Sorry, I forgot, I'm having dinner with Tristan tonight. Let's have lunch, but I do need to go by the cottage for a moment."

"Sure, that'd be fine. Would you like to go to Horden Inn or where we had tea the day we met?"

"Let's go to Talbot's." It was Tristan's day off, so there was no chance of running into him there.

By this time, the dog and cat had lost interest in the human interaction and taken off in the direction of an old thatched cottage down the road, the cat now chasing the dog.

Ryan laughed. "The dog is certainly frightened." He brought his gaze around and studied a building in the distance and nodded toward it. "What's that?"

"It's an old factory that was renovated to house homeless families. It was quite a task I'd say." She stopped and turned toward the building. "Would you like a closer look?"

Ryan raised a shoulder. "Sure, if you've the time before lunch."

"No trouble." April cut across the pasture. She urged Ryan to cross the fence stile as she did.

He was hesitant but followed, looking each way before stepping down to join her. "Checking for large farm animals."

She laughed. "You're not worried there may be a charging bull around, are you?"

"No, I haven't noticed anything in this field—other than sheep." As if he'd conjured up the fluffy creatures, several appeared from a nearby cluster of trees.

"Don't worry, they're friendly beasts."

Nearing the edge of the pasture, they once again traversed the fence and crossed the road toward the building, which resembled a stylish factory-turned-apartment complex. April told him that no expense had been spared to create a welcoming and lovely home for those in need.

An elderly couple exited the double doors and smiled at April and Ryan as they headed for the parking lot on the left. From their other side, a small boy smiled up at his mother as they walked hand-in-hand into the building. April glanced at Ryan and saw a haunted expression pass over his features as he watched the mother and son. His attention shifted to a bronze plaque secured near the entrance, and he paled.

April followed his gaze and read the list of familiar names among those who worked on the housing project—including

Susannah Wilkinson. Even though she cared to know of the connection between Susannah and Colin Heard, she longed to find out what happened between Ryan and his mother. The pain emitting from him at every mention of her now seemed to weigh upon April too.

Chapter Fifteen

Neville, North Yorkshire, England
2016

Colin led the group through the renovated section of the factory. The structure was now sound enough to undergo an inspection, and it was time to do the internal designing, sectioning off rooms, planning details of closets, positioning doors, and decorating. The few families living in the factory had been relocated to the Horden Inn at his company's expense.

"Letice and Susannah have agreed to be in charge of designing the floor plan of the flats, and—"

Vita interrupted, her voice edged with sarcasm. "Why should they do it? We didn't discuss it in a committee meeting."

Colin angled his gaze on Vita. "Letice and Susannah are the only two on the committee who don't work full-time. Besides, Vita, you agreed to organize the decor." Before she could respond he added, "Vita, you work long hours at the gallery. I hardly think you have much time to spare."

Vita didn't argue but said in a huff, "Well, you could have at least brought it before the committee."

"I apologize. I had no idea it would be an issue before Parliament." His voice held no sarcasm but made his point. Vita said nothing. The silence hung like the electrical wires dangling from the ceiling.

Susannah stood straighter and asked, "Colin, wouldn't it be reasonable to include the people that will be living here in the decisions involving decorating?"

He laid a hand on her shoulder, letting it linger briefly. "You're right. I hadn't thought of that. They could voice their preference of colors and styles that appeal to them." His eyes glowed with appreciation as their eyes met. "That's a great idea."

The warmth from his touch was unnerving. She didn't want to pull away, but the contact unsettled her. Not in a bad way, but there were others present, and aware. Relief flooded her when Colin moved on, pointing out different aspects that had been accomplished in the building.

Letice elbowed Susannah's side and whispered, "Good going. Wonderful thought."

But clearly not everyone agreed. Vita pushed past them with a scowl and trailed Colin.

The tour continued without further discourse, with the exception of Tom growing impatient and voicing loudly, "I have commitments elsewhere," before he abruptly left.

A half-hour later, Colin stood in front of the group and thanked them for attending. All dispersed except Susannah, Amanda, Letice, and Vita. Vita kept to the side, still wearing a scowl.

"If any of you have any further suggestions on the renovation, please contact me." Colin looked at each person there. "You too, Vita."

"Colin, you don't have to throw me any crumbs. I want to be a part of this and be useful, but it seems you've chosen who has a say-so—and who doesn't." Her eyes met Susannah's before she walked away.

Susannah made a move toward her, but Amanda held her arm and mouthed, "No."

She patted Amanda's hand and pulled away. "Vita, please wait."

Vita turned her head. "What do you want?" Her tone brusque.

The others stayed within hearing distance.

"No one is trying to leave you out. It's as Colin said, you work so much at your business that he didn't think you'd have the time to do all that's required *and* plan the decor. Letice and I have ample time. I'm sure there are plenty of other things to be done in the next phase."

"Yes, like what? I'd think this would be the end of it once

all is decorated."

Susannah's thoughts whirled trying to come up with something to placate the woman, and the perfect idea came. "What about the grand opening party? That's going to have to be planned, and it wouldn't be intense or time-consuming. Though it's important."

Vita pursed her lips. "Well, yes, I suppose. I am good at entertaining." Her eyes narrowed, and a frown line appeared between her brows. "Why would you care if I was included or not?"

"Why wouldn't I? I don't know you well, but I'd like to. After all, we are Christians in this ministry together, aren't we?"

Vita's shoulders slumped. She gave Susannah a dull-eyed look. "You're right. I'll talk to Colin about the idea, or better yet, I'll bring it before the next meeting." Uncharacteristically, Vita smiled and bid Susannah goodbye.

Susannah returned to the group, their questioning eyes not to be ignored. "Colin, I hope I didn't overstep my boundaries, but I wanted Vita to feel included. I mentioned she could plan the grand opening party." She sighed. "I hope it was all right."

He gave her a slow, disbelieving shake of his head. "Sorry, we couldn't help but overhear what you said."

Amanda's eyes widened. "How'd you manage to break through her ice so fast?"

"She only wants to be included, and the party would be her forte from what I've observed. Remember the veggie and fruit trays at the meetings? She went to a lot of trouble to make those spectacular. Her art gallery is evidence of her artistic abilities." She looked at Colin for approval or denial.

"You're right—and no, it's not a problem. Thanks for thinking of it. The party is a splendid idea, and she'd be an asset in planning it." He nodded toward Susannah and Letice. "Amanda, I'm going to kidnap these two for the rest of the afternoon if they're free and give them the information they need to start."

"Not a problem. I need to go to the church and finish the bulletins for tomorrow's service. Colin, thanks for the tour—and, girls, good luck."

She left, and Colin turned to them. "Well, are you available to be kidnapped?"

Letice sighed. "Well, I'd love to, but I promised my daughter I'd help her pick out the crib for our soon-to-be born grandchild. Sorry—first grandchild trumps all else. Sue, I'll see you at church tomorrow, although I may stop by this evening and bring that book you wanted to borrow."

Susannah lowered her eyebrows and offered Letice a probing gaze. She didn't remember asking to borrow a book. Hesitantly, she replied, "That would be nice." Letice didn't meet her eyes but bid them goodbye.

Colin's eyes brightened. "I guess it's a committee of two this afternoon—that is if you're free. I'm sorry, I should have asked first."

"I am free unless household chores win out over committee planning chores."

"Where shall we go to discuss our plans? All the papers and samples are in my car."

"Do you have an office in Neville?" They walked slowly

from the building, squinting in the bright sunshine. Susannah slipped on a pair of sunshades.

"I do at home, but no one is there on the weekends. Unless I'm entertaining, I don't allow my employees to work weekends. That's time for family and their own household chores." His tone held an edge of teasing at her words, which made Susannah smile.

"We can go to your office if you like."

Colin's step faltered. "It may not be the best place since we'd be alone. We wouldn't want to give someone the wrong idea."

Susannah's face heated. "Oh, I hadn't thought of that. I suppose I'm too old to think along those lines anymore."

His eyes twinkled. "Too old? You're far younger than I am." He opened the car door for her. "At forty-nine, I don't consider myself to be old."

A strange sensation swept over her. She was nearly six years his senior. The words blurted out before she could catch them. "Well, I have you beat by several years."

Colin stilled his hand on the door. "What? That can't be."

Susannah regretted revealing her age, although, why was that? She wasn't ashamed of it. If Colin could be interested in her without knowing her age, being aware of it shouldn't be an issue. Now, remembering the mirror conversation she'd had at Talbot's the previous night, she reprimanded herself. She didn't know if he was interested in her, or vice versa.

She slid into the car. More confident, she addressed Colin as he seated himself next to her and closed his door. "Age is simply an attitude. That is until your body won't cooperate with your mind." She laughed as he produced a feeble smile.

He drove from the parking lot before he spoke. Stopping at the street, he turned to her. "Care to go to the Horden Inn?"

"Good idea. It was the first place I stayed when I came to Neville on my scouting trip with my friend, Diann."

Colin didn't respond. They drove in silence until Susannah couldn't take it any longer.

"Colin, is there a problem with my age?" Her lips quivered. "Do you think someone younger should manage this job?"

"Goodness, no. Is that what you think? I'll admit it was a shock. You look so much younger than I do, so I was taken aback. I certainly didn't mean to make you uncomfortable."

Susannah gazed at her lap, smiling.

Colin pivoted his gaze from the road to Susannah, back and forth. All the while his smile broadened. "Will you let me in on the joke, please?"

"It's too funny. I thought you were a lot younger than me."

"No? Seriously?"

Now, both laughing, the uncomfortable moment evaporated. Parking in front of the Horden Inn, they sat smiling at one another.

Susannah's mood cheered, "So, we have a few years between us. That's not a big deal. I think we're going to be great friends."

Propping his right forearm across the steering wheel, he looked at her, his tone melancholy. "Yes, I suppose you're right."

Susannah read this agreement of friendship as proof that

Colin was not concerned with anything more. She'd been right not to get her hopes up with a new relationship, relief not to be on-stage whenever she was in his presence—always afraid she would say or do something to embarrass herself.

A few minutes later, they were seated with tea in front of them. They chatted easily, although Susannah seemed to be more at ease than Colin. After discussing the vendors that Colin suggested using—all locally owned—Susannah found herself interrupting their meeting. "Colin, have I said something to offend you?"

He toyed with his spoon, scooping more sugar into his tea. "Susannah, I certainly don't want to seem too forward, but you must realize I'm interested in getting to know you and not on a professional or ministerial level . . ." He struggled to continue, running his finger along the edge of the cup's rim. "Nor as only a friend."

Susannah surveyed her cup, unsure how to respond. "Colin, I'm sorry you have a problem with our age difference. I did sense that you were possibly interested in me, but I thought you were merely being friendly to someone new in town."

She looked up to find him staring at her, a strange faraway expression in his eyes . . . not sad or rejected. A slow smile spread on his clean-shaven face, which soon turned to soft laughter, his eyes crinkling at the corners.

"What on earth is so funny?"

"It's incredible how people can have such a misunderstanding."

She shook her head. "I don't understand."

"Neither did I. We both thought the other had a problem with the age difference between us. If two adults are drawn to one another, an age difference shouldn't factor in at all."

She tapped a finger to her chest. "Do you mean that you thought I had a problem with your being younger than me?"

"Yes, I thought you were the one with the issue and wanted only to be friends. I don't mean to be so quick to shove ahead, but I must say I cannot be happier that you're in agreement. The moment I met you, I wanted to get to know you better … and I promise I won't rush. Let's get acquainted as friends first, and we'll see what happens. Fair enough?"

Susannah's heart raced, her face warming. She'd never had a man be so straightforward with her. It was refreshing and hard not to fall into the warmth in his eyes. Swiftly, a mental picture of Colin and Vita dining together at Talbot's popped into her head.

He stopped smiling. His face fell with disappointment. "What's wrong—you don't want to pursue this?"

She stammered. "Well, I, I'm sorry, it's . . . it sounds so silly and school-like." She swallowed hard, and her words rushed out. "What about dinner with Vita last night? She seemed interested in you. And vice versa." She focused on the table and watched as his long, well-formed fingers moved her teacup aside and he gently pulled her hands into his, warm and comforting.

"I had no idea you thought that was a romantic dinner. Sometimes Vita can be very demanding. We did go out briefly in school, and since that time, she thinks she can force her way back into my life. I've put up with it because I think I hurt her when I left Neville to go to university and didn't stay in touch.

I've been trying to make it right with her, but that's about to stop. We obviously don't want the same things in life."

"You certainly don't owe me an explanation."

Colin squinted his eyes. "To be honest, it pleases me that it bothered you. It confirms what I wasn't sure of—that you do want to be better acquainted." He gave a lopsided smile and squeezed her hands.

In the back of her mind, Susannah envisioned the disaster of her marriage to Aaron and how thrilling it all felt when their relationship began. Was this the same start only with another man?

☃

Diann's ringing phone sounded like it would go on forever. Susannah's impatience to speak with her growing with it. She needed advice or a dear friend to listen.

A sleepy voice answered. "Hello."

"Diann, I thought you'd never answer."

"Could it be I had to wake up? Do you have any idea what time it is here?" A long yawn followed, and a tumble of hurried words flowed, "Oh my. Is everything all right?"

"Diann, calm down. Everyone is fine. I need to talk to you."

A flamboyant sigh came through the line. "At five in the morning?"

"I'm sorry. It's a personal problem, and I need advice. I shouldn't have called and bothered you. We'll talk another time."

She started to press the end button when she heard Diann's voice. "Don't you dare hang up that phone! If you're upset enough to call me at this hour, it must be serious. Spill it.”

Susannah held the phone to her ear, silent tears ready to launch.

“Sue, are you crying?” Her voice calm and sympathetic. “Please tell me what’s wrong.”

Susannah’s voice trembled. “Can you come see me? I’ll buy your ticket.” Her words came in gasps now, tears flowing. “Di, every time I’m around him, I’m tongue-tied. Handsome men make me nervous. I’m petrified of a n . . . new relationship.” She hiccupped.

“What’re you talking about?” Diann said through a yawn.

“It’s this guy I’ve met. He’s too good looking, too nice, and too rich.” She blew her nose.

Diann yawned loudly. “And how is that a problem?”

“Di. I’m serious. I refuse to get involved with another man. I can’t live through that pain again.”

“Susannah, you don’t have to marry the guy.” Another loud yawn escaped. “He didn’t ask you to marry him, did he?

“Oh, my word, no.” The thought horrified her.

“What’s the problem? Why can’t you just enjoy his company and friendship? There are a lot worse things in the world to experience.”

Susannah heard a muffled man’s voice ask, “Who is it?”

“Tell Wayne I’m so sorry for waking him.”

“Oh, don’t worry about him. He’ll be snoring in ten seconds.” Diann whispered, “*And* he’s good-looking on top of rich? Please go on.”

Susannah ignored the sarcasm in her friend’s voice. “I

don't know what to do. If I continue the relationship, I'm certain it's going to go south. You see, there's this woman from his past who wants to renew their relationship from years ago. He assures me that they're only friends, but she's a great beauty, and I—I need you to meet him."

It was a long time before Diann sighed with feeling and answered, "Let me see what I can do."

Susannah sighed in return. She identified that tone. Her friend would somehow come through.

Their conversation carried on for another half hour after Susannah had calmed down. After the call, Susannah lounged in her favorite chair, ruminating over the pros and cons of relationships. She struggled with wanting to see more of Colin, yet she pulled back from him.

She prayed for guidance and discernment because once again, the same questions haunted her. Could she truly trust a man once more?

Chapter Sixteen

Neville, North Yorkshire, England
2019

With lunch ordered, April reached into her purse and removed a beautifully bound journal the color of a pale pink rose. There were elaborate swirls of design on the cover stitched in delicate ivory silk threads. Finding it hard to broach the subject, April pushed the journal across the table toward Ryan.

"What's this?" He made no move to touch it.

"I found it among the books at the cottage. It's your mum's journal. I felt you should have it." Timid, April added, "I didn't read it."

His gaze bore a hole through its cover. The stillness was broken by the appearance of the server with their drinks. April gave a polite thank you while Ryan fixedly stared at the table.

"I appreciate your thoughtfulness, but . . . I don't want it." He hesitated briefly. "As cold as that may sound, it's too painful. My relationship with my mother was strained at best."

It all made sense now—why Ryan seemed to lack details about his mother's life. "I see," April spoke gently, watching the drops of water lacing its rim.

He reached for the journal. "You may be right. You've been very kind. I don't want to seem ungrateful." He fingered the edges before placing it on the booth seat beside him.

April was pleased—relieved even. Her face relaxed as she slumped into her seat. "What time is your flight tomorrow?"

He took a sip of tea and leaned back. "It leaves Gatwick at eleven, so I'll have to take the early train and be there by about eight. Guess it'll be an early night for me."

"I suppose this is our last meal together. Please allow me to get the bill. You've been kind, patient, and generous. I appreciate it."

"You don't have to do that, April. It's been a pleasure doing business with you."

"Please let me . . . I want to do something to show how much I value it. I would never have been able to get the cottage without all you've done."

"If it'd make you happy, I accept."

Over lunch, they chatted about insignificant things—the

cottage, life in Neville, the history. Both steered away from the topic of Ryan's mother. Once finished with their meal, Ryan made the first motion to wind down the afternoon.

"It's been a nice day, April. I wish you all the best and hope you have many happy years in Permelia Cottage."

They stood on the sidewalk outside Talbot's, both fidgeting nervously, avoiding the inevitable goodbye.

"It was nice meeting you, Ryan. Thank you for signing the papers in advance of my loan going through so I could go ahead and move in. I hope you have a nice flight home, and that your mourning will be lessened as time goes by. I'll remember you in my prayers."

Ryan muttered under his breath. "Thank you, that's very . . . um . . . caring."

April saw the pain in his eyes when she'd mentioned prayer. Remembering her own now dulled pain, she added, "Ryan, I promise the pain will lessen. I never talk about it, but I lost someone once." She reached into her purse and pulled out the tiny, plastic-encased doll. "This belonged to my little sister."

His gaze lingered on the doll. "April, you don't have to say anything. It's none of my business."

"No, please. Let me explain. Although our situations are different, we have a shared pain in our hearts, except I felt responsible for my sister's death."

His eyes widened, and he shook his head.

"I was only thirteen, and she was but three." She pulled in an unsteady breath. "I was too absorbed in a book when I was supposed to be watching her at the playground. She was a quick little tyke and got out of sight for only a few seconds—but not before someone . . ." April stumbled over the words, her voice heavy with anguish and regret. She closed her eyes as tears pushed through. ". . . hit her in the parking lot. The sound of screeching brakes still unnerves me to this day."

Ryan tenderly grabbed her shoulders and pulled her into his arms. "I'm so sorry. I had no idea."

April shook from the memory of that day as the tears came. His warm, comforting embrace eased the hurt. She lingered in his arms before she slipped away and dried her eyes. "I'm sorry. It's been a long time since I allowed myself to think on it. Time does help. At least with God's strength to hold you. Time will lessen the heartache. That's what I wanted to say before you leave."

One of her hands rested against his chest, his warmth tingling her skin before she let her hand drop. When she brought her gaze up to meet his, she saw a tender look in his eyes.

"April Conyers, you are a kind and compassionate woman. It's been a pleasure knowing you. There's no one else I'd rather have my mother's cottage than you. You'll love it as much as she did, and I hope it makes you as happy as it made her."

April wiped a tear from her cheek, and with a smile, told him goodbye and walked away. Her hands trembled, and an undeniable ache deepened within her as she headed toward Permelia Cottage without him.

☙❧

Ryan opened a newspaper as the train pulled out of Neville.

The sun was rising and cast a soft golden glow over the village. He actually liked it here despite its much slower pace than New York. He understood why his mother wanted to move here. As he grew up, he was aware of her love of England—its villages, countryside, and history. Neville embodied all of it.

His eyes grew heavy with the gentle motion of the train. He was still dozing when the announcement came that they were pulling into Victoria Station, where he would make his connection to Gatwick Airport. Within the next three hours, he would be through security and settled into his comfortable first-class seat headed back to normalcy.

A few hours into his flight, somewhere over the Atlantic Ocean, Ryan was relaxed with a full stomach, and he searched his carry-on bag for something to read. His hand touched his mother's journal. An urge overtook him. He warily pulled it from his bag. His mother's handwriting jumped out to him—bringing back an avalanche of memories. Should he read this? Or was it inappropriate?

The first entry recorded was on the date of his birth.

Today my precious son was born—Ryan Weatherly Wilkinson. I never knew such love until now. I thank my God for giving me such a child. I cannot see that love in Aaron's eyes. He appears to be jealous of my time with Ryan. Why can't he see that this infant is helpless and needs total love and care—from both parents?

The journal moved on day-by-day, skipping months at times. She wrote in some detail about his growth and advanced learning abilities. He skimmed over several months. The next few pages were a bit harder to read, the ink smeared in spots. Ryan noticed the subject and realized the reason for the smudges—tears. They coincided with the date his dad had left them. She poured out her heart on the pages, along with the tears that flowed onto her words. Words that rained out heart-breaking pain. He could barely read from through the mist in his eyes. He was about to slam the book shut when he saw the words that said he had progressed into his teen years.

Susannah had struggled over Ryan's attitude toward her. The words she penned said she felt he hated her, blamed her for his dad's departure. He stared at the back of the seat in front of him. He saw the flight plan on the small screen showing they were now halfway over the Atlantic, to New York. Turning back to the journal, he continued:

Ryan is so angry all the time. It concerns me greatly. I pray for him every day. My heart breaks seeing him this way. Is it my fault that Aaron left? Was I spending too much time taking care of Ryan? I discussed it with my doctor, and he said I was not to blame and that some men cannot manage the competition of a child. They cannot grasp the concept of a child needing so much attention, and they feel left out. I tried to get a sitter one night a week, so Aaron and I could have some time alone, but he always scoffed at that. It was as if he wanted all my attention all of the time or none. Till the day I die I will never understand.

Ryan read on, agonizing though it was. He read about all his antics that hurt his mother in a variety of ways. He wondered why she had put up with him. Why couldn't he see it? Her last entry was the day she moved into the cottage. She seemed truly happy, yet some of her last words were of him.

Getting settled into my English cottage has been one of the happiest times in my life. The only others were when Ryan was born and his childhood, the sweet years. I miss my son and my heart aches. If only he could forgive me for Aaron's leaving. If only I could make him understand that his father was not cut out for fatherhood. He seemed to withdraw even further after Aaron died. It was such a shock to find out he had died and left us so well off. The guilt must have been the reason he had made a will to favor us. I'm so glad we could use some of it to pay off Ryan's student loans, give him a nice, healthy, savings account—and enable me to move here.

He couldn't go on. There wasn't much left to read anyway. The journal was full at this point. There might be another one at the cottage that continued where this one left off—but it would've had details of the short time she lived in Neville before it ended with her arrest.

The arrest that prompted his Aunt Diann to visit his office, a memory he wished to forget. He'd sat in his black leather desk chair in his corner office overlooking Central Park, one ankle rested on his knee, a file folder opened across his bent leg, lost in thought, when his office door burst open and slammed shut.

He'd jumped and swung to face his Aunt Diann's flushed face. She flung her purse onto the taupe leather sofa, fire in her eyes, her voice nearly a scream. "What's wrong with you."

The door burst open again, and his secretary, Janet, rushed in. "I'm sorry. I tried to stop her, but she wouldn't listen."

"It's okay, Janet. Hold my calls, please."

Diann didn't wait for the door to close. "I cannot believe you've done nothing to help your mother. She's in jail, and you haven't even gone to see her, tried to get an attorney, or . . ."

Her voice trailed to nothing, and she broke down. Sobbing, she fell into the chair in front of his desk—elbows on her knees, chin on her chest. Her shoulders shook as tears darkened the carpet.

"Aunt Diann, she knew what she was doing when she stood with that mob. Being part of a riot is punishable with a prison sentence. And, by the way, what are you doing in New York?"

Her head rose, and their eyes met. "I'm not your aunt by blood, but I'll speak plainly. How can you say that with such cold, steady words? I came here to talk about your mother. She worked herself to death to care for you after your father left—never keeping for herself, always giving all her time and resources to take care of you. I'm not saying she was perfect, but you always came first in her life."

Ryan shuddered, the memory eating at him. He glanced around the plane, all the people with their own lives, their own troubles, but how many of them had turned their back on their own mother. What had he done?

He sighed. After his aunt's visit, he'd tried to ignore her, but going out with his friends was not the usual pleasant time he'd anticipated as a diversion. Even dinner with Genevieve, a gorgeous advertising executive, introduced to him by a friend, hadn't made him feel any better.

Now, days after his return to New York the shame of his actions consumed him. His office door banged open to reveal his business associate, Cordell Brimberry.

"Ryan, now that you're back, let's grab some dinner and go to Harper's for some drinks tonight. Genevieve will probably be there." His friend prodded.

The mention of her presence was the deciding factor for Ryan. When they got to the club, Ryan ordered his usual drink, but something about it was off, the whole night seemed off, and he wasn't certain if it was only from jet lag.

Cordell elbowed him in the ribs. "There's Genevieve."

His gaze traveled across to the congested bar to the tall blonde beauty. She'd not seen them yet, and a fleeting thought surprised him. He hoped she wouldn't see him. That was a revelation. Mere weeks before, he'd been more than happy to gain her attention and even planned to ask her out to dinner again when he'd returned from England. But now what? He wasn't thinking straight. It had to be the jet lag, he told himself, before he pushed through the crowd toward her.

Genevieve made eye contact with Ryan and glided through the crowded room to meet him. She wrapped an arm around him and kissed his cheek. "Thought you'd never return," she said with mock exasperation.

He smiled, uncertain what to say, so he awkwardly said, "Well, here I am."

She raised her eyebrows suggestively. "Here you are." With an arm around him, she led him toward a table where Cordell had already joined some of their work colleagues. They sat, Genevieve scooting next to him, and they all greeted one another over the din of music and voices. Their server arrived and took their drink orders.

Ryan had no idea what to say to Genevieve. He ignored her and talked to Cordell on his other side.

Genevieve shifted in her seat until she was hip-to-hip with him and draped her arm behind his back. He glanced at her, and this time his gaze took in the low-cut of her dress. She caught him looking and gave an alluring smile. "Do you like my new dress?"

"Yes, it's—uh—nice."

Genevieve gave a faux pout. "Well, I'd hoped to get more of a response from you."

Ryan noted the emphasis on you but said nothing as an image of April sprang to his mind. How different she was than Genevieve's model-thin figure, tan skin and heavy makeup—nothing like April's dark hair, intelligent eyes, and sense of humor. The women couldn't be more different. But why was he comparing them?

He rubbed his forehead. It was definitely jetlag.

Trying not to hurt Genevieve's feelings, he added, "You look great as always." He read the pleasure in her face.

"I need another drink." Genevieve shot a seductive glance at Cordell, who had just returned from the bar. "Cordell, be a dear, and let me have that." He nodded, and she leaned over Ryan to take it, her face close to his.

"Thanks." She squeezed Cordell's bicep. "My, have you been working out?"

His expression was appreciative. Smiling alluringly, she turned her gaze to Ryan, who wasn't surprised by her flirting. She toyed with any man that came within a ten-foot radius. In the past, he would've ignored her flirtatious attitude, but tonight it rubbed him the wrong way.

Genevieve misunderstood his expression for something else. She rubbed his shoulder. "Oh, Ryan, don't be jealous. I was joking with Cordell."

Her attention no longer flattered Ryan. He steadily grew more repulsed by how strongly she was coming on to him. Was it his imagination she was bolder than usual? Or had he been blind?

"What's wrong with you this evening?" Her look was seductive. "You're normally so attentive."

Ryan reached for his drink and took a sip, giving him time to think of a proper response. He swallowed deeply. "Sorry, I'm tired—it's been a long couple of weeks for me."

Before he could go on, an opening for escape presented itself as one of Ryan's workmates stood and shouted, "Hey guys! Bernie has invited us to his place . . . let's go!"

Everyone stood except Ryan. Genevieve waited for him to stand and escort her out. Instead, he said, "I'll take a rain check. I'm still suffering from jet-lag." He placed a generous tip on the table, returned his wallet to his pocket, and strode to the door.

Boos followed as he waved over his shoulder toward the group, making sure he didn't meet Genevieve's eyes. He caught her reflection in the mirrored wall, and she wasn't smiling. He noticed Cordell move to stand beside her.

ෆᎼᏍ

Ryan locked his apartment, tossed his keys onto the table, and left his shoes by the door. He released a deep sigh and strode to the bedroom to sit on the edge of the bed. He fell back.

Was it jetlag? And why did April's face reappear time and again in his mind's eye? Genevieve was a gorgeous woman, and she was interested in him. He was interested in her. At least, he was before England.

He stared at the ceiling and wondered what had happened in such a short time. First, Aunt Diann's accusations, selling the cottage, meeting April . . . where was his life headed? He'd achieved his goals—a more than successful career, a great apartment, and living in an exciting city with a load of friends and colleagues. Life was full, his career challenging, and his income more than sufficient, yet something had shifted.

Pulling himself upright, he arched his back to work out the kinks. He padded to the kitchen to make a good stiff drink, sloshing a generous portion of whiskey into a tumbler. A large gulp made him cough. The glass clinked as he returned it to the counter and proceeded to the living room. He knelt by his bookcase and ran a finger along the spines of books, but nothing caught his interest.

He stretched out on the sofa and reached for the television remote, and crooked one arm behind his head. Flipping channels, he thought over his sudden aversion to the drink he'd made. That was some of the most expensive whisky available and had always been smooth. Still, it had gone down rough and strong, unlike all the other times.

A show he watched regularly made him pause in his search. It was nothing new, same old plot, cheap language, and scantily clad women. Watching for a while, he realized he was killing time with something that he found neither diverting nor humorous. Sleazy was the word that came to mind.

He returned to flipping channels and stopped on an outmoded show that he remembered seeing with his mother when he was a child. It'd been an old show back then—a comedy in black and white. The remote slid from his grip when he stood. His stomach grumbled as he untucked his shirt, released the buttons on his cuffs and rolled up his sleeves.

The refrigerator revealed sparse contents—milk, eggs, a paltry piece of Swiss cheese, a sad-looking onion, and practically empty jars. The door gave a thump as he let it close. His pantry contained a partial loaf of bread, crackers, and a few canned goods. He grabbed the bread, tossed it on the counter next to the stove, and returned to the fridge. He could make an omelet with what he had. Yes, that did sound good.

An excellent omelet was something his mother had taught him to make—something he'd never forgotten. It was a quick, inexpensive meal, and filling. Cracking three eggs into a bowl, he added a touch of milk and beat the mixture with a fork— adding a little salt, pepper . . . oh, what was it she said would always take it to another level? Oh yeah, cinnamon.

A small pat of butter sizzled in the skillet. In no time, he had an omelet, toast, and a glass of milk. He arranged all on a tray and returned to the sofa. He watched an episode of the old comedy as he ate. Amazed that he found himself smiling at the antics of the characters, it occurred to him that he was truly enjoying a quiet evening alone.

CS§O

April arrived at Talbot's by half six, early for her dinner with Tristan. Anxious to get the evening over, she ordered a cup of tea to calm her nerves when she noticed Hodge approach.

He looked at her, arms crossed. "Hello, my girl. How're you this fine evenin'?"

"Fine, Hodge, fine. Please join me. I'm a bit early. I'm meeting Tristan for dinner."

He tilted his head to one side. "You and Tristan? I wasn't aware you two were an item."

Not wanting to mislead Hodge, she told the truth. "We're only friends, yet he thinks there's more to our relationship than there is. I'm telling him tonight. He's not taken my hints in the past, and it's time to set things right."

"You're doin' the right thing, not leadin' him on and all. That lad is bonkers about you though. You're all he talks about when he's workin'."

The information did nothing for April's state of mind. She felt her face warm.

"Sorry, didn't mean to upset you, but this is best. You cannot go on lettin' him think there's a chance for him if you don't return his feelin's.'"

"Yes, but it isn't going to be an easy task." She sipped her tea and peered over her cup and saw Tristan enter the room.

Hodge followed her gaze and stood to leave. "Good luck, love. I'll be sayin' a prayer for you."

"Thanks," she whispered, and said a silent prayer herself.

"Good evening, April." Tristan leaned in and gave her a kiss on the cheek.

She pulled back out of reflex. He'd never done that before. Anxiety gripped her.

Tristan sat, started to speak, but was interrupted by Effie's approach. "What would you like?"

April gave her order. Tristan gave his choice without touching the menu.

Tristan gazed at April. "You look lovely tonight. Thanks for meeting me for dinner." Now that he had her all to himself, he appeared to be in his element.

April's voice trembled. "Tristan, thank you for dinner. I certainly don't want to put a damper on it, but I can't sit here and eat while I have this on my mind. You've been a good friend since our years in school, and I don't want to lose that— but I must tell you before we go any further—"

Tristan interrupted. "—but you have no romantic interest in me whatsoever." He leaned back and crossed his arms.

April choked on her tea and sputtered. How had he guessed? He wasn't surprised. At a loss, she sat motionless, clutching her tea like it was a life preserver.

Tristan shook his head. "Don't look so shocked. I've known for some time. I wanted to be sure—you know—hear it from your own lips. Also, I ran into Polly this afternoon, and for some reason she came across extremely nervous, so unlike Polly. When I asked her what was wrong, she was evasive." He took a sip of water and gazed at her thoughtfully before going any further. Tristan grinned like the Cheshire cat. "She told me why you agreed to dinner."

April's first inclination was anger at Polly, then she felt complete relief. Possibly, Polly's revealing the truth to Tristan had given him time to calm and realize the truth of the situation.

April sighed. "Well, I guess that leaves Polly out for a secret-keeper."

"Don't be too angry with her. For the life of me I'm not sure why she was so upset that you didn't want a closer relationship with me." He gulped his water and frowned.

Effie appeared with their dinner, giving April time to think. Hesitant to respond any further, she mulled over the implications. They ate silently for a while. They both relaxed and started talking about Polly—how volatile she'd become. They'd all gone to school together, and Tristan and April didn't remember Polly ever having been so touchy. Comparing notes, they realized the metamorphosis had begun a couple of years before—a short time after April and Polly had opened Books–on-the-Green.

Their talk evolved to include the bookstore and what books they were both interested in. Before either of them had realized it, dinner was over, dessert served and eaten, and it was time to leave.

Hodge said goodbye as they left and gave April an understanding wink. Tristan held the door open for her, and they stepped out onto the wet stone walkway. A fine mist still lingered, scenting the air with a fresh scent of rain. Walking silently together down the path, Tristan said, "April, I had a nice time in spite of the outcome regarding our relationship. We'll always be friends."

"Yes, we will." She gave him a hug.

"I wouldn't worry too much about Polly. She's probably been a bit stressed with a new business and all."

"I suppose you're right. It'll be hard, but I may have a talk with her. Possibly get her to see a doctor or something. Stress can kill a person."

Tristan stopped at the end of the walk and faced April. "I'm not sure if I'd suggest that to Polly. She may be offended."

"I'll certainly be praying about it, and her."

"I'll stop by the shop on Monday, and we can have tea—as friends."

April laughed. "Sounds good." Her step was lighter as she walked away, hearing Tristan's laughter behind her. She took out her phone with a sudden urge to call Ryan and tell him what a surprise turn dinner with Tristan had taken.

She froze. What was she doing?

Ryan was someone she'd bought the cottage from and spent a few days with, and that was all. He wasn't a part of her life, she reminded herself, but it was a hard truth to swallow.

Chapter Seventeen

Neville, North Yorkshire, England
2017

Colin paused from addressing the group when Vita strolled in late as usual for the meeting with her signature lavish vegetable arrangement on a large crystal tray. She made a display of struggling with it, her knees buckling slightly under the weight. Tom scrambled to her aid. Her radiant smile praised his chivalry.

Colin continued with updates from the construction site amid clanging sounds emanating from the refreshment table, the crystal ringing out its pleasant tone. Vita sashayed to a front row seat, directly in his line of vision.

Someone chimed in about another factory tour after the meeting. Colin addressed the question, and a motion was made to end the meeting with a prayer for the meal. Chairs scraped across the floor as everyone moved toward the food.

Colin shuffled papers and removed the display board with the renovation plans. Susannah hadn't looked at him—even once—while he was speaking, and he had no idea why. She and Letice chatted quietly at the back of the serving line. He strolled their way, but when Susannah saw him, she whispered something to Letice and headed for the restroom.

He barely heard Letice mutter under her breath. "Stubborn woman."

He joined her in line, and she smiled at him. "Good presentation, Colin."

"Thank you. I hope you all will be pleased with what the crew has accomplished so far. I think they've done an impressive job." Colin peered over Letice's shoulder in the direction of the restroom. He lowered his voice and met her curious gaze. "If you don't mind my asking, is Susannah all right? She doesn't seem herself today, and I think she's avoiding me."

"Oh, I don't think so. She's tired. Hasn't been sleeping well lately." But her expression told him she wasn't telling the whole truth. She turned from him toward the food and began to fill two plates. She shot him a look and said unemotionally, "Wipe that gob smacked look off your face. It's not all for me. One is for Susannah."

"I see." He raised an eyebrow, and chuckled. "There's

nothing wrong with a hearty appetite, even if they're really both for you."

She swatted at him and added good naturedly, "Aren't we cheeky today." Hesitating, she continued. "So, Colin, I noticed you and Vita at dinner the other night. Does this mean you two are an item again—after all these years?"

He opened his mouth to set her straight when a loud pounding stopped his response. Everyone turned to locate the source.

"Listen all." Tom pounded his fist on the table, dishes bouncing. "Let's wind this up soon and get to the factory. I have a full day's work to get done in half a day."

Silence fell in the room, followed by murmurings until Letice declared, "Tom, we just started eating. You can wait a half-hour more." She muttered, "That nutter." Colin bit back a laugh.

Amanda joined in, hands on her hips. "Tom, if you need to leave early, we understand—you don't have to take the full tour. After all, you did leave early during the first one."

Tom glared. Colin remembered he'd been a bit of a hothead in school, and much of that had carried over into adulthood. Tom's jaw clenched.

Vita spoke up. "Don't get your feathers ruffled, Tom. Come sit here—" She patted the empty chair beside her. "—and let's have a chat."

His demeanor shifted. "Oh, all right."

Letice met Colin's eyes and mouthed the word—nutter. She had him pegged for sure. He noticed Susannah sat across the room. He took his plate and headed straight for her.

He smiled when, finally, she met his eyes. "Mind if I join you?"

"No, please have a seat."

He took the seat across from her to offer adequate space. He glanced at Letice, who had joined them, his eyes pleading to not inquire about dinner with Vita again. "I hope you'll be satisfied with the work done at the factory. You'll both be joining in with the tour, right?"

"I would, but I have something else pressing this afternoon. In fact, I better head out now." She looked at her untouched plate of food. "I'll take this with me, Letice." And with a soft smile, she rose from the table and left the building.

Colin had to fight the urge to go after her. Something certainly wasn't right, but he had no right to interfere. They'd only started to get to know one another. They hadn't even been on a proper outing yet, though their unexpected dinner the other night had been wonderful, and she had seemed to enjoy herself. Had he missed something?

◌₃ℰ◌

A knock at the door disturbed Susannah's thoughts as she clipped and arranged yellow flowers into a cobalt blue vase. Dark green stem cuttings slid from her fingers into the trash bin as she walked to the door. She pulled off her muslin apron and tossed it on the back of a chair and opened the door to find Letice. "What a surprise." Susannah waved her into the cottage. She hadn't seen or spoken to her since the meeting two days before. "Please come in."

"Cheers. Hope you don't mind my dropping by." She sauntered over to the sofa and made herself comfortable. "I

212

have something I want to discuss if you have a moment.”

Susannah was halfway to the kitchen when she called over her shoulder. “Would you like a cup of tea?”

“Wish I could, but this will only take a bit of your time.”

Sher turned to see Lettice bite her lip. What was it? She was always thinking of a new ministry project. Not that she minded helping. Susannah settled into the overstuffed chair opposite her friend. “What do you wish to discuss?”

Letice clasped her hands tightly. “First, I have a confession. I prodded Colin about having dinner with Vita.” She held up a hand, palm facing Susannah. “I shouldn’t have, and I could’ve choked Tom because he interrupted Colin’s response, but I only wanted to make certain there wasn’t anything in his manner that suggested he felt something for her.”

She sighed. “I got my answer. He asked if you were okay, said you wouldn’t meet his eyes at the meeting. He practically ran to you when he saw you at the table. If that man’s not interested in you, I’m a codfish.” She drew in a deep breath and continued, “You’re a kind person who deserves happiness. After your impromptu dinner, I thought things were well between you. What’s happened?”

She ran fingers through her hair. “Letice, I . . .” Her head dropped to the back of the chair, eyes closed tight. A single tear fell from the corner of her eye.

“I’m sorry. I shouldn’t have asked. Please forgive me. Your relationship with Colin is none of my concern.” She rose and then knelt beside Susannah’s chair, and pulled her into a hug.

Susannah collapsed into her and began sobbing. “No,

you're my friend, and I need your support." She drew back and swiped a tissue from the box on the side table and dabbed her eyes. "Forgive me for being such a watering can."

"You cry all you want. Makes you feel better." She eased back onto her heels. "Do you want to talk about it?"

How to truly explain the pain she'd been through, caused by the only man she'd ever loved.

She looked at Letice who sat patiently waiting. Diann couldn't be here, and God had placed this precious woman— her new friend—right in her path.

She squared her shoulders. "My husband abandoned my son and me. It broke my heart. He'd never wanted children, and when I accidently got pregnant, he left soon after Ryan was born. I'm not sure I can ever trust another man. It's a struggle I've prayed over for years. Maybe God doesn't want me to have another romantic relationship. If I get too close to Colin, I'm afraid I'll make such a mess of it that he'd leave too." She hiccupped. "I'm aware that's not rational, but there it is."

Letice patted her hand. "My dear, you can't blame yourself for that."

"That's what Diann's been telling me, but I keep telling myself I should've been more careful and not gotten pregnant. It was a total surprise."

"You have to be kidding me. You were married, God wanted you to have your son, and nothing on earth could've stopped that. It was His will."

Susannah's eyes met hers. "That's another thing Diann has been telling me, and I realize it's true, but I'm human. My insecurities surface every time I tell myself that."

"Okay, I'm going to be blunt. For one, stop it. Satan is trying to keep you from moving on. We all get hurt. That's life. Take a chance with Colin. I've known him for a very long time. He's a constant fellow, always dependable and kind. And of all people, he would understand. His wife—" Her words came to an abrupt stop. "I shouldn't be telling you this. It's Colin's place to reveal his past to you. Suffice it to say, he's been hurt too. Give him a chance."

Susannah sighed and silently prayed.

"Now, let's get down to why I actually came over. I'm troubled about the homeless ministry. Vita has slowly tried to push her agenda with this project when Colin is away on business and all."

"Letice, I'm not so sure about getting more involved in this than I already am. Wouldn't you be more qualified—since you've worked with such diverse ministries in the past? And you know Vita better than I do." She exhaled sharply. Vita was a force to be reckoned with—besides, Susannah was a virtual stranger in Neville.

"You'd be perfect. You grasp the ins and outs of this type of ministry, having helped Diann. Certainly, we've assisted some of our members, and non-members, with urgent needs, but this is different. None of us have any experience in this field. Please say you'll think about it at least. You don't have to give me an answer right now."

A sudden thought came to Susannah. "Letice, why I didn't think of this earlier is beyond me. Diann is coming for a visit. I'm not sure when, but she'd have valuable input I'm sure Colin would welcome.

Letice's face glowed. "You're right. See if you can get an exact date, and we'll set a meeting as soon as she arrives." She jumped to her feet and froze. "But how will we manage Vita—once she has her mitts on something it's hard to get her to relent. She's in charge of the flat decorating and the celebration. But that's later on. She's been easing her way into more committees and gradually shoving others to the background. Before long she'll be in charge of everything, and people will be dropping like flies because she's so difficult to work with. We won't have any committees at all."

"Oh, I don't know. Is there someone who can ease her back to her own duties?"

"Perhaps Colin could sort her out. She's always had a thing for him, which seems to continue to the present."

"Yes, but . . ."

She gave Susannah a keen look. "You should call him, see if he'll contact her and smooth her feathers about her assigned duties. Play up the asset she is to the group. We don't need any worries going on with her."

Susannah's stomach tightened. "Worries . . . what do you mean?"

"Now, now, I didn't mean anything by that." Letice jumped from her seat and grabbed her bag. "Let me know when Diann is coming, and we'll have tea and discuss all. Cheers!" Nearly out the door, she called over her shoulder, "And don't forget to call Colin, love."

Susannah stared after her in disbelief. Now, she'd have to bring up Vita to Colin. It seemed Letice had placed her on a slippery slope. After all, she and Colin were only friends.

She rested her head in her hands. Letice was right. Perhaps she was allowing Satan to keep her from moving on. She needed to let go of what Aaron did to her.

Susannah took a deep breath and called Colin. The rings fluttered in her ear repeatedly, not going to voicemail yet. "Hello," an unfamiliar voice answered—a very feminine one. "May I help you?"

Susannah was too dumbfounded to form words.

"Is anyone there?" A moment of silence, a sound of shuffling, and a male voice from the background asked, "Who is it?" The woman replied, "No one there, Colin. Guess the call was dropped."

Susannah punched the end button. A hundred thoughts swirled in her head until she was lightheaded. The woman could be a secretary or business associate? And why hadn't he answered if he were in the room?

More suspicious thoughts crowded their way into her mind. They didn't know each other that well and had no claims on one another. This was why she didn't want another relationship. Pain always seemed to worm its way in. The hurt never fully healed.

The phone's ring jerked her thoughts back. Still clutching it tightly, she looked to find Colin was calling. She continued staring at the screen but couldn't bring herself to answer.

C8ED

Colin listened to the ringing, having redialed the dropped call. He waited patiently for Susannah to answer. He hadn't saved her number yet, but when he checked the call list on his phone, he'd figured out it was she who'd called.

He wanted to ask her to dinner, but he hadn't been out with anyone in several years.

After the divorce, he'd gone out frequently with different women to prove to himself he still could interest women, yet he'd never committed to seeing anyone more than once—until Susannah.

But he had to be cautious. After her indifference at the meeting, he wasn't sure what was going on, and now he couldn't reach her by phone.

A voice pulled him from his thoughts. "Colin, we need to finish if you're going to get this flat on the market soon."

He ended the call, tucked his phone into his pocket, and turned to his assistant. "Yes, Sophie, I want to sell as soon as possible. I won't have need of it anymore. Whenever I am in Paris on business, it'll likely be a shorter stay, so I'll go to a hotel. I'll be spending more time in Neville in the future."

She eyed him suspiciously. "So, what's on in Neville that would keep you there more often?"

"Sophie, you're incorrigible." But he said it kindly. "That's something I'm still waiting to see the outcome. At that time, I'll be happy to share it with you."

She shook her head, short coal black hair swinging from side to side, and grinned sardonically. "Sure thing, Colin. But I have a hunch it involves a very special woman."

Chapter Eighteen

New York City, New York, U.S.A.
2019

"Ryan, there's a call for you," Janet told him as he entered the office with takeaway coffee and his laptop bag.

"This early?" He glanced at his watch to see it was just now eight. He smiled and shrugged. "Business must go on."

Janet's eyes widened. "You're uncharacteristically cheerful this morning, Mr. I'm-not-a-morning-person."

He gave a playful grin. "Droll, Janet, very droll."

Ryan settled at his desk and picked up the phone. "Ryan Wilkinson speaking."

"How are you?" His Aunt Diann's voice sounded so different from their last meeting in this office. "I tried your cell but couldn't get you."

"Sorry, I didn't see a missed call. I assume you got my email." Ryan leaned back and cautiously sipped his coffee.

Diann gave a deep sigh before speaking. "Yes, thank you. And, yes, I forgive you." He could tell she was fighting tears— her voice strained after a brief silence.

"Thank you for agreeing to help clear your mother's name."

"I'm meeting with an attorney this afternoon. The money from the cottage sale should cover the cost. I'll take care of anything more, should there be a need."

"I'm so relieved you're going ahead with this, though it may take some time. Our justice system is painfully slow."

"Aunt Diann . . . I have one of the best attorneys in the city on the case. His name is Vernon Sturdivant and comes highly recommended."

"Will you please call me after you meet with him? I'm anxious to hear what he has to say."

"Sure . . . I'll call you tonight. Guess I'd better get to work, so I'll be able to meet with him this afternoon. Have a good day." He grew silent. "Aunt Diann . . ."

"Yes, Ryan?"

He cleared his throat. "Aunt Diann, I love you."

"I love you too, sweetie."

He heard her tears break free before she ended the call.

CB&ED

Ryan shook hands with Vernon Sturdivant after their initial

introduction. Vernon motioned for him to take one of the chairs facing his imposing black oak desk.

Vernon was an average looking man. He was of average height, weight, build, and had average features. That was his camouflage.

In court, his opponents assumed he was average in every possible way—harmless. They relaxed, let their guard down.

Yet, Vernon was not a man of average intelligence, or talent, in his field of expertise. He knew how to use his powerhouse of knowledge to his client's best advantage.

He casually flipped through a file and stated that he used technology when necessary for backup only. He made a few remarks from what he saw regarding the case and made direct eye contact with Ryan.

"Mr. Wilkinson, I've reviewed your mother's case very closely." He paused dramatically. "I'll take the case, but I must tell you that it will be quite difficult to wipe the slate clean for her. She was caught and recorded in the act of inciting to riot. You're fully aware of the implications?"

Ryan shifted in his seat. "I see, so you don't believe there's much of a chance whatsoever of exonerating her?"

"I didn't say that. I believe it'll be difficult and may take some time. This is a preliminary meeting to see where we're headed. I see the various newspaper clippings here outlining what she was involved in. There were numerous witnesses. We'll have to take this to court in order to clear her name. It won't be something put before a judge in his chambers and decided upon immediately. The laws are shifting rapidly on these types of charges . . . and they are not in favor of the accused I'm afraid. I'm a lot older than you, Mr. Wilkinson. This country is changing—and I must say not for the better."

"Yes, I know what you mean. At least, I do now. There was a time not so long ago that I would've disagreed with you."

"I shudder to think what it will be like when you have grown children."

He'd never given it a thought. Had he contributed to the chaos?

Suddenly coming to mind was the e-mail he'd sent his Aunt Diann before going to England. After their confrontation in his office, his mother's arrest had laid hard on his mind and heart. He struggled with it for days and finally came to the conclusion that he had to try and clear the dark stain on her name.

E-mailing his aunt and apologizing was the first step, and his offer to get legal aid and sell his mom's cottage to fund it. Snapping out of his trance, he asked Mr. Sturdivant what they would do next.

"I'll have one of my assistants contact the witnesses who were there the day of the incident in question and find out why they waited so long to arrest her. Apparently, some time had lapsed because she had time to move to the U.K. We may need to hire a private investigator as well. Do you have a problem with that expense?"

Ryan took a deep breath. "No, sir. Whatever it takes."

Mr. Sturdivant stood and extended his hand. "It was a pleasure meeting with you, Ryan. Please call me Vernon. I can assure you that I'll do whatever it takes."

With sincere gratitude, Ryan shook his hand. "Thank you,

Vernon. I greatly appreciate it."

☙❧

Ryan's hand hovered over the phone. He snatched it up and dialed Diann's number. The piercing ring in his ear gave him something to focus on.

"Hello, Ryan." Diann answered softly.

"Hi, Aunt Diann. Do you have a minute?"

"Yes, are you all right?"

"Yes and no." He paused. "Mr. Sturdivant said this is not going to be easy. That's the nutshell version. He seems an extremely competent man and he said that he will do all within his power to fix this, but that it could take time."

"I see." Diann murmured.

"He said he'd get back with me in a few days."

"I suppose there's nothing else to do now but wait. Please keep me posted. I'll be praying—I know you don't like to hear that—but there it is."

Ryan's voice was barely above a whisper before he ended the call. "Aunt Diann, pray hard."

☙❧

Neville, North Yorkshire, England
2019

"April! Would you get the door?" Polly yelled toward the Books-on-the-Green office. "I heard the bell, and I'm up the ladder."

April pulled her gaze from her bookkeeping. "Certainly.

Headed that way."

She stepped into the front of the shop. "May I help . . ." She met Tristan's eyes.

"Hello. What brings you out so early in the morning?" She caught sight of the burden he was trying to juggle and close the door at the same time.

"I brought you and Polly some tea, scones, and such. Where is she?"

"That's sporting of you. Polly, Tristan brought treats!" She yelled over her shoulder.

Polly's bouncing blonde head peeked around the storage room's door frame. Her face lit like a beacon. "Hi, Tristan. Nice to see you." She practically bounded toward Tristan and took a takeaway cup of tea, snapping off the plastic lid and taking a sip. "Ooh, scones too? You're a love."

Tristan straightened to his full six-foot frame with a gleam in his eyes. "Glad to be of service."

April reached for a tea, relieved Tristan of the box of scones, and placed them on the counter. "I'll get some sugar and milk." When she returned, she saw Tristan and Polly peering into the box of assorted scones, commenting on the different flavors. "Coffee, Tea and Crumpets certainly has a nice selection of pastries, don't they, Polly?"

Speaking through a bite of blueberry scone, Polly mumbled with delight, "They surely do. And they're still warm. You're wonderful, Tristan."

He beamed, a slight blush in his cheeks.

To April, it seemed that Polly had noticed Tristan's actions toward her had changed since their dinner. Polly was the most cheerful she'd seen her in weeks.

She joined them at the counter and listened to Polly and Tristan's chatter while preparing her tea. The door opened to the tinny sound of the bell. She turned to see a tall, well-dressed man enter. He paused inside the door, his eyes taking in the contents of the store.

Polly leaned into April and whispered, "Do you know who that is? He's even more distinguished than his pictures in the papers."

April greeted him. "Mr. Heard, it's nice to see you."

He closed the distance between them. "I hope I'm not interrupting anything important." He glanced at the tea and scones and greeted Tristan and Polly.

"Oh, no sir, not at all." Polly tucked a strand of hair behind her ear. "Would you like to join us?"

April nodded. "Please do."

"That would be splendid, but I've only a short time before I head for London." Mr. Heard turned to April. "I wonder if I might have a word with you—in private." April stammered. "Certainly. We can go into the office. I'll make you a cup of tea, and we'll have a scone."

"Perfect." He nodded to the others, and Polly handed April a few scones wrapped in a napkin.

April led him through the door leading to the office-cum-kitchen and pulled out a chair for him. She filled the kettle with water and put it on the burner. Preparing a cup, she asked over her shoulder, "What can I do for you, Mr. Heard?"

"Colin, if you would."

"Colin, it is." April glanced at him and smiled. "How may I

help you? I take it this visit isn't about a book?"

"No, it pertains to a strange request. Since you purchased Sus . . . Mrs. Wilkinson's cottage, I want to ask a large favor. Please don't think me unethical . . . this is not for me, but for Mrs. Wilkinson."

April whirled, nearly upsetting the cup she'd placed on the table. "What do you mean? Mrs. Wilkinson is dead . . . oh, I remember now. You want to do a memorial for her."

"Well, yes. I do want to do that also, but this is something else. A delicate matter that I wouldn't like to leave this room."

April slid warily onto the chair opposite him. "Yes, I understand."

The whistle of the kettle broke the tension. Standing to retrieve the kettle, she met his eyes. In them, she recognized something she'd seen in her own reflection from time to time—the pain of loss.

Pouring water into the cup, she asked, "Sugar or milk? Or both?"

"A touch of sugar, please." She served his tea, he took a sip, cleared his throat and continued, "April, after I met you and Ryan at the castle, I've continued to be shocked to hear of Susannah's passing."

April heard the yearning in his voice when he'd said her name.

"After she left, Susannah sent a letter to me and to Letice. She didn't know when she'd return, or if she'd return. Until I met Ryan at the castle, I had no real reason to suspect anything out of the ordinary. I've done some investigating and found that prior to her moving to Neville, Susannah had been arrested. After she moved, she was extradited from here to America to stand trial."

"Arrested?" April nearly spewed her tea. Her thoughts flashed to the crumpled article beneath the desk. It had been about Ryan's mother.

He nodded and struggled to go on, his focus on his tea. "The detective I hired hasn't discovered anything else so far. All I'm able to do at this time is to assume she died before it ever went to trial. The strain of it all may have been too much for her." He shook his head. "I don't understand why she never contacted me again after she left. I could've helped her. I would've hired the best legal representation that money could buy. We had grown close, and then she was gone. I never dreamt she was forced to leave."

He sighed. "Nothing in her letter made me suspect anything of this magnitude. She sent me a pocket cross that she said was dear to her and quoted her favorite verse in John." His eyes misted. "I am the way, the truth, and the life, no man cometh unto the Father but by me."

Colin took several sips of tea, and April did too—both thinking in the quiet. The only sound was the plop of water dripping from the sink's faucet.

"April, until I received her letter, I thought she'd left because she wasn't ready to pursue a relationship with me and didn't want to confront me with the truth. I also thought she left to give herself time to think and would eventually be back. She's been gone nearly two years. Scenarios have been running through my mind all this time."

April couldn't keep the compassion from her voice. "Depending on when, or if, she was sick, she may have been trying to spare you from hurt. Who knows, could be she came here to escape the arrest and spend her last days because of an illness." Retrieving a napkin, she dabbed at her eyes. "But what she didn't count on was meeting you."

He grew thoughtful, perhaps weighing the possibilities of what she'd said. "I'm merely speculating. Did you find out exactly when she died?"

"No, I assume the detective will reveal everything when he completes his investigation. He did tell me that there were some issues with the courthouse records, said he'd have to do some digging to find out the details."

April hesitated before asking, "Have you considered contacting Ryan?"

"Yes, I did consider that . . . briefly. I dismissed it. I don't want to bring further hurt to him. Also, since I don't know how long it's been since she passed. If it was recently, it would be all the more painful."

"That's very thoughtful of you." April realized he hadn't stated his request. "Colin, what was it you wanted to ask me?"

"You have Susannah's cottage." The anguish on his face deepened. "If you permit it, I'd like to stop by and look around."

"Of course, you may." Tentatively, she added, "You're welcome to come for lunch. I'm not a fantastic cook, but I know my way around the kitchen. You'd be my first guest since I've moved in."

"That's very kind of you, but I don't want to impose." He quirked an eyebrow. "I'm already imposing by asking to come over."

"It'd be an honor to have you for lunch."

"I accept."

They finished their tea and scones. Colin stood to leave. He stepped back to let April pass through the door first, and gently grabbed her arm, holding her back.

"If anyone should ask about this conversation and my having lunch at your house, would you mind leaving out our discussion about Susannah's arrest and anything connected with that? Tell the truth about my wanting to see her cottage. Several people in Neville already know that we were seeing each other socially. They'll think I'm a sentimental old fossil wanting to relive the past."

"Certainly," she said, laughing. "You're not old."

He shook his head and chuckled. "A sentimental fossil then?"

∽✿∾

Once Books-on-the-Green emptied, Polly trapped April before she could get back to her bookkeeping chores. "Spill it. What did that dish want with you? He's too old for you, but he is very charming, successful, and available. So, what gives?"

"Oh, Polly." April rolled her eyes. "I'll tell you, but you have to promise not to say anything to anyone."

"Well, of course."

"Mr. Heard and Ryan's mother were getting acquainted before she left Neville rather abruptly. He wasn't aware that she had died until Ryan and I ran into him at the castle. He seemed genuinely shocked that she'd passed. Anyway, making a long story short, he knows I bought her cottage and wants to come see it—kind of like going down memory lane or some such. It seems he's a very sentimental man and misses her terribly."

"Wow . . . he's quite a chap." Polly's tone was wistful. "And has a heart on top of all that too."

"Polly, you're such a teenager." April broke out in a giggle, abruptly stopped, an amused gleam in her eyes. "I've invited him to lunch at the cottage."

Polly's eyes widened. "What. You didn't?"

"Yes. It was heartbreaking the way he talked about her. He's in a lot of pain. He brightened when I agreed to the visit."

"You're not afraid people will get the wrong idea? Imagine if the paparazzi got hold of some shots of him going into your cottage. It'd-be all-over England!" Polly grimaced, then her features softened. "Wait a minute. If that happened, Books-on-the-Green would be on the map, and we could be famous."

"Polly!" April shouted in horror.

"Oh, calm down. I'm not serious . . . or am I?" she said sheepishly, wiggled her eyebrows and ducked into the storage room.

April scoffed and returned to her bookkeeping. Polly was back to rare form again. April thought over the conversation with Colin. If she could help ease his pain, she would gladly try, because she understood exactly how it felt to lose someone held dear. She thought of Ryan and hoped, in their time together, she'd been able to lift some of his pain too.

Chapter Nineteen

Neville, North Yorkshire, England
2016

Weeks later, after the unsettling call to Colin, Susannah wheeled Diann's luggage into her guest room. "I'll give you the grand tour in a moment, but first we'll have tea."

"This place is . . ." Diann swept into the room and touched the floral curtains and bent to smell the pink and yellow roses in a white vase at the bedside table. "It is simply unbelievable. And I don't think I've seen any place more, well, *you.*"

Susannah smiled warmly at her friend, who had flown thousands of miles to talk her through her insecurities. It was ridiculous, but since it brought her best friend to visit, she had no regrets. She led the way to the kitchen, and Diann tossed her purse onto the over-stuffed chair by the fireplace, still taking in every inch.

Susannah began to arrange their tea items on a tray when Diann leaned on the counter and fixed her with a point-blank stare. "Okay, out with it."

"What're you talking about?" Susannah turned to remove the singing kettle.

When she returned to the counter, Diann raised her eyebrows and pursed her lips. "You know exactly what I'm talking about—now spill it."

"Oh, Diann." She hadn't thought the inquisition would commence immediately. They'd have tea and tour the house, catch up and much later, talk about the reason behind the visit.

"Don't put me off now. Something big is going on between you and this Colin Heard, and I don't think I've heard the half of it."

Susannah moved toward the small kitchen table and pulled out a chair. "Come and sit." She retrieved the tray of tea items and brought it to the table.

Diann sat obediently and folded her arms, her expression expectant.

"All we did was chat about the factory renovations and ideas on planning what types of flats should be built. It was a dinner meeting, and we wouldn't have been alone if Letice hadn't backed out." She paused, hoping this would satisfy her long-time friend. It didn't.

"And?"

"And nothing. We got to know each other a little. That's all. We'll all be working together on this committee for a while. I'm new to the village, the church, and the community—it's only natural he would want to get be better acquainted. After all, I'm the only new person there." She poured their tea from her favorite pink teapot and fidgeted with all the accompaniments on the tray.

Diann leaned back in her chair and studied Susannah. "You sounded upset when you called—remember, you begged me to come here?" She laughed, the sound musical to Susannah's ears, one of her friend's finest features. Susannah had to smile. Diann was right.

"Yes, Diann, I'm afraid so. What was I thinking? Not your coming here but getting to know Colin—it will only end poorly." Her hand trembled, her cup rattling against the saucer. She took a deep breath and plunged forward with the whole truth. "At dinner, he said he wanted to get to know me better as more than friends."

Diann's face lit up. "Aha, finally. I just had to travel across an ocean and weasel it out of you." Her grin was triumphant. "Sue, don't be so quick to dismiss a possible relationship. From what you've said, he seems like a nice guy."

Sipping her tea, Susannah struggled with how to tell Diann about the phone call. Diann eyed her suspiciously, perhaps seeing the struggle in her eyes. "What else haven't you told me? I can tell when you're distracted." She laid a reassuring hand on Susannah's arm. That's all it took for Susannah to hang her head as tears fell onto Diann's hand.

Diann's voice was soothing. "Come on. You can tell me

anything."

"I called him at Letice's request about one of the committee members." Susannah heard the pain in her own voice. Diann passed her a tissue. "A woman answered his phone."

"Oh." The sound of the ticking clock hung in the silence until Diann asked, "Are you sure she wasn't a secretary or something?"

Susannah looked at her friend, eyes searching for an answer. "I don't think so. She was casual. It wasn't a professional greeting." She nervously folded and refolded her tissue. "And she called him Colin."

∞

Susannah and Diann stepped into Talbot's foyer the next evening and were immediately greeted by Hodge's warm brown eyes. "Hello, m'dears, I think someone's already secured a spot by the window." He pointed in Letice's direction, and she waved them over. "Now, Susannah, who's your charming friend?"

"My dearest friend, Diann Young."

"Brilliant to meet you, my dear. I hope you enjoy your stay in Neville."

"Yes, sir. I plan to." Diann gave him a sincere smile. Susannah recognized the expression—amusement. She had missed her friend and relished their time last night and today discussing Colin, the ministry team, Ryan, and other subjects, catching up on the time they'd been apart. Susannah had called Letice and asked her to meet them at Talbot's for dinner.

Hodge led them to a server who seated them and took their

drink orders.

Susannah introduced Diann and Letice, settled in once their drinks arrived, and immediately moved into a conversation about the homeless ministry. They ordered their food, and Diann shared her experience.

"Diann, you're a wealth of knowledge," Letice said, her face animated. "You must come to our next meeting to offer advice. We would be so grateful."

"Not sure how much help I'll be, but I'd be happy to sit in."

Susannah chimed in. "You'll be a big help." She gave Letice a conspiratorial glance. "We must convince her to reveal the error of our ways."

"Yes, we must persuade her indeed."

Diann laughed and shook her head.

Letice furrowed her brow. "Susannah, by the way, did you ever speak with Colin about Vita?"

Susannah couldn't meet her eyes. "I tried to reach him but was unsuccessful." She glanced at Diann and sent a warning look to keep quiet.

Letice noticed the exchange, her eyes narrowing. "What's going on, Susannah? Has something happened? Colin actually called me yesterday."

Susannah met Letice's eyes. "Why did he call you?" She stammered. "I mean, that's none of my business. Sorry. There's no reason he shouldn't call you."

"He wondered why he couldn't get in touch with you. He said he saw where you tried to call him, and he's been trying ever since to return your call. Said he couldn't even get your voicemail."

Susannah looked down. The arrival of their food came to her rescue—for a few seconds. Resolved to clear the air, boldly, she told Letice, "I did try to call him, as you asked. A woman answered, so I dropped the call."

Letice's eyes showed her confusion. "Whatever for?"

"What?

"Why would you hang up?"

"I was, well, I was hurt by the fact he was with another woman. It seemed we were getting on rather well..." Her voice trailed off as her eyes misted.

"Good grief, Susannah. Colin has business associates all over the globe. Why would you jump to a conclusion like that?" Letice drew a deep breath and let it out slowly. She picked up her fork, but stalled over her plate and muttered, "Sorry, didn't mean to be cross."

Diann plunged in. "Letice, I can answer that if Susannah will allow me." She looked at her friend with pleading eyes. Susannah nodded.

"She's afraid of getting hurt. After all these years, she's still not over everything with Aaron." Diann paused. "The phone call brought back all the pain."

Letice's eyes never left Susannah's. "I'm so ashamed at lashing out like that." She meekly put down her fork and placed her hand on top of Susannah's tightly clenched fist. "I'm so sorry, dear. You've been in turmoil over this. Had I known you were so crippled by it . . ." Her voice straggled off.

Susannah clasped Letice's hand. "It's not your fault. I wish I'd been able to express myself more articulately when we spoke before." Holding back her tears, she told herself that she'd cried enough over her past—and perhaps it was time to move on.

☙❧

"Where is that man?" Letice shook her head. "I do believe he'll be late for his own funeral."

Amanda noted the time and stood, addressing Letice, Susannah, and Diann. "Colin's not always late. It's only five after. We'll get started, and he'll be along I'm sure."

Diann kept glancing at Susannah as if she'd flee the room at any moment. She leaned in and whispered, "Hmm ... tardiness. Strike one for the famous—or infamous—Colin Heard."

Susannah gave a half-smile and shrugged, her attention drawn by the back-door opening, bringing in a rush of cool night air. It was Colin.

Diann nudged Susannah with her elbow, jutting her chin toward the back and shot her a question. "That's him, huh?"

She nodded and pulled her attention back to the speaker. She wouldn't think about the man sitting mere rows behind her.

The meeting droned on, but Susannah hardly paid any attention until Diann was introduced and gave her brief talk. The meeting was adjourned, and warmth on her shoulder yanked her to the present. She looked into Diann's knowing eyes. "Hey, why don't we go get something to drink."

As she rose, Colin's familiar gaze met hers over Diann's shoulder. The soft woodsy scent of his signature cologne met her.

237

Diann turned to follow Susannah's gaze and stepped forward with extended hand. "I'm Diann Young."

Colin accepted her handshake and introduced himself. "Pleasure to meet you." He leaned toward Susannah, his eyes bright. "Good evening. How've you been?"

She tugged on her purse strap. "I'm fine." She blurted out, "I hope your business trip was successful. It's nice to see you." She placed her hand on Diann's shoulder. "Diann, remember, we must run the errand we spoke of earlier." She nodded a hasty goodbye to Colin and pulled Diann to the door.

Susannah didn't turn back. In fact, she hadn't looked at Diann, but swiftly walked toward her cottage with Diann trailing behind. She wouldn't be able to breathe until she entered the cottage.

"Sue, wait!" Diann called.

"No, I'm not going back." Her pace quickened. "I embarrassed myself enough for one evening."

Diann rushed to her side and said breathlessly, "What's wrong with you?" She grabbed Susannah's shoulder and turned her around. "Why—" She jerked her head back. "—you're not crying."

Susannah shrugged. "What of it?"

"You tend to cry over nothing, so I thought you'd be wailing by now."

Susannah huffed. "I'm going home and forgetting this whole wretched evening. I made a fool of myself because of a handsome man. We've only seen each other a few times because he's always out of town on business. And he hasn't asked me on an official anything, so why in the world did I *assume* I meant something to him? That's what I get for letting my guard down like I did with Aaron—and look where that got me." Holding her chin high, she ground her teeth, her voice shaking. "I'm done!"

Diann kept pace with her, mouth open, breathing hard. "I've never seen you so . . . so . . ."

"Determined?" Susannah pushed up the sleeves of her sweater.

"Actually, yes." Diann's eyes widened. "I'm not sure I like it. This side of you is a bit scary."

Susannah plunged her key into the lock of the cottage door. "Oh? Well, you ain't seen nothing yet, sister." She walked through the door, barely missing Diann as she slammed it shut.

They both threw their purses on the sofa at the same time. Susannah's bag bounced to the floor, sending its contents scattering in all directions. The absurdity of the moment struck them as their eyes met, and they burst into laughter. Diann wrapped Susannah into a hug only the best of friends could do.

Diann pulled away, holding her sides while Susannah fell into a chair, her body shaking. "Please excuse me." She swiped at the tears. "I think I've lost it."

Another round of laughter hit her. After several minutes, Susannah tried again, "You know me too well. It's good to laugh again. The old me would be heartbroken."

"You had me going there for a while. That's the most single-minded I've ever seen you, except for the decision to move here." Diann fell into the opposite chair. "And you did it. I admire you."

"Thanks for that." Susannah gave a grateful smile. "How about that tea now since I ruined it for us at the meeting?"

"Sounds good. But I still don't understand why you sprinted out of there."

Susannah paused on her way to the kitchen. "When I asked about his business trip something in me snapped. Even to my own ears I sounded like some jealous fishwife." She shook her head. "What must he think of me?"

She entered the kitchen and put the kettle on. Re-stating the incident brought back the pain. Grasping the edge of the counter, her knuckles turned white. "No, I will not let this eat away at me. I have to move on."

Diann leaned against the doorframe with her arms crossed, watching her. "I liked it better when we were laughing."

Susannah nodded. "Yes, you're right. That felt good."

"Ok, now that's over with, I have something to say, and I'd appreciate it if you'd stay quiet and listen 'til I'm through." Her stare was hard, yet not unkind.

"I think I'd better sit for this." She sat at the table.

Diann joined her. "Yes, I think so because this'll be hard to take." She pointed her finger to the front door. "I want you to go over to Colin's right now."

Susannah started to rise, but Diann shoved her down.

"I'm serious. It's time you confronted your fear. You never fully confronted Aaron, Ryan, and now this. It's time to close some emotional doors. Get everything out in the open, and like you just said—*move on*."

"That's ludicrous. What would I say to him?"

"Tell him what happened tonight for starters. Also, tell him about your fear. Be honest—brutally honest. He can either take it as it is or stop whatever this is between you two."

Susannah toyed with the salt and pepper shakers. "You think so?"

Diann went to the living room and started retrieving the fallen items from Susannah's purse. Once done, she tossed the purse to her and snatched up her own. She grabbed Susannah's forearm and pulled her toward the door. "Come on right now, or I'll disown you."

Susannah started to resist but realized it was no use. She'd gotten herself into this by asking Diann to come thousands of miles to help her. She braced herself and followed her friend down the street toward what she felt would be an emotional disaster.

Dusk settled in around them as they trudged the sidewalks of Neville, Diann keeping a firm grip on Susannah, urging her onward in silence. Diann marched them right up to Colin's front door, and Susannah regretted that she'd pointed the house out yesterday. What had she been thinking?

Diann pounded the brightly polished brass knocker against the heavy wood. "Bet he got it out of some castle," Diann said indignantly. "This guy better be on the up-and-up with you, or I'll have something to say about it."

Releasing Susannah's arm, Diann ran behind the nearest tree. Susannah's mouth dropped. She'd been abandoned.

She began to turn, but when she stepped back the door opened, light flooding the walkway. A pretty young woman asked, "May I help you." Her tone was friendly, welcoming even.

Susannah stammered. "Well, I, um . . ."

"Who's there, Sophie?" Colin called out, growing closer with each word.

Before Susannah could utter another syllable, he stood in the doorway next to the woman. He met Susannah's eyes, his face revealing surprise for a moment. He quickly masked it. "Susannah." Opening the door wide, he waved her inside. "Please, come in."

"No . . . um, I won't intrude on your evening as you have company." She started retreating again.

He moved forward, gently took her arm, and guided her inside. He nodded toward the woman, who closed the door. "Susannah, this is my cousin, Sophie."

"Colin has told me much about you. How you're helping with the homeless ministry and all. How kind of you to volunteer your time. We've been occupied with another project as I work in his Paris office, and he begged me to come home with him to see the progress you've made thus far."

Susannah felt foolish, standing in the foyer with them, the absurdity of the situation pouring over her like an icy rain. She'd been so rash. Sophie sounded like the woman who'd answered Colin's phone. In fact, she was certain it had been her—his cousin.

◌◈◌

Colin watched Susannah's face flush, the same way she'd looked at the meeting an hour ago. He couldn't for the life of him understand what was going on with her, and it hit him.

242

He remembered the call that he'd missed, the calls he'd made to her with no response.

"Susannah, I think we need to talk." He turned to Sophie. "Do you mind, dear?"

Sophie gazed at each in turn. "No. Why don't I pop into the kitchen and make some tea?"

"Splendid idea." Once again, Colin took Susannah's arm. "Why don't we go into my office and take a seat."

As Sophie trotted away, Colin and Susannah went into his office. He motioned for her to sit next to him on a small brown leather sofa. As she sank into its supple softness, she clutched her purse to her stomach.

"Colin, I'm sorry. I honestly don't know what has gotten into me. I didn't mean to barge in."

"You don't owe me an apology. I think I understand. It occurred to me that when Sophie answered my mobile a few weeks ago, you got the wrong idea. That's why you wouldn't answer my calls."

"I'm ashamed to say that's true." She shuffled her flats on the Persian rug, Diann's speech coming back to her full force. She swallowed hard and stared at him. "You'd have to know my past to understand. I jumped to conclusions. Will you please forgive me?"

Colin moved closer and took her hands in his. "There's nothing to forgive. May we put this behind us and start over, please?"

She nodded, and considered their entwined fingers, relishing the contact.

Releasing her, he gently raised her chin until she met his

eyes. "Might we have lunch tomorrow to discuss this further? Sophie is leaving early in the morning."

"I'd like to, but Diann isn't leaving until day after tomorrow, and I can't desert her."

"No worries. She can come along."

Susannah started. "Come with us and discuss this mess I've made? I don't think that's a good idea."

"Why ever not? I'm sure you've already discussed it with her, right?" He cocked his head to one side, warmth and amusement in his light eyes. "After all, I saw her hide behind my tree."

Chapter Twenty

Neville, North Yorkshire, England
2019

April scurried around her kitchen, attempting to make everything perfect for the lunch with Colin Heard. Polly's voice kept coming back to her about what people would think of the situation. What else could she do? She couldn't refuse his request. Lunch was a small offering of consolation for losing Susannah Wilkinson. He'd obviously been taken with her.

She turned down the burner on one of the pots on the Aga—not wanting to burn the delicate herb butter sauce she'd prepared for the haricots verts.

April jumped at the knock on her door. Glancing at the kitchen clock, she saw that he was early. She removed the red toile apron and hung it on the peg next to the refrigerator. She smoothed the wrinkles on her yellow cotton dress and opened the door to Colin, who wore a burgundy cotton shirt and pair of chinos, hands behind his back, rocking on the balls of his feet.

"Good afternoon, Miss Conyers." With a flourish, he produced a fresh bouquet of daisies and yellow roses mixed with sprigs of fern.

"Thank you. These are beautiful." April held the door open for him. As he passed her, she said, "You shouldn't have."

"It was the least I could do after inviting myself here. I appreciate your doing this on such short notice."

"I'll go put these in water. Please make yourself at home."

April watched him move with care into the room as he took in everything that had belonged to Susannah. She headed to the kitchen.

"I see you have all the furniture Susannah had."

Speaking from the kitchen, April said, "Yes, Ryan sold the furniture with the cottage. It was a blessing. I've added a few touches of my own—although I'm not finished."

"Yes, owning one's own home is a work in progress."

"Would you care to take a tour of the cottage before lunch?"

"That would be splendid."

April led him first to the office. His shoulders drooped when he stood at Susannah's desk, and she saw recognition in his eyes as he took in Susannah's books and the mementos she'd collected through her travels. He seemed surprised. "You still have Susannah's personal belongings?"

"Yes, Ryan asked that I get rid of everything except the most personal of things and send those to him."

He studied the items again. "She left everything behind."

⋈

Colin was perplexed that Ryan wouldn't care enough to go through his mother's belongings. Seeing her things brought back the memories of the rare times Susannah mentioned her son. She was proud of his successes, both academically and professionally, yet she had but briefly mentioned their estrangement. His fingertips slid over the small carving of Teotihuacan, the Mayan pyramid in Mexico, and the smooth rock-turned-paperweight that she'd collected from the beach at Dover. His mind wandered, reliving happy times they'd shared.

The tour continued, yet the office, lounge, and kitchen were what touched him most since it was where they'd spent time together. April excused herself to see about lunch.

Colin returned to the lounge, eased himself into the overstuffed armchair, and sighed with emotion. Memories kept surging through him. The few evenings he spent here—laughter and lovely conversation with Susannah about travel and their mutual wish to create memories together in the future. That now seemed so long ago. Too long.

"Mr. Heard?" April stood over Colin, offering him a glass of sparkling water. A sliver of lemon bobbed up and down among the bubbles as she held it out to him. He appeared transfixed by the movement.

Colin woke from his daydream and reached for it. "Oh, sorry. Thank you. Lunch smells wonderful."

"I hope you like it. Most of my recipes are from my mum's arsenal."

Smiling, he said, "She sounds like a collector."

"Oh my, yes, and a fantastic cook. My dad says that's why he married her."

April sat on the sofa next to his chair. She placed her drink on the table between them. "Did you spend much time here with Mrs. Wilkinson?"

He winced. "As much as my schedule would allow. But, yes, I do have nice memories of dinners, conversations, and working on the homeless committee." He sipped the water with a distant stare. "I assumed there would be many more."

April murmured, "Did you love her?"

He stared at his glass, and whispered, "Yes, but I never told her."

❦

New York City, New York, U.S.A.
Several days later . . .

Janet greeted Ryan as he approached her desk. "Mr. Sturdivant called while you were out and asked that you come to his office tomorrow at three." As she handed him the written message, she added, "By the way, someone is here to see you. He's waiting in your office."

"Thanks, Janet."

Ryan was apprehensive about meeting with Vernon, not sure if it would be good or bad news. Now was not a good time for a surprise visitor. "Janet, would you please bring us some fresh coffee—and make it strong."

"Sure thing."

Heading toward his office, Ryan's mind was on the upcoming visit with Vernon. Stepping through the door, he spoke to the back of his visitor's head. "Good morning. May I help you?"

Ryan was astonished to see that the man in front of him was Colin Heard. "Good morning, Ryan. It's nice to see you again."

He shook the man's hand and took a seat at his desk. "To what do I owe the pleasure of this visit, sir?"

"I had a meeting in New York and while in town decided to drop in on you. I wanted to see if your firm could provide fresh insight into marketing strategies for promoting our historic properties."

"We can arrange a meeting to discuss some options."

Colin jumped in. "Are you free for lunch today?"

"Let me see." Ryan rang Janet, who confirmed he had nothing scheduled until two o'clock. Ryan glanced at Colin. "Looks like I'm free—would you like to meet at noon?"

Janet rapped on the door, entered, and placed a tray with two cups of coffee and all the accoutrements on the corner of Ryan's desk and asked Mr. Heard how he preferred his coffee. He replied and smiled as she handed it to him.

"Yes, noon will be fine." Colin stirred his coffee, and gingerly sipped it. "Thanks for the coffee, Janet."

Always confident and never flustered by any of Ryan's important clients, Janet's face reddened. "You're welcome, Mr. Heard." Her fingers toyed with her scarf.

"Thanks, Janet." He sent her a knowing glance, reached for his cup and leaned back in his chair. What was it about this man that had all the women so rattled? "So, Mr. Heard, tell me what it is you'd like for this company to do for you?"

"An ad campaign to promote our U.K. properties in America."

Ryan gave him a sidelong glance. "Couldn't your U.K.-based firm manage it?"

"Yes, I suppose they could, however, I believe that a company located in the target country would be better able to identify with their audience. My U.K. firm understands what drives those in the U.K., but here I gather the marketing approach is somewhat different."

"Yes, I see what you mean. What have been your most successful campaigns in the U.K.? It'll give me a starting point for my lunchtime suggestions."

Colin shared about several campaigns, and half an hour later, he placed his coffee cup on the tray and rose. "It was a pleasure, Ryan. I look forward to our lunch. Why don't we meet at Nonie's?"

"All right. I'll gather my ideas as well as information about this company and the clients we serve."

"That would be splendid. I'll see you there."

Ryan followed Colin to the door. He watched as Colin paused at Janet's desk, thanked her for the coffee once again, and complimented her scarf. Janet blushed. Ryan shook his head and chuckled to himself.

❧

Ryan always tried to arrive before his client to be sure he was seated at a table with a view of the door. Reading body language told him what type of mood a person was in before they greeted him. He was cordial and wanted to get along with whomever he was doing business.

If someone were having a bad day, he could read it in their movements, facial expressions, and tone of voice. He would delay moving into a business discussion right away. Instead, he wanted to offer time to relax and lessen their tension. Life was stressful enough without having to jump from one trying situation to another. Doing business with a new person—or corporation—was taxing, in and of itself. He preferred to try and make someone comfortable first and then address the work.

Ryan entered the restaurant, planning to grab his preferred seat. As he scanned the tables, he was surprised to see Colin already present. He lowered himself into the place across from him. "Nice table—these are most often reserved for frequent patrons."

Colin made no reply. He reached for his water.

When Ryan unzipped his laptop bag, Colin stopped him. "You don't have to jump right into the presentation. Let's have lunch first."

Ryan blinked back his disbelief. He'd estimated Colin Heard as a very astute entrepreneur, not interested in personal connections when it pertained to business negotiation. Returning his case to the seat next to him, Ryan replied, "If you'd rather. What would you like to know?"

The server appeared. "Nice to see you, Mr. Wilkinson." She took their orders with a thank you and left.

"So, you come to New York often?"

"Not often, but I always dine here. I like to go to places I'm familiar with. There is nothing unexpected." Ryan couldn't argue with the thought.

Colin offered, "Why don't I tell you something about myself? You'll have some idea what kind of company I run." Ryan nodded. "First off, I struggled through university. I wasn't all that skilled in academics. Yet, I was determined to finish. I met my wife there, and we married after graduation."

Ryan was curious about this man's career and asked, "What was your first job? Were you interested in acquiring historic properties right away?"

"I started managing a historic boutique hotel near London." He smiled. "Brings back fond memories of those early days. My wife and I had been content. She did the bookkeeping. In those days, we were very happy in our jobs and our life together."

"I suppose that job sparked your interest in historic properties, and—" Ryan was interrupted by a hard clap on his shoulder.

"Hello, old chum." Cordell bellowed, drawing stares from surrounding patrons. He glanced from Ryan to Colin, and Ryan introduced them.

"Pleasure to meet you," Cordell said.

"Likewise. Would you like to join us?"

"Thank you, but no—I'm meeting a friend. Carry on." He

excused himself and walked toward the hostess.

Ryan reached for his glass. "Sorry. Where were we?"

"You asked how I got started. My wife and I were on holiday, driving through the countryside. We came upon this scrubby inn in a charming village. It was a bit ramshackle but had loads of character, so we decided to spend the night. Both of us fell in love with it. It held such history, one of my favorite subjects. All it needed was cleaning and a bit of renovation to bring it to snuff. We approached the owner and asked if he'd consider selling. He did, so we made an offer, haggled over a week, and bought our first inn."

"Do you still own it?"

"No, we killed ourselves bringing it back from the precipice, ran it for about a year, and sold it for a tidy profit. With the funds, we decided to invest in places that people not only stayed in but toured as well—sort of a double-edged investment."

"But you said it had history, why wouldn't you keep it for that angle at least?"

"Well, we agreed that inn-keeping alone was not our forte. Historic properties allowing a few rooms to let combined with touring is more diversified. Even when the rooms aren't let, you have tourists who want to see historic places without always wanting to stay in them."

"I understand."

"Also, we had developed our collection into larger properties."

Ryan smiled. "Like castles."

"Yes. It's a pity that so many of the U.K.'s castles lie in

ruins. There's one in Northern Scotland that was magnificent in its day. One of the twentieth-century owners didn't want to pay taxes on it any longer, so he removed the roof—a property without a roof was dismissed from paying taxes during that era."

Ryan raised his eyebrows. "I'm not big on history, but even I can see that's a rotten shame. Why in the world wouldn't they sell it rather than let it go to ruin?"

"That is an excellent question. I'd love to get my hands on that castle and do it justice—but I'm afraid it's tied up in some possible vacation-flat conversions. They'll most likely turn it into some cheesy, amusement park-type property—" Colin scoffed, his eyes flaming with righteous anger. "—or destroy it and rebuild."

Colin waved a hand, the fire in his eyes cooled. "Enough about me. Please tell me about yourself."

"I don't have such a dramatic history. When I finished college, I started with a small marketing firm in Louisiana, and after gaining some experience, I was hired by this firm and have been here ever since."

"Good for you. You've done well for yourself."

Ryan thanked him, and Colin continued, "As you know, we are more than our careers though." Colin probed gently. "What are your hobbies and interests?"

With a nod of understanding, Ryan answered, "Reading and tennis mostly. Sometimes I go skiing or hiking with friends. I do play the guitar but haven't for a long time."

"You're quite the talented young man. I understand you're an artist as well." Colin paused. "I'm sorry—I seem to remember your mother showed me a sketch you'd drawn. It was quite good."

Ryan's face warmed. He steered the conversation away from himself. "Tell me more about how you came to such success."

"We worked hard and collected a few properties that didn't need much in the way of renovation—doing the work ourselves paid off. Things developed from there into what I have today. It wasn't always easy though. Personally at least."

Colin looked away a moment and back at Ryan. "As the business expanded in ways we only imagined, our marriage suffered. Our reactions to success was vastly different. I returned to Neville for a time and sought out my oldest friend for advice. He reminded me that I was not alone in my struggles, that God was with me. He shared how God helped him through his own difficult time and how he found peace— something I didn't have but very much wanted."

Colin held Ryan's gaze and continued, "With his advice, I spoke with the Vicar at the local church I attended in my youth. The transformation wasn't immediate, but that evening I knelt and begged God to help me. I accepted the truth of His Son and asked forgiveness for my sins. My life has been different from that day forward. Particularly, things I enjoyed before no longer appealed to me. My wife didn't approve. It didn't take long for her to lose sight of why we'd married. She had no direction and travelled frequently with a circle of friends of like mind. During a trip, she met someone and never came home. Had it not been for God, I would be an angry and bitter man today."

Colin cleared his throat. "I'm sorry to have been so open,

but I want you to know where my priorities lie."

Ryan's response was slow in coming. He recognized the anger and bitterness Colin spoke of. He had carried it with him for decades. Ryan avoided Colin's eyes. To his relief, the server arrived with their food.

Ryan reached for his fork, and set it down, as Colin bowed his head and said a brief blessing over their food. "This looks great. I didn't have time to eat a proper breakfast this morning."

A pressing question came to Ryan before their business continued, "Mr. Heard?"

"Please call me Colin. Mr. Heard sounds like an old man." His laugh was somber.

"All right . . . Colin. But is what you shared your way of saying you won't do business with a company that isn't Christian-based?"

"Oh, heavens—no. That's not what I meant at all. I want every company to be aware of my standards and that I'll not compromise them. God comes first in my business as well as my life."

"I see. And I now understand why you were friends with my mother."

Colin's fork was halfway to his mouth when he stiffened. He returned it to his plate and looked at Ryan. "I hesitate to bring up your mother again, but since you broached the subject . . . had she been sick for long?"

Not anticipating the question, Ryan took a bite of food for time to think of a response.

"I'm sorry," Colin said, his concern genuine. "I shouldn't

have mentioned it. I imagine it's still too painful to speak of."

"Yes . . . it is." Ryan relaxed, able to avoid the subject.

"Would you tell me about your career? It must be going quite well to have reached the level you're in. Do you wish to remain in your current position or advance further?"

"I'm happy where I am for the moment. Perhaps in a few years, I may want to make a move. It depends on what the company offers."

Colin smiled. "You have a bright future ahead. I can tell."

Ryan smiled back, and they chatted over the remainder of their lunch, keeping the conversation on a lighter level. Once the plates had been cleared, hot tea—ordered by Colin—and dessert delivered, it was time to get down to business.

"Mr. . . . . hmm, Colin, we can start with demographics if you'd like. What is your target market?"

"I'd say niche marketing. Perhaps garden clubs—most of our properties have extensive gardens. Next, it would be history buffs, genealogists, and historical societies."

Ryan added, "Travel agents should be included. With the advent of the Internet, a lot of people assume they're extinct—when in reality they still provide a valuable service, especially to those who are too busy to plan a trip."

"Good point. I suppose some of that knowledge comes from your mother's experience."

"I suppose." Ryan said and went back to business. "What would your expectations be regarding an increased revenue timeline?"

"Would a ten percent increase within six months after the campaign has started be feasible?"

"That would depend on how you want to market it—television, newspaper, radio, Internet, direct mail."

"In your experience, what combination would be more effective?"

"Target audience would determine that."

From his laptop, Ryan presented a preview of his initial plan, which he and Colin discussed over the next hour. They parted with another meeting scheduled at Ryan's office in two days. At that time, he would have a rough marketing proposal in place for Colin's review.

Walking back to his office, Ryan reflected on what Colin shared about his experience with past anger and bitterness involving his wife. Where did his stem from exactly? His father's abandonment played a large part in it. But did it go further, and he blame his mother? Was that why he was antagonistic toward her?

CS&O

"Aunt Diann, what else can I do at this point? The attorney is investigating every possible angle," Ryan assured his aunt that afternoon. "His researcher may have found some court documents that could help the case, and he said he'd be in touch as soon as he knows something more."

Her voice choked on tears. "Oh, Ryan . . . it's hurting my heart that your mom has been accused of something that was, in reality, exemplary. She was standing up for innocent lives. Don't you see it?"

Had she asked him that question a few weeks ago, he would've responded "No," but, today, he wasn't sure. Was abortion wrong? His mother and her friends called it murder—even if within days after conception—and were vocal about it to the point of imprisonment.

"Ryan, are you still there?" Diann's voice was gentle.

"Yes, I'm here. I'm not sure what to say right now. She didn't do anything wrong—but it's against the law to do what she did."

He heard the struggle in her voice to remain calm. "Sometimes the law doesn't stand for the right thing. There's a higher power than man's law." She hesitated. "Please call me when you have more news . . . and Ryan, thank you for doing this. I love you."

"I love you too, Aunt Diann." He ended the call and let the phone slip from his fingers onto his sofa. What else could he do for his mother? The question that kept haunting him was why he hadn't tried to help her from the beginning of this horrid debacle?

Chapter Twenty-One

Neville, North Yorkshire, England
2016

"I don't think you two need me here." Diann pressed her lips together. "Although, I appreciate your invitation, Colin. I'm intruding."

Susannah saw the smile creep over Colin's mouth. He tried to hide it with his napkin. "I at least owe you a lunch considering that Susannah wouldn't have come to see me had you not marched her to my door."

Susannah's shoulders fell. Colin gave her a comforting smile. "I'm sorry. I didn't mean to embarrass you. It's just that I'm grateful Diann urged you to talk to me."

She swallowed the lump in her throat. "I feel so utterly foolish about all of it."

Diann patted her shoulder. "Don't fret. It's all said and done and see how much better things are. You and Colin are still friends, and all is forgotten."

Colin nodded. "I'm indebted to you, Diann."

"By the way, I'm here to set Colin straight." Diann's mouth curved into a wicked grin, a gleam in her eyes.

Susannah tensed, uncertain what would come out of Diann's mouth. She was known to be outspoken. "Oh, please, Diann. Don't say anything."

Diann finished. "—to embarrass you?"

"Well . . . yes," Susanna whispered.

Colin's eyes shone with amusement. "Susannah, don't worry. I'm ready for the inquisition and happy to oblige. It's commendable to have such a caring friend." He looked Diann squarely in the eye. "I'm ready, your Honor."

Diann turned her gaze on Colin. "I understand you've been married before." Diann tilted her head. "Why did it end?"

Susannah's mouth dropped. "Diann."

"Right to the point, I see." Colin took a deep breath. "No, that's fine." He cleared his throat. "My wife—ex-wife—felt she'd outgrown our marriage. Her interests changed, but mine didn't. I rather like living a quiet life. She wanted more excitement than running small inns, and as our profit increased, she craved the life money could buy and found someone who shared that opinion."

Diann's nose wrinkled. "I'm sorry, Colin."

He nodded. "Thank you. Next question."

Susannah broke in. "Diann, this isn't necessary, and it's way too intrusive."

Diann's expression was unreadable, and she plunged ahead. "I don't believe all the junk about opposites attract. Do you share the same interests, goals, values? I don't mean to say you have to like everything the other likes and so on."

Colin's eyes turned to Susannah. "I believe we do have a lot in common even though we've not known each other long. We can take our time and get to know one another better. I find Susannah a charming, caring, godly woman. If something is important to her, it will be important to me. Communication is key, but faith in God's Son is uppermost. If each one grows closer to God first, they will grow closer to one another."

Susannah's eyes never wavered from Colin's. Her appreciation for him was strengthened by his sincerity. She noted the way he sometimes moved his hands as he spoke, the slight curve of his mouth when he grew amused, and the way he ran his hand through his wavy hair when nervous.

Diann cleared her throat. She grabbed her purse and rose, placed a hand on Susannah's shoulder and said, "I'll see you back at the cottage. My work here is done."

After she left, Colin smiled at Susannah, amusement in his eyes. "I like her. She gets right to the point." He reached across the table and took Susannah's hand. "And now I will too. Would you have dinner with me tomorrow night?"

☙❧

Perched in her now favorite overstuffed armchair, Diann's gaze moved to Letice who sat cross-legged on the rug in front of the fireplace, and to Susannah on the sofa, her legs stretched the length of it, her back against the arm.

"Diann, I'm going to miss you." Letice sighed. "It seems like I've known you all my life. And calling me Letty—I love it—I've never had a nickname before."

She took a sip of tea and looked at the other woman affectionately. "Letty, it's been a pleasure. If it weren't for my husband and family, I'd move to Neville in a heartbeat."

"It'd be wonderful having you here." Susannah blinked rapidly. "I may start crying . . . in fact, I *know* I will tomorrow when we take you to the train station."

"Sue, please don't start." Diann sat upright; her teacup tipped precariously. "I will if you do."

Letice stood. "Will you two stop it. I'm going to start blubbering, and Susannah knows I have a low threshold for weeping." She took her cup to the kitchen and called over her shoulder. "Anyone for a refill?"

No one answered. "Splendid. I guess this means the remainder of Diann's stay will be spent with tears flowing."

"No, we're not going to do that." Susannah swiped at her eyes and stood. "Let's get ready and go eat at Talbot's to enjoy our last night together." She went to her bedroom.

Diann followed but paused at the kitchen entrance. Leaning in, she spoke softly, "Letty, would you do me a favor?"

"Yes, dear." Letice gathered the dishes and began to wash and dry them. "What's on your mind?"

She moved into the kitchen and kept her voice low. "I want you to keep an eye on Sue for me, she tends to get morose from time to time, and it takes a friend to get her out of the house to cheer up. Not leaving the house for days at a stretch, she gets bogged down in genealogy, writing her travel articles and editing photography."

Letice paused from her chore and watched Diann. "I'd be happy to. We'll have a lot to do with the factory renovations and such. In fact, we do have that meeting this weekend."

"Thanks a million. I knew I could count on you." Diann dragged the toe of her shoe in imaginary circles on the floor. "I should be a bit jealous of you."

Letice's eyes widened. "What in the Queen's land for?"

Diann laughed nervously "Well . . . only that you seem to have replaced me. You and Sue have become very close. Honestly, I'm glad she has someone like you. I'm too far away to be of much use except by phone."

"That's very decent of you to say. I have become close to Susannah, but you'll always be her oldest and dearest friend. I'm honored the two of you have included me. You've both made me feel more than welcomed—like we're sisters." She gave Diann a quick hug."

"Letty, you're a sweet lady, and I thank you for our new friendship. Let's stay in touch."

Susannah strolled into the kitchen, and Diann startled. "Okay, what are you two conspiring about without me?"

Diann glanced at Letice, who had picked up on her signal. They rushed to Susannah to grab her into a group hug.

"Oh, you two. Stop this." Susannah withdrew from their arms. "Now I am crying."

Letice smiled. "We need a name for our trio of friendship."

"Oh, how silly," Diann exclaimed. "I feel like we're in grade school again."

Susannah started laughing—one of those contagious laughs that was hard to end. Before long, they were all three hysterical, on the verge of tears. Letice choked out through her giggle. "I'm famished . . . let's go eat." Their walk to Talbot's turned some heads on Neville's sidewalks with their excited chatter. Diann was in the middle of a story about their Horden Castle tour when they arrived at the inn's front door.

After greeting Hodge, settling at a table, and putting in their orders, Letice looked at Diann. "I wish you could stay longer. We need all the help we can for the new homeless flats. Although, we certainly appreciate the input you've given us thus far."

Diann toyed with her napkin. "I'm glad I could help. I'll only be a phone call away." Determined not to give in to emotion, she continued, "Everything has been wonderful— the castle tour, the meetings, meals with you two . . ."

She would greatly miss Susannah and her new friend, Letice, but foremost in her mind was Susannah's burgeoning relationship with Colin Heard. The man seemed genuine, but he was a businessman and grasped how to present himself in the best light. She wanted her friend to be happy, and she prayed that Colin was an answer to that prayer.

Chapter Twenty-Two

New York City, New York, U.S.A.
2019

Ryan settled himself into his desk chair for the morning. He had a lunch meeting with Vernon Sturdivant to discuss the next phase of the case. Lost in thought, he jerked at the sound of his intercom. "Yes, Janet?"

"Ms. Genevieve Lee is here to see you." Janet's singsong tone alerted Ryan of what she thought of Ms. Lee.

Hesitantly, Ryan replied, "Send her in, Janet, and will you please confirm my lunch reservation at one?" Confirming an appointment was Ryan's way of letting Janet know to repeat the request within earshot of his waiting client.

Ryan stood as Genevieve opened the door and sauntered in. He didn't come around the desk to meet her. "Good morning. To what do I owe this pleasure?" He motioned toward one of the chairs facing his desk. "Please have a seat."

Her face puckered. She made a show of crossing her long, shapely legs as she sat, her dark blue skirt slipping up. Her gaze bored into him. "Ryan, what on earth have I done to make you no longer interested?"

Ryan opened his mouth and closed it. He didn't have the answer. It wasn't that long ago he'd made advances toward her, and she'd responded in kind—until he came back from England and no longer wanted to pursue her.

She crossed her arms. "Well, are you going to answer me?"

He refused to hurt her feelings. "Genevieve, you've done nothing wrong. I . . . I find you extremely attractive."

"BUT . . ." she raised her voice, dark eyes cold, unforgiving.

This was a side of Genevieve he'd not seen. At times, she'd been surly toward waitresses—especially attractive ones. "To be blunt, I'm no longer interested because I don't think we have enough in common."

Her appearance morphed into ice-laced haughtiness— words coming out slow, drawling. "I see." She examined her nails, rubbing a thumb over them one at a time.

"I don't mean to be abrupt or rude, but you did ask, and I won't lead you on. It wouldn't be fair to you—or to me." Ryan gave her what he hoped was a presentable smile. "I hope we can part as friends."

The silence was thick. Genevieve's incredulous expression told him she couldn't fathom that any man wouldn't fall all over himself for her.

Ryan stood and repeated, "Again, I hope we can part as friends, Genevieve." He extended his hand.

Genevieve pushed herself from the chair, using the arms as leverage, eyes not leaving his. She reached out as if to accept his hand but, instead, slapped it. So violent was the move that Ryan had to stop himself from retaliating with a biting comeback. "I take that as a no. Goodbye, Genevieve."

No sooner had she walked from his office, cool as a glacier, his phone rang. "Ryan, what did you say to Ms. Lee? She was as red as a lobster."

"Oh, that. She asked me to marry her, and run off to the Galapagos Islands, and I said no."

Janet laughed. "I've always said you should've been a comedian. Why didn't you tell me to mind my own business?"

"I wouldn't dare. Besides, you know all my secrets." Ryan cut the call. A joke was one way he covered tension. At least Genevieve was one source of it he wouldn't have to deal with any longer.

◦◦◦

Diann yanked boxes from the storage closet of her home office. "Now what did I do with that business card?" One shoebox-sized container had a label clearly marked England.

"Thank goodness. Here it is." She placed the box on her desk, tossed the lid aside, and shuffled through brochures of Horden Castle, Talbot's Tavern, and various places she and Susannah had visited on their initial trip. More memorabilia followed from her return visit to see Susannah in her new cottage. She'd been happy with the exception of the continued estrangement with Ryan. That was the greatest source of pain in Susannah's life, and Diann was concerned about her health. Her heart hurt to think of all Susannah had gone through in past years.

Tears threatened. She couldn't go on remembering. Focusing on the good days should be uppermost in her mind—and the fact that Ryan was helping her to set the record straight about his mother's innocence. After their confrontation in his office, his attitude had started changing. When he came back from England, it had progressed. She kept praying.

The box was nearly empty, and the card hadn't surfaced. Coming to the last item, a puff of breath expelled, followed by a deep sigh. What could she have done with it?

Plopping with a thud in her desk chair, she leaned back and prayed. "Lord, if you want me to do this, please let me find it."

Diann reviewed each memento before carefully returning it to the container. Overwhelmed with the prospect of searching elsewhere, she reached for the lid. A piece of paper jammed inside it caught her eye. The card.

She closed her eyes and said aloud, "Thank you."

That evening, Diann sat at dinner with Wayne and discussed Ryan's meeting with the attorney, their telephone conversation, and the way God had delivered the card into her hands.

"Don't you think that's a sign God wants me to contact Colin?"

Wayne chewed thoughtfully for a moment as his gaze held hers. "Honey, I'm not sure Ryan would want you to do that.

You should ask him first." He reached for another roll and held it like a baseball. "These are the best rolls you've ever made."

"Oh, Wayne. You know those are frozen rolls I bought at the store."

He smiled, bits of roll stuffed in his cheeks like a chipmunk, knowing it would make her laugh.

She shoved his shoulder. "You're so silly."

"So, whatcha going to do about dishy Colin?"

A laugh burst from her, remembering how she'd told him what some of the women in Neville called Colin Heard.

"I don't know what to do. I should call him. He may not help, and that may be a letdown for Ryan." She bit her bottom lip, deep in thought, and picked up the card on the table, turning it over in her hands, and deep within her she felt an even greater urge to call him. For Susannah.

"Diann." Wayne placed his hand on her arm. "Let God handle it."

⋘⋙

Ryan and Vernon finished lunch and discussed minor things about the case—trial dates, witnesses, etc.

"Vernon, you seem to be avoiding the most important issue of this case. What did your investigator find? You said on the phone that he'd returned from Louisiana with his evaluation. Do you have bad news?"

Vernon said flatly, "Actually, it's quite the opposite—yet, there may be a small glitch in the process."

Ryan rubbed the back of his neck. "Like what?"

"It seems there were a few other arrests within days of the event. They were only held a short while, paid a fine, and released. End of story. Well, end of their stories. Your mother's name sort of fell through the cracks, and the prosecutor handling the case got in a bit of hot water because your mother wasn't among those arrested at that time. The prosecutor was in the district attorney's office trying to make a name for herself, fresh out of law school. She was determined to make amends for her error and keep a mark off her record."

Ryan tensed. "So, where does that leave us?"

"At first, the prosecutor had difficulty finding your mother because she had moved to England. Once she found her, the attorney used it to her advantage and said your mother fled the country to avoid prosecution. That heightens the sentence on any given case. Therefore, the result being your mother's prison sentence instead of a slap on the wrist, a fine, and released like the others."

"I see." He swallowed a lump. "What next? How do we clear her name?"

"Trial is the only way unless we find a judge willing to view the evidence and hear the witnesses in his chambers. Laws have changed drastically in a short span of time, and some are unwilling to bend. They may look on this case as being too little, too late."

Ryan's hands squeezed into fists beneath the table, his mother's face in his mind, her voice urging him on. "Do whatever it takes, Mr. Sturdivant. I owe it to her." And far more, he thought.

Chapter Twenty-Three

Neville, North Yorkshire, England
2016

Colin Heard's sleek sedan pulled up in front of Susannah's cottage. Humming a tune from the radio, he slid out of the car and sprinted along the stone path. After one knock, a voice called for him to come in.

He opened it to Susannah pulling on a light sweater. She looked at him, smiling. "Right on time. I like a man who's punctual."

Colin gave her a quick kiss on the cheek. "In a hurry?"

Grabbing her purse, she slung it over her shoulder and shrugged.

"Hungry?" Colin teased her.

"I am. Letice and I went to Northallerton today and did some research for the flats." She turned and darted toward her office, calling out over her shoulder, "Just a minute. I almost forgot something."

Returning with a folder full of papers, she handed it to him. "I thought we could go over these at dinner."

"So, you mean I have to work for my meal tonight?"

Susannah laughed, which pleased him. "Yes, I suppose you do, sort of, except you're buying." She cocked her head. "And don't give me that impish grin."

His laughter rang out this time. "You, my dear, are incorrigible." He gently took her arm and led her out the door.

Their drive was spent listening to classical music and discussing Colin's latest purchase—a 500-year-old historic inn near Salisbury.

"I'll complete the paperwork sometime next week. Would you like to go with me?"

"I'd love to go, but I'll be out of town a few days next week. I'm taking the train to Scotland to research for a travel article." She pulled out her phone and showed him the dates on her calendar.

He eased the car into a spot at the restaurant's car park and asked her to repeat the dates and entered them into his phone's calendar. "I'll be gone that week as well."

"We should make the best of tonight." He draped an arm on the back of her seat and fixed a steady gaze on her. Her intake of breath was audible. He smiled, and they both jumped as a loud thump sounded on her window.

"Hey, you two!" Letice called out with a wave, beaming as if she hadn't seen them in years. Amanda stood at her shoulder, eyes downcast.

Colin let out an abysmal sigh and exited the car. Susannah had already emerged when he reached her side.

"Evening, ladies," he said, attempting to keep his agitation at bay. Talk about timing. Susannah offered a strained smile.

Letice's voice came between winded breaths. "What a coincidence. I sprinted across the lot to catch you. What brings you two to Northallerton?"

Amanda's cheeks flushed. "Sorry to bother you. Letice saw you and insisted we pop over and say hello."

Letice shot Amanda a glare. "Oh, don't be ridiculous. They don't mind at all. I see Susannah brought the research from today. So, see, they're discussing it over dinner."

Colin glanced at Susannah, who hadn't said a word but clutched the folder like a life preserver. He placed a hand at the small of her back. Susannah's face showed relief at his nearness.

"Yes, we're reviewing it at dinner."

"Splendid." Letice chimed in. "We can get a large table, so we can spread everything out."

Amanda and Letice stepped out, expecting them to follow. Colin took Susannah's arm and led her to the restaurant, trailing the chatting women. He offered an apologetic look and whispered, "Sorry, I think we're trapped."

Susannah gave a nervous laugh and squeezed his arm. He placed a hand over hers with reassurance. All he wanted was time alone with the wonderful woman beside him. Would it ever happen?

◌◈◌

Susannah's train ride from Northallerton to Edinburgh was uneventful. She'd decided to break her journey halfway, in Edinburgh, for a light lunch at her favorite tearoom. The trip continued back at Waverley Station to board the train to Aberdeen and switched to a bus that hugged the eastern coastline of Scotland. Sandy beaches came and went as the bus wound its way to its final destination of Cruden Bay.

The gentle swaying of the bus left Susannah groggy after hours of train travel. She'd spent some of the time alternately texting Colin, Diann, and Letice and the remainder making notes for her article.

Long grass blowing in the wind along the North Sea's scenic coast seemed to wave hello to her. Many years had passed since her first visit to this part of Scotland where more of her ancestors had lived. It pulled her in as if she belonged there—the same way Neville did.

How different her life would've been if she'd moved here instead. She exhaled as thoughts of Colin filled her mind. He seemed perfect—and though he obviously wasn't, she prayed fervently that her heart would not be broken again. It was the unknown she feared. She thought she knew Aaron by the time they'd married. It didn't take long for his true nature to appear.

Cruden Bay came into view and past it, Slains Castle, its reddish stone glinting in the midday sun, mesmerizing her. As the setting of one of her favorite novels, it had captivated her, leading her to research its history.

This time, instead of a fleeting tourist trip, she planned to thoroughly explore and spend three days getting familiar with the castle and its surroundings intimately.

After checking in at the St. Olaf Hotel, she ate a quick lunch in their small dining room, her table by the window overlooking the golf course. From her upstairs room, she glimpsed the castle in the distance, perched on the cliffs as it had for hundreds of years, vast and imposing, a sentinel along the rugged coast with waves crashing beneath it. What an impressive sight it was.

Susannah set off with her journal, bottled water, snacks, and other necessities in her bag. She walked through the village, past shops and the historic tavern. It was a long, yet pleasurable stroll that joined a path within a small wooded area, and crossed fields to end at the cliffs.

The remainder of the afternoon she sat among the ruins facing the sea, scribbling furiously as the words came upon her like a flood. She consulted her previous research to blend it with her surrounding observations. Envisioning women in long dresses moving through the castle's now abandoned passageways, their skirts swishing, brushing the walls with each step. Seagulls screeched into the wind, swooping into the surf below the castle in search of a meal.

The sun began its decline behind her, leaving shadows, darkening the interior of the castle. Rising from her stone perch, she gave one last glance to the open sea to the east. The sun had nearly set before she reached the St. Olaf. She glanced behind as a temporary goodbye to the castle, a dark hulk on the cliff top.

The next morning, she lounged in bed longer than she

should've, and a relaxed breakfast left her invigorated for a full day of exploration. She ordered a take-away lunch, so she could spend the whole day out.

Her plan was to walk through the village shops, taking pictures and interviewing the locals before returning to the castle. A glance out the window overlooking the beach revealed the wind more active than the previous day. She grabbed a gauzy purple scarf and entwined it around her hair, tying a loose knot under her chin. The interviews, a cup of Earl Grey at the Kilmarnock Arms Hotel, and a brisk walk across the fields energized Susannah to head to the castle again.

After a couple hours of work, she had dozens of detailed photographs and a rough sketch of the castle's floor plan. Her article would highlight the castle, an unofficial tourism destination the world had almost forgotten. Perched on the sill of the huge open window watching the sea, she sat with the wind whipping her scarf as she ate her sandwich.

Occasionally, the murmur of disembodied voices walking the ruins broke her concentration—tourists. She watched a couple stroll hand in hand along the castle's outer wall. The woman shaded her eyes and pointed far out to sea. Susannah squinted, the image reminding her of Aaron in the first—and only—sunny days of their relationship as they explored the Azores together.

She stood, brushing crumbs from her lap. She wouldn't think of him, not in this beautiful, peaceful place. Not today.

Packing her trash, she reclaimed the camera for one more shot of the room. In her mind she visualized it as a parlor, or possibly a library—although it would've been the floor above as the lower floor held the kitchen, servants' quarters and storage rooms. It most likely had been filled with darkly carved furniture lit by a warm glowing fire. She glanced to the brilliant blue sky where the upper floors were, so long ago. Through the paneless window, she took one last lingering look out to sea, studying the waves thrashing the rocks far below.

"Searching for a ship?"

The deep male voice startled her. She sank onto the sill, her legs weak, and grabbed the window's rough edge.

With wide eyes, she met Colin's gleaming gaze and wicked grin. "Colin Heard, you scared the life out of me."

He shoved his hands into his pockets and pulled a face. "I didn't mean to frighten you."

"You were off the mark a bit. I was so lost in thought..." Her voice trailed off as she regained composure.

"Sorry." He came to sit beside her. "I thought it'd be a nice surprise."

"It is, but aren't you supposed to be on your business trip?"

"Actually, no." He rubbed his jaw and looked out to sea a moment, and back at her. "I made that up when you told me your dates. Spur of the moment decision." He gave her an innocent smile. "A romantic gesture, I thought, but nearly scaring you off a cliff was certainly not my aim."

She shook her head with a grin. "Well, you achieved that whether intended or not. You're so funny."

"Funny?" He gave her a playful shove with his shoulder, his broad smile reaching his eyes.

She turned to look at the rolling waves. From her peripheral vision, she saw him follow her gaze.

"Frightened of heights?"

"Not so much. I do have a healthy respect for them though." She lightly shoved him back. "You?"

"Not at all. Used to hang glide a bit when I was younger."

"You didn't?" She raised an eyebrow. "I suppose I shouldn't be surprised."

Through a wide grin, he said, "Yes, young and stupid, I might add. Won't be doing that again. Learned my lesson." He rolled his sleeve to his bicep and presented a nasty scar on his right forearm. "Had a foul run-in with a tree coming down that broke my fall and my arm."

Gently, her fingertips touched his scar, the sensation of the firmness in his muscular arm beneath leaving her short of breath. "I'm impressed. I've never been that brave. Born a chicken."

Colin laughed. "No harm there." He stood and helped her up, not releasing her hand. Warmth spread through Susannah's hand. She picked up her bag and fidgeted with the strap.

"How about a stroll along the beach and dinner tonight?" He asked, his voice at her shoulder, his nearness both welcomed and unnerving. "I'm staying at the Kilmarnock Arms. I could collect you at half seven. Where are you staying?"

She steeled herself and met his eyes. "That sounds perfect. I'm at the St. Olaf. I was about to leave when you startled me. I need to return to the village to take more pictures and interview a few more people. Walk with me?"

He squeezed her hand, led her through the castle's

shadowed halls and into the soft waning light as they strode toward Cruden Bay.

ଔଓ

Colin sat in the lounge at the St. Olaf perusing his phone when Susannah walked downstairs. He met her eyes and stood. "You look nice. I'm glad you took my suggestion of wearing comfortable shoes."

"Since it's all I brought, I had no choice." She returned his smile. "This is a business trip. And since I spend a lot of time on foot, I always bring two pairs of comfy walking shoes."

"Smart girl."

She raised her eyebrows. "Haven't been called a girl in decades."

"Pity, that. You still look like one." He gave her a roguish wink.

"Flattery will get you nowhere, mister."

"Pity that, as well." He smiled. "Dinner?" He claimed her hand to lead her away when he turned and grabbed something she hadn't noticed on the table. "Almost forgot my torch."

"What's that for?"

"It's almost dark. We'll need it to walk to dinner."

She narrowed her eyes. "You're scaring me again."

"Properly so. Wait and see."

Once they reached the shops, Colin pulled out a long strip of fabric and told her to turn around.

"You are joking, right? A blindfold. Seriously?"

He nudged her. "Yes. Please hush and play along. I won't

let any harm befall you."

Her head slanted. "How do I know that? I mean, how do I identify you're not another Jack the Ripper." She teased. "After all, I don't truly know you."

He covered her eyes with the cloth and tucked her arm in his. "Stay close, so you don't trip. Let me guide you. This is going to take a while, so please be patient." He paused. "Wait, where'd I put my knife?"

Her laughter rang out, and she squeezed his arm.

He whispered in her ear, "Although, I could carry you."

She whispered back, "We don't have time to take you to the hospital and have dinner."

"Hardly," he responded and smiled broadly.

The walk was long, over uneven terrain. "We're almost there. Just a few more steps." He told her to stop, released her hand and moved behind her. He put his hands on her shoulders to angle her slightly. A gentle breeze rustled the hair at her neck, bringing with it the scent of the ocean, and he let the blindfold slip away.

"Bon appétit," he said, crossing his arms with satisfaction at her shocked expression.

She covered her mouth and stared. Her lower lip quivered. "Colin . . . I . . ." She sniffled, her light eyes gleaming with unshed tears. ". . . I'm not certain what to say."

He turned to take in the scene he'd made just for her in the castle's parlor. A large tartan blanket was spread across the ground. Flickering candles in glass jars rested on every available stone surface—the window opening, vacant spaces in the walls, tucked into corners, and on the blanket among the display of food and a bottle of sparkling water with two crystal stemware glasses. He may not be an interior designer, but he had to admit the scene held every bit of romance and tranquility he'd hoped to create.

"Do you like it? Is it over the top?"

Susannah gingerly stepped toward the blanket and looked at the thick cushions on either side of the food covered with a linen tablecloth.

She turned to him, and he could see the depth of emotion she was fighting back. She sniffed again and swiped at her eyes; her voice affected. "Colin, no one has ever done anything remotely—" She broke down.

"Please don't cry." He moved to her. "I simply wanted to show you how much I care for you. I don't mean to rush anything."

He met her eyes. She offered a gentle smile as she dried her tears and gave a soft laugh. "Colin, I'm beyond pleased." She wiped away a tear and moved to sit on a cushion. "But it's breathtaking, literally."

He sighed with feeling. "You scared me this time. I thought you didn't like it."

She sent him a disbelieving stare. "How could I not? This is phenomenal."

He poured her a glass of water, the tiny bubbles dancing in the candlelight and watched her take in the room, still in astonishment.

"How did you do this? And when?"

"After I left you to your interviews, I did a little research of my own. It is true that money can buy you about anything. Sad to say." He shrugged. "Seeing your face was worth every pound."

He took a sip of water and smiled over the rim. "You're not getting off too easy." He surveyed the room. "We have to clean this up."

Susannah's head lifted from peeking beneath the linen covering. "What? And you said I was incorrigible."

He smiled warmly, content and relaxed in her presence, and longed to see her so happy every single day if he could have any part in it. The room radiant with candlelight and the sound of the waves below the castle set the backdrop for what he hoped was the beginning promises of love.

Chapter Twenty-Four

New York City, New York, U.S.A.
2019

Colin's cell phone rang at six in the morning. He struggled to open his eyes and look at the clock by his bed. He groaned, reached for the phone, and mumbled, "Colin Heard."

"I'm so sorry to wake you." The feminine voice sounded genuinely regretful.

"Pardon me—who is this?" He sat upright. "Is there a problem?"

"Colin, it's Letice. I hate to be a bother, but Amanda and I have a question. I lost all track of the time difference between Neville and . . ."

"America?" He finished for her.

"Yes, I wasn't certain what city you were in, so I couldn't calculate the exact time difference."

"No harm done." He rose, strode to the window, and opened the drapes. "What do you need?"

"We have the plans complete for the playground and wondered when you'd be back. We want to start on it right away and wanted to know if we could e-mail them to you for approval. Would that be possible?"

She stopped long enough to take a breath. "When are you coming back?"

"I'm not certain—but, yes, e-mail the plans. I'll go over them today and be in touch. Although, I'm sure you two did a wonderful job."

"Thank you. Sounds splendid." She paused. "Do you have much business to take care of in America?"

Colin's lips curved slightly. "Not much—some loose ends to tie—I'll be home soon. Take care and let me know if you need anything else. Goodbye."

"Goodbye, Colin."

Colin knew what she was about.

Ever since he'd revealed Susannah's death and meeting Ryan, Letice had acted strangely. She'd wanted any information she could find out about the mysterious circumstances behind Susannah's departure from Neville, which was nothing to speak of, at least that's what he'd told her. He wasn't sure she could handle the news of the arrest.

First, he had to do what he'd come to New York to do— discover the full truth.

How had she died?

⊂ఠ⊃

Tristan slowly opened the door of Books-on-the-Green careful not to disturb the tiny bell. He succeeded, and repeated the process in reverse, crept behind Polly, who knelt putting books away.

He whispered at her ear. "Hello, Polly."

Polly screeched and jumped at the same time, turning, fists at the ready.

Tristan backed up so fast that he stumbled over a box and fell flat on his back.

"Tristan. What in the Dickens are you trying to do to me? You almost got a busted nose—are you daft?"

He moaned. "Oh . . . my back. I think I hurt something."

Polly dropped to her knees and mothered over him. "Oh, no. Can I do something to help? It serves you right—sneaking up on me like that." She sat back on her heels.

"Hey. How about some compassion here? I could be seriously injured."

"I'm sorry. Let me help you." She put an arm around him, carefully helping him to sit.

The door opened, and April entered, her eyes widening at the sight of Tristan in Polly's embrace. "Well, well, while the cat's away . . ."

Polly scowled and released him. "He's hurt, you dolt." Tristan winked at April over Polly's shoulder.

"Oh, Polly, you don't know when you've been had." Tristan shot her an irritated look as she walked to the counter and busied herself with tidying it, turning her back on the pair.

"April, what's wrong with you?" Polly's voice held genuine concern.

"Polly, please. Tristan's fine. He's having a bit of fun with you."

She turned to Tristan, who had returned to his prostrate position, and stared at him with a probing glare.

Finally, he couldn't keep up the farce any longer. He broke into a wide grin. "Sorry, Polly. April's right. I didn't mean any harm. I was trying to be funny."

Polly leaned back on her haunches and slugged Tristan in the shoulder. He yelped and grabbed his arm. "Hey, that hurt."

"Good." Polly rose and stood over him with a wide stance and reddening face. "You twit, you should be ashamed."

Tristan burst out laughing. "You look quite comical, all red-faced and standing like a Roman warrior."

Polly stomped off toward the kitchen. Tristan heard the kettle crash into the sink, water running, and the kettle slammed onto the burner.

April laughed. "Sounds like we're having tea."

He sat up. "Should I stay, or am I in danger?"

She gave him an apologetic expression. "Go browse some books, and I'll test the waters for you."

CB&EO

April found Polly at the table waiting for the kettle to boil, her expression unreadable.

"Polly, Tristan was only having a laugh. Give over. He

teases those he likes." April reached for three cups and put them on the table in front of Polly with a clink.

Polly eyed the cups and looked at April curiously. Her chin propped on fisted hands. "Did you invite him to stay for tea?"

"Not yet. I thought I would." April sat in the chair opposite Polly. "What's going on with you? I thought you liked him. You certainly thought I should date him."

After studying her empty cup a moment, Polly's eyes misted. "You honestly don't have a clue, do you?"

"What? My middle name is clueless." She hoped to elicit a smile from her friend, but Polly's face remained taut. April could tell that she was struggling with something but couldn't bring herself to admit it. "Polly, we've been friends since primary school and have always been able to communicate well, that is, until the past few months. And I've no idea why you've been so angry—" April crossed her arms. "—out with it, Polly. What's going on?"

"Oh, all right." Polly peered over April's shoulder, and she gasped.

April turned to see Tristan hovering in the doorway.

He cleared his throat. "Sorry, ladies, but I'd like to buy this book—unless you want me to nick it rather than break up your conversation."

Polly rose and retrieved the now whistling kettle. Talking over her shoulder, she told Tristan, "Take the book. Pay later. Just leave."

"Polly, don't be rude. Tristan's a friend and a patron of this shop." April turned to Tristan. "Tristan, I'm sorry—I don't think Polly is feeling well right now. I'll walk you out." She led

Tristan from the room.

Tristan called out behind them. "Bye, Polly. Nice to see you too."

"Oh, Tristan. Don't antagonize her. I don't know what's gotten into her, but I mean to find out before the day ends."

"All right." He reached for the door and paused. "Start me a tab." He held the book out.

"Heavy reading, indeed," April teased, noting the book was a collection of superhero comics.

"I need a break from uni. Studying is about to do me in."

She smiled meaningfully, nodded as they said goodbye, and he left the shop, the book tucked under his arm.

After scribbling the book title on a notepad, April returned to the kitchen to find Polly sipping tea, and her own cup was filled. April sat and took a sip, her eyes on Polly, who was meticulously folding and re-folding a napkin.

"You're not leaving this room until you tell me what's going on. If I have to bodily pin you to that chair, you will spill it—post-haste."

Polly looked at April, her eyes brimming with tears. "I'm in love with Tristan. All right? I have been for years."

April nearly dropped her teacup. "Did you just say what I think you said?"

"Please don't toy with me."

"I'm not." April swallowed. "I just find it hard to believe. You've been trying—for months—to get me to go out with Tristan. Why didn't you tell me the truth?"

Her eyes held sorrow. "Because I thought he was in love

with you."

"He only thought he was because he misread our friendship since we were in nappies."

Polly appeared thoughtful. "He did seem to get over your rejection pretty quick, didn't he?"

April laughed. "If I wore my feelings on my sleeve, I'd be hurt by how fast he's moved on."

Polly's posture relaxed, and she nibbled on a biscuit. "I suppose you're right."

"Tell him how you feel, Polly. I think you two would get on well."

Her eyes widened in horror. "Oh, no—I couldn't do that. If he had any feelings for me, he wouldn't have pursued you."

April shrugged. "You can't be sure until you tell him. But, first, you need to lighten up with him."

Polly pursed her lips. "How so?"

"Tristan loves a laugh. He can get a bit carried away but play along. Give him tit-for-tat. He'll love it."

Polly twisted and folded the napkin again. "I'll give a try."

"That's the Polly I know and love." April held up the biscuit tray. "Now, how about we polish these off and get back to work."

Grinning, Polly grabbed a few and shoved several into her mouth, the light in her eyes warming April, sparking her new determination to bring Polly and Tristan together.

CB&SO

April bent over the open oven door to check on her herb-roasted chicken and vegetables when the knock at the door startled her. She closed the oven and strode to the door. Her parents huddled under the tiny overhang. She ushered them inside. "Oh my, you'll be soaked."

"Not to worry, love. Your little roof kept us dry." Mrs. Conyers gave April a peck on the cheek and a robust hug. She glanced around the room. "I'd forgotten how charming this place is."

Mr. Conyers repositioned the package at his hip, which suspiciously resembled groceries. "Hallo, duckie," he said, kissing her cheek, "Something smells lovely."

"That it does, C.C." Her mother smiled in approval. "Need any help?"

"No, thanks, Mum. Everything is under control. Dinner should be ready in twenty. Please have a seat, and I'll get you something to drink."

C.C. Conyers followed his daughter to the kitchen and placed the package on the table with a thud. "Here you go." His whisper was conspiratorial. "Your mum insisted. She's worried you're not eating well. She believes you may be scrimping on things to save a pence."

"Oh, Da. That's ridiculous." She shook her head and unpacked the groceries. "Her heart is in the right place, but I'm fine." April handed him a stemware glass of water. She carried two more glasses into the lounge area.

"Here you go, Mum." She handed off the drink and eased herself into the overstuffed chair. "And thanks for the groceries. That was very thoughtful, but you didn't have to do it."

"I know, dear, but you look like you've lost weight, and I

won't have you going hungry."

April watched her father roll his eyes as he expelled a humph before seating himself on the sofa next to his wife. He placed a reassuring hand on her shoulder. "Love, our girl can take care of herself. You've taught her well." Mrs. Conyers kissed his cheek.

April watched her parents, admiring their genuine affection for each other. They seemed so suited. She longed for that kind of relationship with a spouse. In God's timing.

The oven timer rang out, drawing April from her thoughts. "You two stay put while I get everything on the table." She winked at them. "It's time for me to wait on you for a change."

April prepared the table with an ivory and pink checked tablecloth. Each place setting held bisque plates with gold edging and crystal stemware. A large platter supported the roasted chicken surrounded by glazed carrots and rosemary potatoes. Another serving dish held green beans glistening with a touch of olive oil and sprinkled with chopped herbs. Fresh yeast bread rounded out the meal. It was perfect.

She called her parents to eat. Once seated at the table, she asked her father to say Grace.

Bowing their heads, Mr. Conyers began, "Lord, we thank you today for the provisions you have blessed us with. We thank you for such a wonderful daughter and for providing her with this splendid home, this meal, my lovely wife, and the wonderful life you've given us. Amen."

April and her mother echoed, "Amen."

Mr. and Mrs. Conyers savored their first bite and complimented April to the point of embarrassment.

Conversation floated from one subject to another, finally moving to the purchase of Permelia Cottage.

Reaching for another serving of vegetables, Mrs. Conyers remarked on the cottage's furnishings. "I must say the previous owner had a wonderful sense of style." She added, "And you've certainly put your touch on the place as well. With equal good taste."

"That would be the mother of the young man I met at the shop. Wouldn't it, April?" Her father took another bite.

"Yes, Ryan Wilkinson. You met him at the shop when you brought over my smashing sign."

Mrs. Conyers watched her daughter. "Ah, yes, your father mentioned a rather fine young man he met that day."

Mr. Conyers eyes widened in horror. "My dear, I said no such thing. Men do not use the term fine when speaking of other men."

"Sorry, dear. You did say he was a rather nice-looking chap though and wondered if April had taken a fancy to him."

"Da. Did you say that?" April exclaimed, equally horrified.

He pushed a green bean around his plate with his fork. "Well, I did think I sensed some type of interest there." He abandoned his bean and glanced at her. "From both of you. Sorry if I was mistaken."

"Yes, you were. I merely purchased the cottage from Ryan, and that's that." April's hand trembled as she reached for her water. "Ryan is a nice enough fellow, but it's clear he's really struggling with his mother's death. It was very painful for him to sell her cottage. He seemed withdrawn. A lot on his mind and perhaps in his past too."

"He seemed nice to me," said Mr. Conyers.

"I have a feeling he needs prayer. We should pray for him."

"Certainly, we will, dear. You may depend on us," Mrs. Conyers said genuinely.

"Thanks, Mum."

After tea and cheesecake, Mr. Conyers stood and stretched. He patted his stomach. "Lovely dinner." He glanced at his wife. "My bed is calling to me."

"Da, it's only half seven." April laughed. "It's been nice to have you over. Let's do this often."

"Certainly." Mrs. Conyers stood with her plate and headed for the sink.

"No, Mum. I'll take care of it. You go on home."

"So quick to get rid of us, are you?" Mr. Conyers draped an arm around April's shoulders.

"You're such a joker. I'll see you at church on Sunday."

"Bye, love."

As April locked the door behind them, she heard her mum say, "Lock tight now, dear."

She called through the door, "Yes, Mum." She smiled all the way back to the kitchen, shaking her head.

Once April cleaned the kitchen, she went into the office and sat at the desk. The box in front of her contained a few small mementos she had carefully packed. The items had belonged to Ryan's mother, and she thought they may be of sentimental value. Also enclosed was a book she'd purchased at Horden Castle. She hoped Ryan would like the little souvenir. She also added a short note of thanks for all he had done to help her buy the cottage.

Memories of the week she'd spent with him rushed back. She was unexpectedly pressed with the need to pray for him. She slid to her knees and asked God to touch his heart, protect him from all forms of harm, and lead him to Jesus.

Now engulfed with peace, she rose and continued the packing and labeling of the box. Yes, she felt much better after placing Ryan in God's hands. Who knew if he had anyone else praying for him?

03 80

New York City, New York, U.S.A.

2019

Ryan checked his mail and found a small package. He didn't remember ordering anything. He armed it up and headed for his apartment. He sorted through bills and advertisements, pausing at the package with an international stamp. Turning it over, he noticed it was from the U.K.

He retrieved a bottle of water, stalling, his gaze fixed on the package across the room—fearful of what it may contain. As he walked by the table, he grabbed it, and strode to the sofa and plopped down. As he ran his fingers over the carefully scripted address in April's careful handwriting, he wondered how she was and if she was still liking the cottage—his mother's cottage.

After ripping the paper off, he opened it to reveal a tour guide his mother had penned, a few of her travel mementos, and a souvenir book about Horden Castle. An envelope tucked inside exposed a note.

Ryan,

I'm enclosing a few items of your mother's that I thought you may want. Merely mementos, but I thought you might like to have them. Also enclosed is a book about Horden Castle that may be of interest to you, especially since your ancestors walked the halls and grounds very much as we did that nice day. I enjoyed our tour and hope you did as well. I trust you are well.

May God bless and keep you,
April

Ryan stared at the note. He read it again and tried to ignore the ache in his middle. She was a kind person. That's all it amounted to. Yet, he'd never met a woman like her.

He tossed the empty box onto the coffee table and jumped from his seat so sudden he felt a brief wave of dizziness. She was a total stranger. They'd had a business arrangement, and that was it. He stormed off to the bedroom, placing his bottle of water on the mantel as he passed. The phone rang while he changed into sweatpants and a t-shirt.

"Hello." He paused with the t-shirt still over his head, the phone pressed to his ear.

"Hey, old man. Haven't seen you in ages." The voice paused. 'Well, since I ran into you at Nonie's."

The voice was muffled by the shirt, so Ryan pulled it down and repositioned his phone at his ear. "Cordell—is that you?"

"Yeah. Why don't you join us at Harree's?" He was yelling over the din of voices and booming music in the background.

"I'm already in for the night." Now fully dressed and sitting on the edge of his bed, Ryan frowned at his reflection in the mirror.

"Come on, man . . . the gang misses you. What happened to our friend, Mr. Wild-and-Crazy?"

"Cordell, I'm not into that right now. Have a good time, and I'll see you in the office on Monday. Bye."

He ended the call, fell back onto the bed, and stared at the ceiling. Life was not the same, and he wasn't certain when the change began—nor did he know exactly what the change was.

Chapter Twenty-Five

Neville, North Yorkshire, England
2016

The back room of the soon-to-open Tea & Scones filled with laughter. Letice and Susannah studied the menu they'd devised. There would be plentiful, yet manageable, items for Letice's new tearoom.

Letice narrowed her eyes. "By the way, you never told me the juicy details of your run-in with Colin in Scotland."

Susannah shifted uncomfortably in her seat. "You and Diann should've been sisters."

"Come on, give me the goss." Letice leaned in, her forearms resting on the table.

"If you insist." Susannah recapped Colin's surprise candlelit picnic at Slains Castle and their romantic walk along the beach.

"He did what?" she exclaimed, mouth gaping, and recovered. "That'll be a fly in the ointment to Vita. She came by and showed me the research she'd done with the homeless housing. She fished for info about you and Colin. If he'd have her, she'd be all over him in a minute."

Susannah made a rapid change of subject. "Letice, this tearoom is going to be amazing. I can't believe the work you've done on this old shop. It's so inviting, and you've captured the essence of the nineteenth century—a leap back in time."

Letice gave Susannah that I-know-what-you-just-did look. She took the hint though and dropped the Colin subject. "Yes, well, except for the plumbing." Letice's hazel eyes flashed with amusement. "I couldn't have done it without you, Susannah. You've helped, encouraged, and even pushed me past my comfort zone."

"I haven't done anything that a friend shouldn't do. To see you fulfill your dream makes me so happy. And proud of you, too." She tilted her head back. "Although ..."

Letice's eyes narrowed again. "Have I forgotten something? What' wrong?"

"No, I was thinking I've earned a few complimentary raspberry scones for my efforts."

She grabbed her forearm. "For all my life."

"Let's not get ahead of ourselves. I don't want to see my ninety-year-old friend hobbling down the street to bring me scones in my dotage."

Letice shook her head. "Hey, don't be cheeky. Besides—" She waved to encompass the room, "—this place may not even make it, after all."

"Don't be absurd. It will." Susannah's chin jutted out as she crossed her arms. "I finished my article on Neville for a travel publication, and I mentioned the most promising new tearoom in all of Yorkshire."

C3&0

After weeks of traveling on business, Colin was glad to return home. He'd missed seeing his friends, and most of all, he missed Susannah. They'd communicated via e-mail, phone, and text messages, their relationship more promising with each passing day.

But he'd grown concerned when the previous week resulted in unreturned messages. In their months of friendship, she hadn't done this except when she'd mistaken the identity of his cousin—a tricky moment, though they'd come through it well, thanks to Diann's intervention.

He stepped from his car and approached Susannah's door, knocked, and waited. No reply. He pulled out his phone and tried to reach her once more. No answer. He could hear her landline ringing from inside.

Looking around to see if he was being watched, he stooped to move a small rock in her flowerbed, which concealed her emergency key. Once inside, he moved toward the kitchen, calling out to her. No response.

A teacup and plate sat on the table. There was tea still in the cup, cloudy from sitting out too long, one of the biscuits on the plate had a bite missing. The chair stood a few feet from the table, positioned as if someone had merely stepped away for a moment.

He strode to her bedroom, calling her name once more. A scattering of clothes lay on the bed, dresser drawers hanging ajar. The closet door stood open, revealing several bare hangers. Next, he went into her office and found on the desk a rough draft of the Cruden Bay travel article she'd written. A few printed photographs from the trip littered its surface. He picked up a picture of Slains Castle and thought back to their dinner that night. A perfect night.

He'd enjoyed her company and holding her hand with the sound of waves and wind around them. She'd seemed to take pleasure in the night as much as he.

Replacing the photo, he noticed two envelopes propped against a tape dispenser, one addressed to him, the other to Letice. His fingers shook as he tore open the envelope, the sound ripping the silence. A small object fell out and pinged along the flagstone floor at his feet. Stooping to retrieve it, he found it to be a small silver pocket cross. Inside the envelope, he found a card.

Colin,

My life has taken an unexpected turn. I'm not sure if I'll return to Neville. It's out of my hands now. If my situation changes, I'll contact you. I know you, of all people, will respect my privacy. It would be best if you forget about me. Just let me go.

Susannah

Weakness overtook him, and he stumbled into the desk chair. He squeezed his eyes shut, not knowing what to make of it. It appeared that she'd left in a hurry. But why? Where?

He thought of Letice. Grabbing his phone, he frantically called her. "Letice, we need to talk," he said, his voice brittle.

"Colin, what's wrong?"

He ran his fingers through his dark hair—he had no voice.

"Are you there?"

He steeled himself and said with a tremble in his voice, "Letice, you need to come to Susannah's right now."

She gasped. "Colin, you're scaring me. What's happened?"

The note slipped from his fingers onto the desk and, with tears in his eyes, he said, "She's gone."

Chapter Twenty-Six

New York City, New York, U.S.A.
2019

Colin strolled down the sidewalk snaking through Central Park. The early morning air had a crispness to it. He breathed deeply and slowed his pace, taking in his surroundings. He lowered himself to a park bench beneath an immense beech tree.

A man of stocky build, gray hair, and plenty of muscle approached him. He had a gleam in his eyes that defied his powerful physique, a quality Colin found both menacing and jovial.

"Good morning, Mr. Godwin." Colin stood and presented

his hand. "Trust you're doing well today?"

"Well enough, Mr. Heard." Scott Godwin presented Colin with a large brown envelope.

"All you asked for is here, except . . ." He paused while a young man in an expensive suit strode past.

"Yes, Mr. Godwin?" Colin took the envelope but made no move to open it.

"Except I can't find any record of Mrs. Wilkinson's death." He rubbed a hand over his face.

"I don't understand," Colin said, skeptical. "What does that mean?"

"It's possible she didn't die in Louisiana. She was extradited to the U.S., but she did go through customs in New York and stayed a few days here before she was sent to Louisiana. With the new privacy laws in place, it's become increasingly difficult to search out certain records. Those files are protected. Although unlikely, it's possible she died en route. Yet, I can't locate any record of that either. All seems kinda strange to me."

Colin grew silent. He glanced at the package. Mr. Godwin cleared his throat.

"Mr. Godwin, thank you for your time and efforts. I have all the information I need. You've been very thorough given the brief time allotted." He reached into his pocket and removed a plain white envelope and gave it to the man. "You may count it now if you'd like. I've included a bonus."

"That won't be necessary, Mr. Heard. I trust you. There was no need for the bonus—but I thank you all the same. Doin' my job."

"Thank you, again." Colin stood, clutching the brown envelope.

Later, at his hotel, he walked to the large window overlooking Central Park. He could see the bench where he and Scott Godwin had met. He stretched out in the comfortable armchair next to the window. Still gazing over the park, he reached for the envelope. He stared at it and wondered if he should open it at all. Was this an invasion of Ryan's and Susannah's privacy? He desperately wanted to discover what happened. Why had she left? He rose and paced the room.

What had caused her to move to Neville and leave her new life there? What drastic event had caused her to go? Had he pushed her too fast?

No. He would never believe that she had left because of him. However, there was one thing he was certain of. He grabbed his phone and called Ryan's office.

"Hello, Janet. This is Colin Heard. Is Ryan in?"

"No, sir. May I take a message?"

He slumped onto the sofa. "Yes, please. Will he be free for coffee sometime before lunch?"

"I'm looking at his appointment calendar, and he does have a free hour at ten this morning. Would that be convenient for you?"

"Yes, will you have him meet me at the coffee shop on the first floor of your building, please?"

"Yes, sir—my pleasure."

He heard the smile in her voice. "Have a nice day." Colin propped his elbows on his knees and let his wrists hang limp, his head bowed. Why had he pursued the investigation? He had to unburden himself to Ryan. Maybe he should've never come. He desperately needed to know what had happened to this woman he'd grown to love.

◌◦◌

Colin chose a booth at the coffee shop, his eyes focused on the door. He sipped his Earl Grey, trying to get his thoughts together on what he'd say to Ryan. He wasn't sure how his confession of snooping in his mother's business would go.

He let out a low sigh when he saw Ryan approaching. "Good morning. Thank you for meeting on such short notice." He hoped the lump in his throat wasn't evident in his voice.

Ryan lowered himself into the booth. He opened his mouth to speak when the server approached.

"What will you have, Ryan?" The server smiled broadly.

"My usual, Cindy. Thanks."

"So, what do you have on your mind? Advertising is still working on your project, so I don't have anything to report."

"That's fine. I'm here about something else." Colin placed a white envelope on the table and slid it forward.

"What's this?" Ryan didn't reach for it.

"A letter that I hope you'll read when you're alone. Right now, I need to say something to you." Colin cleared his throat and was about to begin when Cindy came back with Ryan's coffee.

"There you go."

They thanked her and returned to their conversation.

"I need to apologize to you."

308

Ryan brought his gaze from the envelope to meet Colin's eyes. "What for? I don't understand."

Colin looked away, searching for the right words to begin. He said a silent prayer for strength. "Ryan, I must ask your forgiveness for something I've done. After I spoke to you at Horden Castle and found out that you were Susannah's son, so many unanswered questions bombarded me. I was a man obsessed to learn the truth. I even hired a private investigator." He reached to the booth seat and produced the larger envelope. "This is his report. I haven't opened it." He pushed it toward Ryan. "I couldn't."

Ryan stared at it, his forehead wrinkled.

"I don't expect you to understand my feelings toward your mother. We were getting to know each other when she left, but I did care for her." He stared intently at Ryan, searching his eyes. "Will you forgive me?"

Ryan reached for his coffee and took a long drink but said nothing. He studied Colin. "Why are you asking for my forgiveness?"

"Because I've intruded upon your privacy. This is about your mother's memory, her life, of which I have no claim other than friendship. Remembering her the way she was in Neville should be enough. We had some pleasant times together." He realized the sadness in his eyes was unmistakable. He felt the depth of her loss within his very soul. "To tell you the truth, Ryan, her leaving nearly undid me."

⊂◈⊃

Ryan was silent a moment, taking in the man's sorrowful expression. He shrugged. "Mr. Heard, I seriously don't know what to say. I'm not angry with you, nor do I think you need my forgiveness. It is I who should . . ." How could he possibly tell this man—a stranger—what he'd put his mother through? And he would have to tell him everything in order for him to understand. He wasn't prepared for that.

Ryan rose without warning. "I—I forgive you if you feel you need it. I respect what you're saying—and admire your business acumen. But it's too difficult for me to speak of my mother." He picked up his takeaway coffee. "If you'll please excuse me. My ad department will be in touch. But I—I just can't talk about her now." He turned to leave.

"Ryan." Colin grabbed the envelopes and stood, thrusting them forward. "Please take them. You can throw away the report if you wish." He touched the smaller envelope. "But please read this."

Ryan hesitantly took them. "All right," he said softly. "Have a good day, Mr. Heard. Let's not bring this subject up again ... please. If I decide to discuss it, I'll let you know."

"Fair enough. I will look for your marketing proposal. We can work via e-mail for now."

Ryan paid for his coffee, and walked out into the bright day, a beam of light reflecting off the side of a bus, the sound of the city surrounding him—horns blowing, the buzz of conversations along the sidewalk, a faraway siren. He stepped briskly toward the park rather than his office. He dropped the large envelope into his bag. He wouldn't open it.

Chapter Twenty-Seven

New York City, New York, U.S.A.
2019

LaGuardia Airport offered its usual flurried atmosphere. Loud conversations in multiple languages engulfing the air, attempting to invade Ryan's train of thought on the upcoming trip. Vernon and Ryan checked in for their flight and made it through security with time left to discuss the case over coffee. During the flight, they didn't engage in conversation. Ryan read a book, and in no time, the flight was touching down at their destination.

Outside baggage claim, Ryan and Vernon waited on the curbside for Diann to pick them up. Ryan took in the typical Louisiana, late-spring afternoon. Bright pink azaleas bloomed profusely, fragrant drooping white clusters of the fringe tree dotted the landscape, and rose bushes lay heavy with nearly opened buds.

Introductions done, Diann asked, "Ryan, would you and Mr. Sturdivant prefer to come to my house for dinner? Or would you like to go to your hotel?"

"I'm beat. I think I'll order room service and crash for the rest of the evening. Is that all right with you, Vernon?"

"That's fine. I'd like to go over my files one last time before the trial." Vernon's voice held fatigue as well. "Thanks for the invitation."

"I understand. We can do it later in the week, depending on how long the trial goes." Diann's voice quivered. "Hopefully it won't be long."

Ryan noticed the anguish in her tone and felt deep guilt that he was the cause of her sorrow. Diann wouldn't feel this way had he been kinder to his mother and stood by her when the whole thing began.

The car stopped, and Ryan became aware of his surroundings. They'd arrived at the hotel. Vernon struggled with his luggage as Ryan got out of the car. Diann opened her door, but Ryan stopped her. "You don't have to come in. We'll see you tomorrow at the courthouse."

Vernon stepped to the window. "It was a pleasure to meet you." He strode to the lobby, leaving them alone.

Diann reached into her purse for a tissue. Ryan saw what was about to happen. "Aunt Diann, please don't be upset. It'll all work out. You wait and see."

Dabbing at her eyes, she looked at Ryan. "Do you think

so?" She sniffled.

Her pain hurt his heart, stabbing like a dull knife. It was so hard to hold any semblance of control when she looked at him like that. "Yes, it will," he said with more conviction and control than he felt. "We'll meet you at the courthouse at two tomorrow." Ryan reached into the open window and squeezed her shoulder.

"Are you sure you don't want me to pick you up?"

"No, we'll take a cab."

Diann offered a final fleeting glance, and he watched her drive slowly from the parking lot.

As Ryan unpacked, he noticed the envelope Colin Heard had given him in New York only two days before. He ignored the larger envelope and reached for the smaller one. The feel of something small and hard within it grabbed his attention. The overused cliché of "curiosity killed the cat" came to mind. He released a sad laugh and thought how true that could be.

He tore into the envelope and removed a single piece of paper. When he unfolded it, a small object fell to the floor and bounced on the carpet. It was a small metal cross that looked vaguely familiar. He held the cross and opened the paper.

Ryan,

Please accept this pocket cross as a gift. Your mother gave it to me in much the same way I'm giving it to you. It was enclosed in the final letter she left for me when she disappeared from Neville. She was a strong Christian woman, and I admired her a great deal.

Please don't be offended, but I can see that you are

struggling with God. You remind me of myself many years ago. I gave up the fight and followed Christ. My life has never been the same. I don't want to go back.

In John 14:6, Jesus told his disciples, "I am the way and the truth and the life. No one comes to the Father except through me." Ryan, I always wanted total control over my life, not wanting to relinquish any of it to anyone or anything. I struggled constantly. Selfishness was my god until I met the real one. And, no matter what, I have an unmistakable peace and fulfillment.

Colin

Ryan stood motionless in the middle of his hotel room, clutching the cross and the letter. His mind wandered through scenes of his childhood—he and his mother kneeling beside his bed for nightly prayers—his small hands as a boy holding onto this very cross, the cross he'd refused the day before he left for college.

The letter fluttered to the carpet, and he fell to his knees. His fingers closed around the cross. Letting his head drop onto the bed, he felt completely drained—physically and emotionally. His guilt of how he'd treated his mother for so long pressed down on him. He'd shut her out of his life as an adult and not stood by her when she'd needed him the most. It was all too much. His resolve broke, and he started to pray.

○§○

The next morning, Vernon and Ryan exited the hotel lobby and entered the waiting taxi. The mid-day air was clammy against Ryan's skin. He'd forgotten how the humidity weighed on a person. Or was it a dreaded fear of what he was about to do?

The cab ride lasted about twenty minutes, yet it seemed only five. He didn't want to do this, but he must. The time had come. He and Vernon discussed the sequence of events that could occur, as the air conditioner pushed coolness into their area. His heart pounded in his chest with the rhythm of the tires as it met the expansion joints on the bridge.

The taxi door slammed. Vernon paid the driver as Ryan stepped onto the sidewalk.

"Ryan, are you okay?" Vernon's voice was laced with concern.

"I'm fine . . . a bit nervous." That was the first time he could ever remember confessing any weakness aloud.

"I understand. But we must have a first-hand account of what happened that day—and thereafter."

"That doesn't make it any easier."

"Yes, well, follow my lead." Vernon offered Ryan his most confident grin. "This isn't the first time I've been down this prickly road."

Chapter Twenty-Eight

Neville, North Yorkshire, England
2019

Colin stepped off the train in Neville, his mind still in a whirl from his hasty trip to New York. He hoped he'd done the right thing by giving Ryan the letter and the cross. That young man needed God so desperately it hurt Colin to his core. If only Susannah could've seen her son come to God before she'd died. That hurt him even more. He prayed that Ryan would seek God for himself.

Forcing composure, Colin entered the tea shop to meet Letice and Amanda to start planning Hodge's 100th birthday celebration. He had volunteered the use of Horden Castle for the party. Hodge was a man to be admired, and Colin wanted everything done in a very special way. Hodge's family had been a part of Neville's history for more than three hundred years, and the whole village should be able to join in the celebration.

As soon as Colin walked through the door, they waved him over.

"Good afternoon." Letice spoke cheerfully. "How was your trip to the States?"

Colin diverted his eyes briefly. "Fine—quick." He turned to Amanda and noticed April was at the table as well. "Hello, April. I didn't know you were working on Hodge's party."

"Yes, sir. I also wanted to visit Letice's tearoom. Isn't it splendid?"

"It certainly is. She did a wonderful job renovating this place. Sorry, I've been away so much and haven't had an opportunity to enjoy it."

April tugged on her necklace. "So, you recently got back from America? Were you on vacation?"

"A business trip. A hurried one at that." He sat in the vacant seat next to Letice and poured himself a cup of tea. "All right, ladies, what do we have in the works for Hodge?"

April looked over the fireworks details. She had a friend who owned a fireworks business and offered them a bargain.

Colin folded his hands on the table. "That sounds like an impressive, and professional, display. I'm certain Hodge will be excited to see it. I was fortunate to see one myself while in New York ..." His voice trailed as he inadvertently revealed where he'd been.

April's eyes widened. "Did you see Ryan?"

Colin turned away and fumbled with his cup.

Letice took the opportunity to ask her own question. "So … your business took you to New York. Did you happen to go to Louisiana as well?"

"Letice!" Amanda's face looked stricken, appalled at her boldness.

"Oh, give over. I wanted to know if he found out anything about Susannah. How she died and all. She was a good friend, and let's face it, she left in the strangest possible way," she said miserably, and crossed her arms.

Colin saw April studying him. He traced the rim of his cup. The quiet settled on their table. He sighed. "I'll not lie to you. My hope was to see Ryan and find out what happened to her. I was deceitful and have apologized to Ryan, revealing my intentions, which left me knowing no more now than I did before. And no, I did not go to Louisiana. There was no point."

April gently asked, "And how was Ryan?"

Colin noted the concern in her voice, saw it in her eyes. "He's a very confused young man. As I told him, I believe he's struggling with God. He refused to talk about his mother. I didn't press him."

"Oh," was all April managed to say.

Letice chimed in. "Colin, I'm sorry. I didn't mean to pressure you. I want to know what happened to Susannah as much as you do. Why was she so secretive about her departure? Why didn't she stay in touch? It's all so peculiar."

Amanda cleared her throat. "We need to move on. Not only is it depressing, but we don't know any more now than when she left. We must pray for Ryan and let God take care of it, all right? Let's discuss the party now."

Everyone nodded in agreement and returned to the business of the day. By the end of the meeting, they were all in a lighter mood. Letice and Amanda excused themselves, leaving April and Colin at the table.

"How about one more cup of tea? I'm not quite ready to leave."

"Sure, that sounds nice." She chewed on her lower lip, looking pensive.

Once their tea was refreshed, Colin opened the conversation. "I have a reason for keeping you." He paused, struggling for the right words. "You're obviously concerned for Ryan, so I gather you two became close while he was here."

She shook her head. "He's a very private person, not sharing much about himself. He was anxious to get back to New York."

"I'm sorry. I assumed by your reaction that you were somewhat close. We had a couple of meetings—mostly business-related. I met him to apologize for seeking information about his mother." He continued, emotion thickening his voice. "I tried to share my faith with Ryan. That's all I could do. I left it to God."

April's eyes misted. "Mr. Heard, I'm glad you did. Judging from your success, I think Ryan would look up to you. You may be the exact person God put in his path to reach him. I'll pray that your words will remain on Ryan's mind and heart."

"Call me Colin, and thank you for that. Perhaps that's what compelled me to go to New York after all. God has a way in dealing with us, and sometimes we don't even know it."

April met his eyes and gave him a small, sincere smile. "Yes, He does, Colin."

☙❦❧

Vernon and Ryan approached the outer gate of the prison. After showing their credentials, the guard pushed a button. The gate clicked open with a loud buzz. They followed the same procedure through a second gate. Each gate was connected to a tall chain-link fence topped with rows of barbed wire encircling the compound and a building of gray concrete.

Inside the structure, they approached a window and presented their identification again, this time placing it in a drawer. A guard waved them through a metal detector and asked them to surrender the contents of their pockets. The items were placed in baskets behind a counter. They searched Vernon's briefcase thoroughly, checking every pocket and crevice before returning it to him.

Ryan's mind whirled at the order of events leading up to this meeting. He took deep breaths to steady his nerves. A guard unlocked the door and led them down a long narrow hall. At an intersection, another guard intercepted them guiding them farther into the facility. He placed them in a small room with a table and three chairs, one chair facing the other two. A large one-way glass covered most of a wall.

Vernon and Ryan seated themselves side-by-side. Ryan's hands trembled. He clasped them in his lap and was still looking down when the door clicked open. In his line of vision, he saw two pair of feet—one the guard's black military-style boots, the other pair belonging to someone wearing bright orange pants. There was a gentle clink of metal from chains around the prisoner's ankles.

Vernon cleared his throat but remained silent.

Ryan's gaze rose to the body of the prisoner—the handcuffs on slender wrists, hands loosely clasped. It was almost too much for him. He'd never been in a prison in his life. What was he doing here? Why hadn't he let Vernon take care of this alone?

But deep within he understood he should be here now, it should've been years earlier. He swallowed, steeling himself, and forced his gaze to meet the prisoner's—and peered straight into the hazel eyes of his mother.

Chapter Twenty-Nine

Louisiana, U.S.A.
Present Day

The courtroom crowd was sparse. Coverage had been minimal by the media. Ryan sat behind the table where his mother and Vernon Sturdivant were seated. He held the pocket cross, fumbling with it, silently praying. The bailiff announced for all to rise and introduced the judge. The jury followed, and the trial commenced.

In no time, the opening statements were given, and the prosecution called Susannah Wilkinson to the stand. Walking to the front of the courtroom, she exuded confidence and strength as she was sworn in. Ryan was proud of her—it seemed—for the first time in his life.

Ms. Lola Percy, of the prosecution, began to grill her. "Ms. Wilkinson, what exactly were you doing in front of the Timlee Clinic on the third of May?"

His mother spoke, her voice faltering. "I was merely trying to talk to each of the women going into the clinic." She looked at her lap.

"And what exactly did you tell them?"

"That they did have a choice. That they didn't have to abort their babies. I wanted them to know there are many couples who would love to give their child a home." Her shaky sigh was audible.

"Did you say anything about religion or your faith?"

"I only asked if I could pray with them, and they agreed."

Ms. Percy threw a sidelong glance at the jury and faced Susannah again. "I see. So, you caught them at a vulnerable moment and pushed your religious beliefs on them, did you not, Mrs. Wilkinson?"

Vernon stood and called out, "Objection, your honor. She's badgering the witness."

The judge looked at him, then at Ms. Percy. "Sustained. Counsel, conduct yourself professionally, or I will cite you for contempt."

Ms. Percy scowled and reluctantly asked another question, "Why weren't you arrested with the others?"

"I was off to the side speaking with a young girl and her mother when the police came. When we finished talking, I went to my car parked along the road. Before I discerned what was happening, I heard glass breaking and I saw an elderly woman get hit by a rock and stumble. I rushed toward her and tried to catch her, and that's when the smoke bomb exploded."

His mother sighed with feeling. "It was chaos. I barely got her out of the crowd to a nearby bench. I checked her arm, but it was only bruised and scratched. I walked her to the bus stop to make sure she was all right. I returned to my car to leave and saw people being arrested. It all happened so quickly. But I was not part of that violent group. It's an approach I don't believe in."

"Mrs. Wilkinson, what did you do then?"

"I was frightened." Her face etched with pain, and Ryan ached to take her hand. "I sat in my car and prayed for a few moments before I left."

Ms. Percy's shrewd eyes narrowed at his mother, and she glanced at the judge. "No mention of religion should be made, your honor."

Ryan noticed the judge conceal a smile. "Isn't that why we're here, Ms. Percy? You are trying to prove that Mrs. Wilkinson was using religion to sway someone's rights and that she ran in order to avoid prosecution. Am I correct?"

Ms. Percy stammered. "Well, yes . . . but . . ."

The judge frowned. "Please continue, Mrs. Wilkinson."

"As I said, I was in my car praying and asking God what I should do. After a few minutes, I left."

"You went home and forgot about it?" Ms. Percy asked.

"I went home, but I have never forgotten about it. I did go on with my life, though."

Ms. Percy tented her fingers, tapping them against her lips. "Was going to England a way to move on with your life?"

"I'd planned the trip for some time. Long before this happened. I've wanted to move to England for many years. A dear friend helped me with the decision." Ryan followed his mother's gaze to see Diann in the courtroom sitting beside Wayne. Diann gave her a reassuring smile.

"Your move to England was not to escape arrest?"

She responded emphatically. "No, not in the least. I had no idea I was under any type of suspicion as I was not part of the violence. And I was unaware of the warrant for my arrest until they knocked on my door in England and forced me to return to the U.S. They brought me before a judge and said because I had left the country, I had no rights and would not receive a trial—but go straight to prison."

"I don't understand, Mrs. Wilkinson. Did they not allow you an attorney?" Ms. Percy asked with an air of disbelief, her resolve cracking slightly.

Ryan watched his mother fight back tears, her chin trembling. He shifted in his seat and wished there were something he could do.

"No, they didn't."

"Ms. Wilkinson, I find that hard to believe. Do you have any proof?"

The judge then addressed her directly. "Mrs. Wilkinson, are you saying that you were not given any occasion to contact an attorney or family member?"

"Well, initially, I was allowed one call. I left my son a message but didn't hear back from him." Her eyes focused on the floor. "I had no way of knowing whether he'd received the message. After two days, I asked to try again but was not allowed." She blinked several times and continued. "Had it not been for a friend who saw a writeup in the newspaper about my extradition . . ." Her voice broke.

Ryan noted that she didn't mention their estrangement, for which he was grateful.

The judge didn't press for further details. He looked at the prosecuting attorney and asked, "Ms. Percy, would you like to explain what has happened here? Everything Mrs. Wilkinson has said can, and will, be substantiated. She has no reason to lie, knowing that it can be proven."

The room erupted with loud murmurs, and the judge tapped the gavel a few times for silence. He thumbed through the file in front of him. "It seems there were a few other arrests within days of the event. They were only held a short while, paid a fine, and released." The judge gave Ms. Percy a piercing look. "Why is there no mention of Mrs. Wilkinson's name?"

She squared her shoulders. "I have no idea, your Honor. Except, at a later date we viewed the video surveillance and found Mrs. Wilkinson to be a part of the violence that ensued. Your Honor, I certainly do not know what this is all about. No one is ever denied a phone call or representation. I'm sure Mrs. Wilkinson is mistaken. No one would allow her rights to be violated. The system works." Her tone was confident.

Vernon objected again.

The judge responded, "Overruled, Mr. Sturdivant. Let's see what evidence Ms. Percy has, although you should have been apprised of any evidence in advance."

"Thank you, your Honor." Ms. Percy waved in the direction of an assistant who dimmed the lights and turned on an overhead screen, which She pointed to. All heads turned. "If the jury would please watch the video from the security camera outside the clinic on the day in question."

The video showed the crowd, calm at first. An obviously pregnant woman approached the front of the clinic. As she passed in front of the protesting group, one of the women gently grabbed her arm, but she shrugged it away. The woman would not let her pass, clearly attempting to force the woman to listen to what she was saying. An instant later, several police cars pulled up. A rock sailed through a windshield. More rocks followed, flying randomly in all directions. Chaos broke out, people running helter-skelter. From one corner of the frame, Susannah came running across the scene, thick smoke covered the footage. Once the smoke cleared, police were making arrests.

Ms. Percy turned toward the judge. "As you can see your Honor, Ms. Wilkinson was running into the thick of things, anger clearly evident on her face." She tossed her folder onto the table and turned to look at the jury, and to the judge. "Your Honor, this is why Ms. Wilkinson has been charged with disturbing the peace, rioting, obstructing public passage, leaving the scene of a crime." She ticked each charge off a finger for emphasis. "And, finally, fleeing the country to avoid prosecution."

The judge didn't respond for a few moments. He tapped his index finger against his chin. "Well, Ms. Percy, do you have any witnesses? Or does the prosecution rest its case?"

"Yes, your Honor. But I reserve the right to question the witness that the defense calls."

"Duly noted. Mr. Sturdivant, you may call your first

witness, or you may proceed in questioning Mrs. Wilkinson since she has already been sworn in."

"Thank you, your Honor. I would like to question Mrs. Wilkinson."

She inhaled deeply, the rise and fall of her chest evident. She tried to maintain eye contact with Vernon.

Vernon attempted a reassuring nod. "Mrs. Wilkinson, will you please tell us exactly what happened that day—in your own words?"

"Objection, your Honor. That question's been asked."

"Overruled. Let's see what Mrs. Wilkinson has to say without the segmented questioning, shall we?" He smiled smugly and turned to Susannah. "Please continue."

Her smile was forced. "As I said, I was about to leave when the violence began. I don't believe in forcing my views on anyone. It was at that time I saw rocks being thrown, and the elderly woman hit by the rock and the smoke happening. I helped her to a bench and made sure she was all right before I took her to her bus stop. That's where my involvement in this ends. I don't know anything past that until the authorities came to England and forced me from my home and brought me back here."

Ms. Percy rose from her seat. "Your honor, the video does not show any of this occurring. We only have her word."

"Ms. Percy, why wasn't the video viewed at the onset of this case? When the first arrests were made?" He leaned forward to peer at her sternly.

She rifled through her file and stuttered, "I—I'm not certain . . ."

"What I think, Ms. Percy, is that someone dropped the ball on this and saw an opportunity to make a name for himself . . ." he emphasized, ". . . or herself."

"May I speak your honor?" Vernon asked, lifting a file folder.

"Yes, Mr. Sturdivant."

"Your honor, I hold here a file containing evidence that the investigator assigned to this case made a grave error and overlooked obvious evidence."

Ms. Percy stood abruptly, arms crossed. "Your Honor. The prosecution was not apprised about this so-called evidence."

The judge's eyebrows pulled together. He nodded at Vernon and replied to his unanswered comment, "How so, Mr. Sturdivant?"

Ms. Percy's composure evaporated. "Your Honor, objection."

"Ms. Percy, do you want to be found in contempt? Overruled." He turned back to Vernon.

"First of all, Ms. Percy has seen this evidence and found it to be inadmissible as hearsay. I disagree and would like for you to review it. I have a witness's deposition that can corroborate Mrs. Wilkinson's testimony about the violence she was not a part of."

The judge opened the file and read it. Clearing his throat, he proceeded to tell all present that the elderly woman Susannah assisted had passed away, but that her daughter agreed to give a deposition stating what her mother had told her. "She states the events that occurred were as Mrs. Wilkinson's testimony states and were not a part of the violence in any way."

The judge closed the file. "I'll allow this as evidence."

A low buzz of voices sounded in the courtroom. Jury members glanced at one another, their faces anxious.

Ms. Percy rose. "Your Honor, this is hearsay. This should not be admissible since it's from a third party."

"Ms. Percy, I understand what you're saying, but why should this not be admitted? This third party was not directly connected to the occurrence, but the series of what happened there was relayed to her by her mother—not some stranger off the street. She didn't know Mrs. Wilkinson. Therefore, I don't think she was swayed one way or another."

The judge turned his attention to Vernon. "Mr. Sturdivant, would you like to question Mrs. Wilkinson further or call any other witnesses, or close?"

"Your Honor, I would like to ask Mrs. Wilkinson one last question if I may."

The judge leaned back, propping an elbow on the arm of his chair. "Continue."

CS&SO

Susannah swallowed hard, her eyes clouding, knowing what was coming.

Vernon moved to stand in front of her once more. "Mrs. Wilkinson, why was speaking to these women at the clinic so important to you?"

Her head hung. After a moment she raised it, her gaze fixed on the closed door at the back of the room. She couldn't tell her story if she made eye contact with anyone. "I had been married a couple of years when I found that I was pregnant. My husband didn't want children though. He was adamant about that. When I unexpectedly became pregnant, he gave me an ultimatum." She straightened and didn't dare look at anyone, especially Ryan. "End our marriage or have an abortion."

A few quiet gasps, some sniffling, and a cough echoed through the courtroom.

She brushed a tear from her cheek. "I refused. I would never do that to my child." Her voice cracked, she cleared her throat and continued, "I've been an advocate for the helpless ever since."

"I have no other questions, your Honor. The defense rests." Vernon returned to his seat.

The judge couldn't take his eyes off Susannah. "Yes, well ... Ms. Percy, do you have any further questions?"

Her eyes icy, she said, "No, your Honor."

"Bailiff, please return Mrs. Wilkinson to her seat."

Susannah allowed herself to be guided from the stand, her attention on the floor, heart pounding—her spinning thoughts, and the closing arguments a blur. Ryan had said Vernon Sturdivant was the best lawyer in New York, and she hoped he was right.

"The jury is dismissed to come to a verdict."

The bailiff asked all to stand, and Susannah gathered enough courage to glance behind her at Ryan. His shoulders tensed, and he stared at a small object in his hands that glinted in the light as he turned it over and over. He fumbled and almost dropped it. But Susannah had recognized it as the cross—the same one she'd tried to give him but eventually left it for Colin. How could that be?

Before their eyes could meet, the bailiff gently led her away. Looking over her shoulder, she caught a glimpse of Ryan and Vernon in deep conversation, Diann's hand gripping Ryan's shoulder.

As she walked, she prayed. God, please let the truth be enough.

Chapter Thirty

Neville, North Yorkshire, England
Four months later . . .

April stood in the middle of the wide-open expanse of green in front of Horden Castle. It was a perfect morning—mild temperature, no humidity, slight breeze. She prayed it would hold out for the remainder of the day and night for Hodge's big celebration. She couldn't imagine how they had kept it from him. But, somehow, everyone had been tight-lipped.

"April!" Letice called out from across the green.

Letice and Amanda, along with Vita and others, headed her way loaded with boxes of paper lanterns, torches, and lights.

"Good morning, everyone." April relieved Amanda of a box. "I can see that you all are ready to get to work."

"Thanks, dear. I should've listened to Colin and only carried one."

April laughed. "Where is he? Did you leave him to carry everything else?"

Vita smiled. "We should have. He's so bossy."

"You don't mean that, Vita." Letice pinched her lips together. "He is in charge of this."

"Yes, well, he's an okay egg." Vita strutted away toward the castle gardens.

Horden Castle and its grounds were about to become a beehive of activity. Dozens of people clustered around. It appeared to April that the entire village of Neville was chipping in to help Hodge celebrate.

As April fell into line behind the others, she spotted Colin coming her way. His arms loaded with more boxes. She rushed forward to help.

"Thank you." He rearranged the remaining two boxes and took in the scene before him.

"You've done a lot of work these past weeks in my absence. I appreciate it."

"You're welcome. I adored it. And I've not done any more than the others—including you." She grinned smugly. "It's taken a village."

He laughed at her joke. "Yes, it has. And I haven't done all that much. I also hate that I've been away from the expansion plans for the housing project. I've been told you're involved now as well and even started a little library in the common room."

"Yes," April said, her face heating. "Books are my specialty, and I had no idea you could use another person until Amanda brought it up. Next thing, I'm knee-deep in committee meetings."

"That sounds like her. She knows good help when she sees it." He motioned toward the decorating underway. "Speaking of help, we'd best get going to have everything ready for this evening."

April nodded, yet something in his expression didn't match his cheerful manner. His face was sad. "Are you well?"

He stared into the distance. "Oh, it's just that I know Susannah would've liked to be here. She and Hodge were dear friends. They actually met the first time she came to Neville. I believe he may have played a part in why she chose to move here."

"Perhaps. He's a lovely man, isn't he? I never met Mrs. Wilkinson, yet everyone that did seems to have nothing but nice things to say about her."

Colin stared at the castle. "Yes, she was a very nice woman and would want us to pull out all the stops for Hodge. So, I say, let's get on with it, shall we?"

"Yes. For Hodge." April offered a soft smile. "And Susannah."

Colin echoed her words, his voice lingering on Susannah's name.

⊗

The evening turned out as flawless as the day had been.

Hodge's grandson, and Colin, led the man of the hour, blindfolded, onto the castle grounds just before sundown. He was positioned among the hushed crowd on the patio, so when he opened his eyes, he would be looking into the crowd and the breathtaking sunset.

His grandson whispered into his ear, "Are you ready?"

Hodge's wrinkles deepened as his smile widened, eyes nearly disappearing. "Yes, I am."

The blindfold was untied, and the entire crowd yelled, "Happy birthday, Hodge!"

He brought his hands to his cheeks, his mouth ajar and looked around at the faces of his family and friends with the castle and the English sunset as the backdrop. Tears glistened in his eyes as one by one, people greeted him with hugs, back slaps, and their best wishes. Colin clapped him on the shoulder and gave him a microphone.

"I realized somethin' was goin' on, but I never imagined it would be so grand, especially for the likes of me." He beamed. "I so appreciate this wonderful surprise, and I want you all to have a good time. I will. I won't go on any longer with my chin waggin'."

He reached for his handkerchief and blotted his eyes. "I love you all. Now, I would like to give thanks before we dig in." Bowing his head, he began, "Lord, thank you for these wonderful people, for the food, and the perfect weather. Thank you for givin' me one hundred years on this earth, and for givin' me eternity in Your home." He passed the microphone back to Colin who stood by his side and observed the joy surrounding him.

Letice, Amanda, and Vita came forward to give him a hug and wish him a happy birthday. "What a great birthday gift. Hugs from the lovely ladies in Neville."

"Why, Hodge, you scoundrel." Vita lightly pushed his shoulder. "Is that all you wanted for your birthday?"

"What better to ask for at a hundred?" He grinned sheepishly. "I'm the most blessed man in all of England."

The sun now gone—thousands of tiny white lights illuminated the trees, topiaries, fountains, and walls. The entire castle gardens appeared like a nocturnal fairyland. Light reflected in the water of the moat and the fountains throughout the grounds. The torches made a backdrop behind the refreshment tables, highlighting a massive feast of platters loaded with roasted meats and vegetables. Cheeses, breads, and crackers were artfully arranged with garnishes of fresh herbs. A gigantic punch bowl was filled with Hodge's favorite drink, a pineapple and orange concoction.

Several guests had already loaded their plates and sat at tables near the entrance to the garden-patio. Colin watched April smile from across the crowd at Hodge and the other women as she wandered to the other side of the garden. She gazed at the large fountain, lights dancing across the water.

⁂

April admired the fountain while sipping on a glass of Hodge's punch. A nudge to her ribs from behind made her jerk and almost spill punch on her party dress.

"Oh!" April whirled to face her assailants. Tristan and Polly burst into laughter. "You two are a riot," she said sarcastically. "So now I guess I have two pranksters to deal with." She propped one hand on her hip in mock disapproval. "A real pair you are."

Tristan draped an arm on Polly's shoulder. The two, as a couple, was something April was going to have to get used to. She was thrilled at the prospect.

In fact, the whole evening seemed to brim with promise, like anything could happen. She caught a glimpse of Hodge surveying the sea of party guests, noticing his look of admiration. He stood near the entrance to the patio and garden grounds, his head turning toward the approach of two latecomers still in shadow on the dimly lit walkway to the castle. She saw his face shift to one of utter disbelief, and he held out his hands with a broad smile.

CฆEา

Colin was closing in on Hodge at the exact moment he turned and opened his arms toward two stragglers entering from the castle's front. With Hodge's position on the rise of the courtyard, Colin couldn't see who was walking toward him until he saw the man lingering back against the wall.

He stood motionless, his mind whirling with possibilities, long-held dreams that had no hope to come true. Was this one now—an impossible, heart-wrenching dream? He found he was holding his breath, his hands clenched at his sides. He listened, and watched the scene unfold before him as Hodge embraced the last person he expected to see. "*Susannah,*" he whispered as his vision blurred. He shook his head and looked again as he strode toward them, barely making out what was being said.

"Oh, my dear." Hodge croaked through tears. "It's so good

to see you. I knew you'd be back."

"Oh, my friend," Susannah said, tears shimmering on her cheeks. "It's so good to see you too."

"Please come." Hodge turned and waved for Ryan to join them. "Everyone is here now."

Ryan shook Hodge's hand. "It's nice to see you again."

"You too, my boy." His aged eyes shone with happiness and perhaps a touch of mischief. "April is around here somewhere."

Susannah turned, and her eyes met his. He didn't hesitate as long purposeful strides carried him toward her, his pounding heart masking all the sounds around them. He stopped in front of her, studying her face. She was really here—alive.

Her eyes filled with fresh tears, and Colin hesitated no longer. Tenderly, he folded her in his arms and kissed her. Everyone exploded into applause. He pulled back but didn't release her. He gazed into her eyes and said, "I should've done that a long time ago."

She nodded and smiled through the crying. "It doesn't matter now, Colin. We're here together at last." She drew him closer and whispered, "Right where we belong."

෨෩

Polly gasped, leaned toward April and pointed to the edge of the castle grounds. "Look who's here."

April followed Polly's gaze and brought her fingers to her lips as she saw Ryan shake Hodge's hand. Ryan surveyed the gardens until he met her gaze and smiled. He waved and strode toward her while Tristan led a protesting Polly away.

April sipped her punch, trying to think of something to say. She smiled as he stopped a few feet in front of her.

"It's so nice to see you again."

"You too." She stammered. "Would you like some punch?"

"I would love some. But, first, I'd like for you to finally meet my mother."

April's mouth dropped. "Your mother?"

"Yes. It's a long story. One I'd like to tell you over dinner if that's all right."

April studied him, noting a new lightness about him from his eyes to his posture. She remembered what he'd said about reading other people. And if she were to read him at that very moment, she would say he had found peace.

He stepped closer and took her hand. She looked into his eyes as he placed a small cool object in her palm and pressed her fingers around it.

She glanced at her hand, slowly opening it to reveal a silver pocket cross, and his transformation made sense. She smiled at him. "Dinner at Talbot's tomorrow night?"

He gave a nod and took her other hand in his as the night sky lit up with a boom, sprays of sparks and brilliant color cascading over Horden Castle. The display reflected more than fireworks in the fountain's gleaming surface but an image of love, forgiveness, and reconciliation.

THE END

PERMELIA COTTAGE

Acknowledgments

Having such a widespread support base has made my writing journey a pleasure. God has graciously placed so many wonderful people in my life to encourage and give me direction.

My first writing partner entered my life in 2007. Morgan Tarpley Smith is a great friend, encourager, and fellow writer. She also graciously formatted this book. Thank you, Morgan.

In 2016 I met Tammy Kirby at an ACFW (American Christian Fiction Writers) meeting. Our friendship has grown around our writing projects and research trips to the U.K. Thank you, Tammy, you have become a wonderful friend.

There are so many to thank that I don't have room to list everyone. Just a few I'd like to acknowledge are my husband

Max, my son Daniel, my mother, two unique aunts, beta readers—Donna, Eileen, Jo, Morgan, Pam, Tammy, and Wanda.

I'd also like to thank Jessica, the owner of Blue Cottage in Wiltshire, England. In 2013 I had the pleasure of staying in her 16th century cottage. She kindly gave me permission to use the photograph I took of her charming cottage for the cover of my first novel. Although the interior layout differs from Permelia Cottage, Blue Cottage was an inspiration for me. If you'd like to vacation there, contact Jessica at thebluecottage.co.uk

Thank you, Vikki, for a lovely cover. Book cover design is by Victoria Davies at vcbookcovers.com

Author's Note

This story has been on my heart for a long time. I've struggled with writing it because I've longed to write historical fiction, but God impressed upon me I should publish this novel first. Only through His grace and prompting has it come to fruition.

Now, onto the historical novels I've been hoarding in my head, and in my heart! I hope you have enjoyed Susannah's and Ryan's story and the way I intertwined them.

Sometimes God places us in circumstances that are difficult—just to get our attention—sometimes to make us grow, or to draw us to Him. This story is about these things. God knows what it will take to get us to follow Him. He gives us many chances to seek Him for eternal salvation.

Please forgive me for any errors regarding legal issues, Britishisms that may be inaccurate, and the poetic license I've taken in telling this story.

Bedale, North Yorkshire, England is the fictional Neville. I have visited Bedale on two of my trips to England because some of my ancestors lived there centuries ago. The area which encompasses Bedale has a population of over three thousand, therefore I changed the name because I wanted to condense it into more of a small country village.

Also, there is no rail service (except via the scenic, and historic, Wensleydale Railway) into Bedale, so I created one that travels to Northallerton, which has a larger population, to give my characters more ease of transportation.

Blue Cottage inspired Permelia Cottage, although I changed the floor plan. It's in the tiny village of Ebbesbourne Wake, Wiltshire, England. I hope you enjoyed the story and that it touched your heart.

God bless,
Carole

Carole Lehr Johnson is a veteran travel consultant of more than 30 years and has served as head of genealogy at her local library.

Her love of tea and scones, castles and cottages, and all things British has led her to immerse her writing in the United Kingdom whether in the genre of historical or contemporary fiction.

Carole is the author of two inspirational novels set in England, *Permelia Cottage* and *A Place in Time*, and the novella collection, *Their Scottish Destiny*. She is a member of the American Christian Fiction Writers (ACFW) as well as the president of her local chapter. She and her husband live in Louisiana with their goofy cats.

For more information, visit
www.carolelehrjohnson.com

Sign up for Carole's newsletter on her website for updates on her next release, U.K. travel features, recipes, book recommendations, and more.

Books by Carole Lehr Johnson

Permelia Cottage

A Place in Time

His Scottish Destiny *Novella*

co-authored with Tammy Kirby